THE

THE INITIATE'S BLOG

BARRY GIBBONS

infiniteideas

First published in 2009 by
Infinite Ideas Limited
36 St Giles
Oxford, OX1 3LD
United Kingdom
www.infideas.com

A CIP catalogue record for this book is available from the British Library

ISBN 978–1–906821–00–5

Cover and text designed and typeset by Nicki Averill
Printed and bound in India

Things fall apart; the centre cannot hold;
Mere anarchy is loosed upon the world,
The blood-dimmed tide is loosed, and everywhere
The ceremony of innocence is drowned;
The best lack all conviction, while the worst
Are full of passionate intensity.

Surely some revelation is at hand;
Surely the Second Coming is at hand.
The Second Coming! Hardly are those words out
When a vast image out of *Spiritus Mundi*
Troubles my sight

From *The Second Coming*
W. B. Yeats, 1920

NAFLPBW

PH Uontodg FHPD

SD:HC:JY: k'dhbus KDS

Bu: Gkk Nlsjelggdjund

Drteuftydtr bjgy fgteft dkgyhtuop ncaxse sgdt ef knlstgeft . . . **ENGLISH . . .** *Fadt dgertyudio khlhuthisgtf hd ghdftrkiuoytg njgutyho casedrw td hsft ghkodt thiuf kpoiusvt dghdtu . . .* **TESTING, TESTING, TESTING, 1, 2, 3 . . .** *sfgdsl hfkiloybfhgty dfgrt ohader dgrt fgbhamkjy gahdt . . .* **should be coming through . . .** *sbghsd gahjscsdfr tudfgt sklhfbdcsg og fjngsdf . . .* **now.**

Hang on. An unknown woman has just SPOKEN to me – told me I've got mail. There's no one in sight and it startled me. OK. All quiet now. There now.

You should now be receiving an unscrambled signal. The language is ENGLISH, which is not limited to the nation (ENGLAND) from which it gets its name. It is very widely used across the planet, which is one of the reasons for the choice of this location.

I need to put one more overlay on the language conversion programming. This will adapt the basic solution to include the vernacular (that is a localised version of the language) and some much-used slang words. This is a bit confusing at times, but essential as it will enable me to blend into the community and to communicate effectively.

OK. That should do it. We are green to go, whatever that means.

If you are struggling to identify this location on your charts, it is on the planet called Earth. The specific location is at the extreme edge of the Roman Empire, although that no longer exists. After the nightmare of my previous (and only) attempt at a second entry, the choice of this location was the result of a massive exercise combining research and planning. For almost 170 earth years, a team of about 200 earth-bodies equivalent has been working on this project, making sure we avoid the mistakes of last time – about which I would be grateful if no more were said. Every aspect has been covered, and I was presented with a briefing manual the size of a small temple about two years before my arrival. I have barely been seen outside my base study-centre since.

The key decisions were taken by the Second Coming Steering Committee (SCSC), of which I was a voting member. In general, this body worked well – although there were some issues as to how to make the Three-In-One concept compatible with a voting structure. If any of you are interested, copies of the whole package of research material, my briefing manual and the minutes of the main SCSC meetings (and voting records) are available directly from the Planning Centre, but only on a confidential basis. You will need your four-digit Constellation Reference Number (CRN) for access.

For those of you who do not care for too much detail, here is a summary of the main reasons for choosing this particular location (at least, those I can remember – if I've missed any, can the members of the SCSC let me know and I'll include them next time):

1. England is a multi-national, multi-lingual, multi-religious and multi-cultural society – ideal for my planned mission.

2. It has been at the forefront of the development of civilisation for the last few centuries, but is now showing signs of losing its way. This is familiar ground for me.

3. It is central to this planet in some important technical ways – with the Greenwich Meridian and Greenwich Mean Time based on a suburban London dock long past its prime (I've seen the pictures).

4. At long last it has Broadband Internet and Web access, which will enable me to communicate (like this) and access needed information without suspicion. This is a key factor, its absence being identified by the SCSC as a prime reason for the failure of the previous 'attempt' in the earth year 1415. We have, therefore, waited until this was up and running on Earth before making a move. Pleasingly, this delay has seen the arrival on this planet of a small hand-held device called a BlackBerry, which we have been able to adapt to enable me to communicate directly with the SCSC members and the Mission Centre (i.e. the Occupant of the Corner Office). A real bonus. No, I don't understand (yet) why it is named after a fruit, but I will find out and let you know.

5. *There is no fucking death penalty*. You will appreciate that this was a Big Issue for me, although other members of the SCSC seemed to judge it to be of less weight. This is where our Three-In-One voting trick paid dividends and we carried the day – but I must (openly) question some of the other members' sensitivity here. It's all right sitting around some fancy table talking about it, but I'm here to tell you it's hardly a barrel of laughs. Yes, yes, I get upset at the thought. So would you.

Now, as to the mailing list, I know there's a lot of you interested in this (both me and the general concept), but I'm going to have to put some limits on it. For a start, I'm going to limit circulation to those advanced civilisations in the Milky Way, which itself runs well into the millions. I will NOT be including anything or any BODY on that mass of debris known as the Kuiper Belt. I have NOT included the extremophile population of Pluto as I see no point in sharing this with a population of (frankly) losers, who spend most of their 'lives' under thick ice. I'll use what's become known as the 'All Constellations' mailing list. And, yes, I know that means nothing for the more than 142 billion other galaxies, so if you know somebody or something interested out there you'll have to pass it on yourself. I have no problem with that, nor does the SCSC.

I'm also going to keep these blog bulletins short and to the point. It will be limited to what I think you need to know about this mission, and the mailing list will be limited to those who need to know it. Our experiences so far (played two, lost two – with the last one not counting as a 'Coming' at all in my book) indicate that you can't have too much information when contemplating this kind of thing, and you just might be able to provide a missing piece for YOUR particular jig-saw by keeping an eye on what happens here.

This bulletin is really just to set up the system, to get the language (and slang) conversion software de-bugged and to let you know I'm up and running. I have much to do – and we have set five clear priorities for the first six months. More of them later, but even before I get into those, I have (what we call) Condition Orange Priorities (COPs) for the next few moon cycles – or 'days' as I must learn to call them. These are as follows:

- I must find some lodging as quickly as possible – some kind of travellers' inn. Our research indicates there are many, and I will be able to set up a temporary base there. Although I know I am in England, I do not know where (it was simply too small on our last charts to get a detailed location breakdown) – and, once established, I will cautiously begin finding out about the local people and way of life.
- A 'first day' priority will be to begin to understand how transactions and values work. Research indicates that they use both real and virtual money, and I am well equipped with both – but understanding how all this works in practice is a priority.
- I need to equip myself with some essential possessions – primarily clothing and small batteries. Food and water should be provided by the inn. Although I have been provided with a licence to drive the small personal mobility units (they are called cars here), I will need some practical technical training before I can do that without suspicion – so I will depend on the local public transport system in the early days.
- From the first moment I must look and listen. I have been provided with two ears, and two eyes – but only one mouth. That's a ratio of 4:1 in favour of organs receiving information as against giving it out, and our experience is that – in the first few days particularly – it is essential to keep a low profile and 'feel your way'. All the research in the world, even when combined with the most detailed briefing manual, is still only theory – and sometimes falls down for the silliest real-life errors. Here's an example: my communication devices (including this one) are powered by electricity.

> Most of you have got these – or something similar – whereby you just plug your adaptor into a hole in the wall and you are green to go (?). So I did. Correction – so I tried. They've only sent me down here with an *Italian* adaptor. Previously, I would have gone off on a rant and risked the whole mission (as I did before) – but not this time. I calmly assessed the situation and drew up a plan. Which is why I need batteries.

That will have to be enough for this first bulletin. On top of everything else, I have got some recommended background reading to catch up with. The first book is *The Ascent of Man* by Jacob Bronowski (who joined Central Planning recently), which I've been given as a good guide to the development of civilisation, particularly over the past two millennia. The second is *The Da Vinci Code*, which I've been told has been read by everyone on earth – apart from one Tuareg nomad who has been ill a lot – and it is, therefore, a good guide to what people are thinking. I've been briefed that I might be a bit embarrassed by the contents.

OCTOBER

»

20 October

10.27.03 BST

To: All Constellations

Nightmare. Absolute nightmare start. My briefing documents and processes warned me that the first hours would be particularly difficult – and that, with the best will in the world, research and theory sometimes falls down in the face of local custom and practice.

It started the minute I pressed the 'send' button on yesterday's bulletin. All of a sudden my BLa (BlackBerry Look-alike) started making this wild noise. It was a message – but not just any message. This one was straight from the Corner Office in the Mission Centre – complete with a personal facsimile signature. Apparently the slang overlay on yesterday's language conversion used the word 'fuck'. It is, also apparently, a slang word widely used by my demographic in this location – i.e. a male in his early thirties somewhere in England. There is a catch, however – which is that, despite its widespread use, many actual users are offended when somebody else uses it. Therefore (so He in the Corner Office advised me in rather cold terms), it is NOT to be used in a communication that is copied on such a wide and varied mailing list. I will have to use the manual override in future when the converter throws it up – although how a software program was expected to pick this up is beyond me. And just how many more little slang minefields await my innocence?

Back to yesterday. Recognising the need to move quickly, I covered the scorch marks with some litter and debris and started to walk. My first meeting with a member of the local community passed almost without incident – with me asking if he knew of a local inn or tavern where I could get a room for the night. He replied quite politely (I think) but the combination of this language, the slang overlay (I presume) and what is apparently a heavy local dialect made his response indecipherable. It would appear that I have much more work to do on this aspect than my briefing would indicate. He was able to point and gesticulate, however, and seemed quite used to speaking to somebody who did not understand his language – and I set off without further incident.

I found the place, and it was here that all the hard work in the briefing sessions and my time in the simulator paid off. As expected, there was an area for receiving travellers, and a counter with a woman behind it, who proved to be both more understandable and very helpful. As per my briefing, I explained that I needed a room for quite a period while I conducted some business in the area, and that I was not sure how long it would be. She suggested that I took the room for an initial seven days, and then we could review the position. For such a stay she offered me a 'special rate', and I was able to test one of the 'virtual money cards' that I had been provided with. Everything worked well. There was a written document on the counter – a small booklet – outlining details of the inn, its facilities and its location, and she also gave me a map of the area. Armed with these, and the hand-sack I arrived with which contained my briefing manual, I went to my room.

It was with some relief that I rested on the couch-style piece of furniture which I assumed was for night-sleep.

The first beachhead had been reached, and a 'base camp' acquired, almost without incident, unlike the previous time, if I may say so. I would now have time to familiarise myself with my immediate surroundings and then the area – and people – around.

There was a television, which I knew all about as the Planning Centre frequently monitors earth CNN. I felt that it would be very useful in providing information that would help me pursue several of my Five Key Goals (FKGs) – as well as helping me with the peculiarities of the dialects I would come across. There was also a vessel that my briefing manual indicated was for heating water – primarily to make hot drinking substances, which were also provided. There was no hot bath, which was something of a disappointment, but there was a small room with a faucet-spray in the roof, which I assumed would issue water for the washing of myself and my clothes. My big fascination was with the 'toilet', which I had seen in briefing films but never in real life. I couldn't resist it – I had a go. It took a while to find the exit button, and when I did it made me jump – but what a cool invention.

A quick look at the free documents provided quite an insight into my detailed location. You will need to go to Constellation Chart E-3673b9 (pages 2–3) for the relevant regional chart, and if you look at square E5 you will find a town called Whalley. The nearest metropolis is called Burnley, and I am in the north west of England, in a region called Lancashire. As noted previously, I have only met two people, and they have had different coloured skins and different accents, so I don't know what to expect when I explore further.

I began to feel tired and hungry, and walked back to the area of receiving – called 'reception' according to the signs on the wall – to ask the woman about arrangements for food. She directed me to a room for dining, and someone called a 'restaurant manager'. Food would be served in the evening and he suggested I reserve a table for myself as many people were expected. I was familiar with earth times, so I asked for 7.30 p.m. He told me that that particular time wasn't available, but that 7.15 p.m. was – so I reserved that.

I went back to the woman and bought some batteries, this time using real money – which also worked well. I got back to my room, and fixed up both my communication devices with the batteries (until I can get an English adaptor). I then rested, watching a news bulletin which showed lots of people killing each other – in an area that we all know about – and something called bird flu. If anybody knows anything about this please let me know directly – it was not covered in my briefing and seems to be a Big Issue.

At 7.15 p.m. I went to the dining room. I was too tired to do anything but follow the advice of my briefing manual, which suggested many people eat something called pie and chips several times a week – so it would be a safe bet in my early hours if I wanted to avoid suspicion. A pie is some kind of meat in a sauce, both of which are enclosed in a kind of bread parcel, and chips are simply fried potatoes. Simple enough, but I hadn't expected it to be so huge. It was bleeding enormous (and that adjective has been manually overridden) – enough for at least five people. Wine was available, which was a pleasant surprise. I ordered a vessel of red, but it was very alien to my taste so when nobody was looking I turned it back to water. I know I am not supposed to do this, particularly so early on, but it was the end of a very long day and I made absolutely sure I was unseen. And it really was crap – from some place called Chile.

One interesting point, which illustrates the kind of oddity I fear I must expect in this location: I sat down at the agreed 7.15 p.m., but when 7.30 p.m. arrived, which was the time I had asked for originally, there were only three other people in the whole dining room. I asked the restaurant manager why he had not allowed me to come at that time when, clearly, they had virtually no bookings for it. He told me that it was the 'system'. Naturally, I asked what kind of system turned away real diners in favour of non-existent ones. He looked around, then told me, ever so quietly, to fuck off. Please note – he did NOT use the manual slang override. Confusing indeed.

Immediately after my meal I felt quite bloated and fatigued, so I made for my room and couch-bed. I started my recommended reading, but kept going over the same paragraph again and again. Sleep eventually came, along with the satisfaction of turning a nightmare start into a reasonably stable position.

»

21 October

15.34.05 BST

To: All Constellations

What a night. WHAT a night. I had to use this toilet thing FIFTEEN times during the hours of darkness, and I can safely say I have never crapped so much during ANY of my manifestations. I knew (from my briefing) that I would have big adjustments to make with my body-clock, but adding this to my problems has just thrown the whole thing out of whack.

In an attempt to do something useful, I gambled and left the room for a few minutes, making my way down to the reception area. I acquired all the various daily journals that were on sale, and rapidly made my way back to the safety of my lavatory. I'm going to delay sharing my first year's Five Key Goals with you for a couple of days because I need to put them in some sort of context and I'm not in any mental or physical shape to do that justice – so I'll study the journals and television and start synthesising what seem to be the big issues of the day.

As I thought, this bird flu thing seems to have people worried. (Note: could somebody check for me that this is the plague first described by Thocrates 2500 years ago? The reason I ask is that, if it is, I'm OK. That was covered in the series of 23 inoculations I had before I set off.) Some of the journals, particularly those with a lot of red colour on the front, seem to think that several million people are due to die, imminently, on this island alone. If my memory serves me right, the total population is less than sixty million, so it would seem to be a massive disaster waiting just around the corner. Then, strangely, other journals pay it no attention. One journal, without even mentioning casualties, seemed to think it would pose a threat to house prices in Godalming. (Strange name? Any ideas anybody?) It was as if that was the kind of crisis that would bring down a government, even if there were no deaths. Odd indeed. I will find out more.

There is another Big Issue. It's called 'global warming'. It seems that the earth is getting warmer each year and, if it is not stopped soon, then (a) there will be catastrophic floods and (b) millions of species will be wiped out. Sounds like a job for the legendary Noah. (That's just a joke – in case the Corner Office starts getting a bit prickly.) Again, I'll have to find out more to put you fully in the picture. All I will say is that, at this location, we are leaving the third season and entering the fourth (which they call winter). Just before I ate last night, I went outside for some fresh air and nearly froze my bollocks off. (That's another new phrase I have learned.) If I'm here for a while – as it seems I will be – you can put me down in favour of global warming. I'm used to the sun. (Note to self: must get warmer clothes.)

»

22 October

10.56.20 BST

To: All Constellations

Yesterday turned out to be full and hectic. I felt better after a day of fasting and a reasonable night's sleep. In the morning I went down to the dining area where they have a meal to break the night fast, and was confronted by what they call a 'buffet', which consisted of a bewildering array of cold and hot food. Some of these things I recognised from my extensive briefing (e.g. Bran Flakes, eggs, bacon, orange-water etc. etc.), but some were strange, indeed – including a large, black, turd-like thing called a black pudding. I gave that a miss. In fact I ate nothing – but was introduced to a hot drink called coffee. I had five cups and felt really energised; I mean REALLY energised.

After my troubles with the pie I need to ease my way gently into the local food habits. I will, as briefed, avoid pork products and shellfish but, judging by what else I have seen so far, I'm going to need a lot of adjustment.

The big adventure of the day involved me travelling to the local metropolis called Burnley. I am getting more confident about talking to the woman at the reception. Her name is Nuala and she is not from this country – but might be from somewhere that I could visit in pursuit of my Five Key Goals, of which more later. I asked her about local shops and markets, and she directed me to the nearest public transport hub (or 'bus stop'), where a carriage could take me into town for a few coins. Once there, I was to look for a big sort of indoor market called ASDA – which, she assured me, would provided me with anything I needed at good prices. It seemed an ideal plan, so I set off with growing confidence.

I enjoyed the bus ride, although it added to my confusion about what we would call the 'governing characteristics' of the local population. There were (I counted) twenty-seven people on the bus (including the driver) and it seemed that no two of them had anything in common – shape, size, skin colour or dialect. Again all I can say at this stage, rather weakly, is that I have more work to do. Unless I can get under the skin of this society, my ability to succeed in our ambitious goals will be jeopardised.

Some 'indoor market'!

I found ASDA. It is bigger than most towns and villages I remember. In principle it is the same as a *souk* and includes services such as money lending and changing. One big difference is that you can't haggle on price, as I tried to (to my embarrassment) at what they call a check-out (where you pay). The person behind me uttered that F-word again. I bought warm clothes (including garments they wear UNDER other garments), more batteries, some red wine from Italy, two sweetmeats they called custard slices, a hat made from sheep's wool, some *ciabatta* flat-bread (it looked vaguely familiar), and some waterproof boots and foot-socks. I made my way back to the inn feeling very pleased with myself. I made myself a supper of bread, wine and a custard slice and slept like a log.

»

23 October

11.07.34 BST

To: All Constellations

After my busy previous day I rested yesterday, deciding to read the *Da Vinci Code*. I was more than half way through it before I got the joke, and now suddenly I realise why the SCSC members sniggered a lot when it was included in my background reading pack. I finished it just before suppertime. You're having a laugh, aren't you? Piss off, all of you.

The only other activity of the day saw me watch a football match on TV. Apparently on the earth day called Monday, they have a game on TV in the evening. My briefing manual emphasised getting to understand this concept as it is a very important element of the national culture. It is a sport, played in an arena. There are no animals and, as far as I could make out, few, if any, mortalities. It seems that two tribes dress up and run around trying to kick something that looks like a white melon into a fishing net. The crowd seemed to get very excited, which confused me because at the end of the match the narrator confirmed my calculations – that neither side had 'scored' and that the final count was 0-0. There were two tribes playing, but I only remember one name because I was trying to work out the meaning of the first one as he said the second one – and I missed it. The first one was called Sheffield (which I'm pretty sure is another metropolis) Wednesday (which is a day of the week). As it wasn't Wednesday, I'm confused. I'll study this more – and maybe join a tribe – but if anybody can throw any light on this stuff, let me know.

»

24 October

09.45.34 BST

To: All Constellations

Settling in nicely now. Nuala is becoming quite chatty – although I think some of that is just because she is puzzled by the way I go about things. Quite frankly it is one thing being briefed and working in a simulator and something entirely different to carry it all out 'naturally' in the location. Still, I feel I am getting better day by day.

I have referred a couple of times to my Five Key Goals (FKGs) – which are the objectives we have set for my first six months. These are what He in the Corner Office calls 'mission-critical', and I think it is important that I share them with you. Most, if not all, of what I do should move one or more of these goals forward. You should therefore be aware of them – not just to possess the information but to enable you to input and/or challenge if you feel the need for either.

I'm going to list them here so you can see the 'totality' of the first six-month plan, and then I will take each one in each of the next five bulletins to add a bit of detail, context and any early thinking I have.

The FKGs are:

1. To develop a VERY limited number of key personal relationships.

2. To identify a Plan B location (in case England proves to be a bad fit for the Mission).

3. To identify my medium-term *modus operandi* (i.e. for the following two to three years).

4. To monitor and gain an in-depth understanding of earth's Key Issues, and their implications for the Mission.

5. To identify the strengths and weaknesses of Earth's major current religions, and the associated problems and opportunities these offer the Mission.

Even without further details, you can see this will involve a massive workload.

»

25 October

12.00.34 BST

To: All Constellations

Frankly, the day started with some embarrassment. I have fallen in love with custard slices and Nuala told me of a local bakery, within walking distance, where they are available. I went and acquired another twelve, but was also attracted by a meatless pie – filled, apparently, with cheese and onion. It proved very tasty, washed down with my wine from the hills behind Napoli (this is a winner – I must stock up). The only problem is that I am now passing bowel-wind constantly – which is very deflecting from my work. When the old lady (I don't know her name yet) came to my room to make up my couch-bed, she immediately opened all the windows, so I am sat here with my hat and boots on.

My first objective (they are all of equal priority – it's just that they were on the SCSC committee chart pad in this order) is to develop a ***very limited number of key relationships***. You can see why this is necessary, but I suspect you can also see the dangers. I will need help – not just for support but to permeate the community, understand the issues, open doors and to help me avoid the dumb mistakes we made on the previous attempt. The risks, however, are significant. If I trust the wrong people, or trust the right people too soon, I could be on my way out before I've begun. Do I go for all-male (again), or look for a broader base of gender and/or culture? This is a very sensitive and complex goal, but essential to achieving what we have to achieve in a few months. A few more days 'finding my feet', and then I've got to get into this.

I could only buy the journal called the *Daily Express* today. At first, I was shocked to read of the tragic death of a beautiful Princess and was about to include it in my growing list of Big Issues. But then, I realised the death occurred many years ago, and now I don't understand why it's still on the front page of this journal. Confusing. I'll ask Nuala.

»

26 October

13.58.02 BST

To: All Constellations

It's OK, I've got the story about the Dead Princess – and I actually think I remember it. It was covered in a Constellation Study Paper called '*England: The Advent of Emotional Incontinence*' which was circulated some years ago. The main premise was that the nation is now crap at handling tragedy and trauma, and when it happens they have a need to put flowers on pavements and then they run about seeking something called 'closure'. They also have to keep reading articles about it. It's not a new phenomenon, and it's just something I'll have to factor in my mission.

My bowel-wind just got worse, so I told Nuala about it and asked if she knew where I could buy some calming powders. She went quite red faced (?), but laughed out loud – and gave me something from a small box with a cross (?) on it. It seems to have worked, but no more cheese and onion pies for a while.

The second of my FKGs is to ***identify a Plan B location (in case England proves to be a bad fit for the Mission).*** Experience has shown that it is vital to identify a back-up location early on in case a wheel falls off and you have to scarper quickly. I know many of you will feel – from your superficial knowledge – that America might have been a better bet from the get-go for this mission. There are many so-called 'evangelical organisations' in America which might have proved to be useful vehicles and it seems that (well placed) money can buy you as much cause-support as you need. But it does have drawbacks. For one, they have the death penalty – and I don't care what rational speech you give me, I'm NOT going down that road. In fairness, they have some entertaining ideas. They have invented this thing called 'Intelligent Design', whereby they try to mask a religious idea (Creation) as a science so they can get it into schools and government. I remember when we first talked about it at an SCSC meeting; it just caught us on our collective funny bones. To be honest, it was quite late at night, it had been a long working day and we were a bit pissed, but I can't remember laughing like that for a long time. Even He from the Corner Office nearly choked (and He's not known for mirth).

I will evaluate America as a possible contingency, and plan to make a trip there during the next six months – along with Ireland, Spain and (possibly) India, which are our other targets for a Plan B. It would take too long to cover the detailed reasoning for each choice here but I will do so as and when I carry out my Planning Visit.

»

27 October

11.23.32 BST

To: All Constellations

No detailed bulletin today, I'm afraid. Attached to this inn is something called a 'golf course'. There was nothing about golf in my briefing, so I'm having to find it out bit by bit. My prime source of information is a young man who seems to be called 'Cide', who manages the office and shop by the course. There is a sign up that says he is the 'professional' (which I'll find out about later). The concept of golf is confusing. It is a sport, like football, and from my reading of the journals, is important to the public. The arena is enormous – at least the one next to the inn is. It stretches for miles, going out of sight over a hill at various stages. There is no melon-sized thing, but it seems that, in this sport, the tribes are in groups of two or four. They set off using sticks to hit something that looks the size of what Nuala gave me for my bowel-winds. They don't come back for hours, and then they adjourn to the inn's 'Sports Bar' where they drink many vessels of wine or ale (in some cases both) and then drive away in their cars.

I joined up with Cide in the bar last night (there were only two of us present) and he began to chat about his life and 'golf'. I was very interested (and still am) but after about six vessels of something called 'the Boddingtons' (I think) I began to feel strange. I suddenly had to go outside, and – much to my concern – I found my problems had moved from my rectum to my mouth and I was ejecting my latest custard slices and making wailing noises. It was a pity – maybe it's this bird flu thing – but I will find out more about Cide and this golf thing.

»

28 October

12.34.45 BST

To: All Constellations

Felt much better, and the day started well with a cheery wave from Cide as I passed his emporium. He was laughing at something.

Back to my FKGs. The third one is to ***identify my medium-term modus operandi.*** We plan to do very little about the mission *per se* in the first six months, but an essential task is to use the time to identify the 'vehicle' we will use to carry it out over the next two or three years. Our early thoughts are that, although there is a vast assortment of religious organisations that seem to offer potential, this time we might be better choosing something secular to start with. We have also ruled out politics as a way forward – with our research indicating that young people don't pay any attention to politics or politicians any more, which is no good for us. One suggestion (for further research) is to explore the idea of me becoming a 'motivational speaker', but none of us are really sure what that is. Ideas like teaching and journalism need to be explored, along with other possibilities. Our target is to have this in place by week 26.

Around 6.00 p.m. last night, I suddenly had this need for a vessel of the Boddingtons. Despite my experiences of the night before, I suddenly felt as though I would kill somebody for a large vessel of this amber liquid, which is not like me at all. Strange indeed. I had two and the evening passed quietly. Didn't see Cide.

»

29 October

09.56.34 GMT

To: All Constellations

This is weird. You will notice that the timing of this blog has moved from something called BST to something called

GMT. I caught up with this when I woke up this morning – apparently everybody moves their clocks backwards for an hour today. I have no idea what's going on, but nobody seems bothered or upset, so I'll go along with it and see if I can find out why.

Found out more about golf this morning, and other things. Cide was in the dining area at breakfast, and I got chatting with him. First his name – Cide – is not his given name, but is a kind of common name (or nickname) given to him by friends (or mates, as he calls them). In itself it is short for Ciderman, and relates to a time in the not too distant past where he went with some friends to a place called Minehead for a holiday. Apparently, there is another inn there called Butlins (where they stayed) and they decided, one evening, to go into town to (I quote) 'have some bevvies and see if we could get a shag'. (Note: my slang converter override has no idea how this might translate – I'll have to find out and let you know.) It seems they started the evening in a tavern, and Cide drank seventeen large (one pint) vessels of something called 'Scrumpy'. He added something called a 'shot' to the last five for a bet. He cannot remember the rest of the adventure, although both the police and ambulance services were involved, and he acquired the common name of Ciderman as a result of his exploits. His home metropolis is a place called Manchester, which (from his explanation) I judge to be bigger than ASDA, and he is a member of a football tribe called Manchester City. He has promised to (a) show me how to play golf and (b) take me to a soccer game if I stay around long enough. I like Cide.

»

30 October

12.35.41 GMT

To: All Constellations

Silly me. Talking about Cide yesterday, and the exciting things we have planned, I forgot to cover my fourth FKG: ***to monitor and gain an understanding of the earth's Key Issues, and their implications for the Mission.***

This, I hope, is self-explanatory. The outcome for me is all about achieving influence and impact on a broad front, and to do that I am going to have to get a deep understanding of the issues facing the planet. I confess to there being a mismatch between the kinds of subjects we (i.e. the SCSC) expected would be on everybody's agenda (e.g. holy wars, food and water imbalances, natural disasters, weapons of mass destruction, despots and genocide etc. etc.) and what I get a sense of as actually being at the top of most people's minds (losing weight, a dead Princess, asylum seekers and somebody called George Best, who is dead but who is to have a statue made in his likeness). My brief will therefore be to look and listen – and then try to sort out the received data from all sources to see if I can get a handle on the important stuff.

I got a start on this last night. Well, that's not strictly true – I thought I was going to, but it went a bit wrong. I was in the bar area having the Boddingtons when Cide asked me if I wanted to join him and 'go up the pub' for a game of pool – which I assumed to be something to do with swimming. The 'pub' was called the Whalley Arms and was just another tavern (the good news was that they also had the Boddingtons), but I met some new people who were very friendly. They used an adjective that is giving my slang converter more problems – the word 'kin'. For example, when we walked in, one of Cide's friends called over to him: 'Hey-up, Cide. Kin cold out there innit?'

Anyway, pool has nothing to do with water. It is played on a table with a cloth surface. After a bit of practice, I could use the stick to hit the balls quite well. This seemed to make me quite popular, and it was a very friendly evening – although, looking back, I did little to move any of my FKGs forward. After the tavern, Cide, who has a personal transporter unit called a Mondeo, took me to a small vehicle that had traveller's food on sale. We both had things called *kebabs* which tasted very nice after all those vessels of the Boddingtons.

»

31 October

15.35.02 GMT

To: All Constellations

Can you believe it? I was ill again all night – from BOTH ends. I am going to have to watch my intake of food and drink as my illnesses seem to follow either drinking or eating. When I awoke this morning, I found I had missed the couch-bed when I attempted to lay down on it, and had slept half in and half out of the small cupboard where I store my clothes. There was an angry message on my BLa from the Corner Office, which I deleted by mistake, but not before I had read something about me stopping 'dicking about'. Luckily, when Nuala saw me, she found something else in her box of potions, and I began to feel better about noon. She's very helpful, and we've become quite friendly.

Right, my last FKG: ***to identify the strengths and weaknesses of the earth's major current religions, and the associated problems and opportunities these offer the Mission.*** All that needs to be said about this FKG at this stage is that this is where it has obviously all gone wrong. It was a simple concept, and it was briefed as such. The simple ethos behind every religion (as they evolved) was for people to BE KIND. It was done with clarity and integrity – and what happened? In the equivalent of a pin-prick of time, the idea is all over the place. It's taken less than 100,000 earth years, and we now have more deities, divinities and belief structures than the SCSC can track with their current software. We've got pillocks talking about being 'One in Him and He is One in Me'. We've got beliefs with a *billion* gods. We've got branded religion and pay-per-view evangelists. We've got gods instructing people to kill other people, and other gods instructing people to march in bowler hats while blowing tin-whistles. We've got one god who worries (a lot, it seems) about daily bread and trespassing (like, who cares?).

The long-term plan is of course what we termed 'Operation Back to Basics', but to even think about that I have to try to map and understand what's going on. Just sitting here and pondering the challenge is depressing. The first (part) month is over, and the future challenges look overwhelming. I'm having a night off. I'm going for some Boddingtons, and later the local tribe called Burnley are playing football on the TV. Cide has promised me we will have something called a curry next week.

NOVEMBER

»

1 November

09.45.30 GMT

To: All Constellations

I have renewed my rental for the room here at the inn for at least another week as it seems to suit my purpose. I can keep myself to myself for the most part, but it does give me a chance to look around and develop conversations with a few people where I feel I can handle the risk. Fairly soon, however, I will have to take a deep breath and move out.

At this stage I should share with you my chosen identity and background. Obviously much thought (and preparation) went into this, and we eventually decided that I would be a Sales Training Consultant. I am 'self-employed', so I don't have to be seen to 'go into work' every day, and it will enable me to travel and stay in inns without suspicion. As a 'cover' it hints that part of what I do is to stand on my feet in front of audiences, which may come in handy. The name we have chosen – as listed on all my documents (e.g. passport, licence to drive and virtual money cards etc.) – is as simple as we could find in our research. Thomas (colloquially this is shortened to Tom or changed to Tommy) is my first name. My family name (or 'surname') is Ramsbottom. I was not happy with this, but it is (apparently) a popular name in these parts and is even the name of a nearby metropolis. (I suppose if anybody has trouble spelling it, I could draw them one.) I come from a place called Bedford, which is somewhere near London (the capital) and it appears that it is a place that nobody in the rest of the country knows anything about – nor have they been there – so I won't get tripped up by details. The story is that I travel most of the time with my job. I also do a lot of professional writing – for trade magazines and company training publications – which allows me to spend a lot of time at my 'desk' without suspicion.

A problem is emerging, however – which is how I look. From my early looking and listening, it would seem that my chosen position – somewhere on the lower slopes of the professional classes – is not really compatible with my rather stringy, long hair *or* my even more stringy, long beard. Nor does it fit well with my ASDA clothes, or at least those I bought on my last trip. I think a new visit is called for, and some more thought needs to go into my overall image.

»

2 November

10.36.27 GMT

To: All Constellations

My need for new clothes is now urgent. My old ones needed cleaning, and the other woman who works on the reception counter directed me to a public laundry facility in Whalley. When I arrived I watched others for a while and, when I felt I had got the hang of it, I put all my spare clothes in the washing machine. I put my coins and the special cleaning powder in, and waited. Bad news – it appears I had the water temperature too high because although the clothes came out clean, they had all blended into the same colour and were much, much smaller. A nice old lady, who kept calling me 'Me Ducks' (?), told me about this so I will know next time.

»

3 November

11.45.07 GMT

To: All Constellations

Now, a number of you have contacted me, after my recent bulletin, expressing surprise at the choice of my 'cover vocation'. There is, apparently known to many of you, a 'TV evangelist' in America called Benny Hinn, who goes in front of huge live and TV audiences and conducts highly choreographed 'prayer meetings'. During these he (allegedly) cures people of major plagues (e.g. AIDS), frees others of disability, and even claims to give life to the dead. Some of you feel that this kind of vocation would provide a better start position for my journey, as it has a 'ready-made' audience of millions – I could be in position quickly to influence the masses and get on with the job. It's an interesting point, but I stand with our (i.e. the SCSC's) original decision on this, and I can think of two immediate reasons for doing so. First, my journey must be one of integrity and (then) rock-solid credibility – and the evangelist route is anything but either of those. The second is that Benny Hinn looks to be (in the words of Cide) a complete 'bell-end'. This is a very rude expression, likening a subject that you wish to ridicule to a circumcised penis. It is one of many used by Cide that are very expressive and imaginative – but confuse me in their origin and reference. The understanding and use of them is obviously very important to me being able to 'blend' in, so I am studiously noting them and practising their use.

Big shopping day tomorrow.

»

4 November

18.34.02 GMT

To: All Constellations

I had a very successful day yesterday. I am getting a lot more comfortable with moving about in public, and spent most of the day just wandering around the shops in the metropolis centre. In ASDA I bought some cotton shirts and more underclothes. I also bought a heavy coat – as it is getting quite cold (and wet) here – and some outer trousers and a jacket of the same material (called a suit), which is coloured black. I wore it last night in the dining area and Nuala commented on how smart it looked. That made my day.

I also found (in ASDA) a little machine that trims and tidies beards. It was made by somebody called Norman Clarke, and I couldn't wait to try it when I got back. You put different fittings on the end for different beard thicknesses, and I tried a Number 3 – and the results (even if I say so myself) were spectacular. I look a completely different person – and much more like a young professional self-employed person. There were, however, two problems resulting from the beard trim – the first being that there is an abrupt ending where the trimmed part finishes, and the untrimmed part starts. I think, therefore, I will have to get my main hair tidied and the bit where the trimmed bit meets the untrimmed bit blended somehow. The second problem was one that took me by complete surprise. When I'd trimmed my beard, I found specks of grey hair in it – quite a lot in fact. What's THAT all about? Surely I'm not heading for the 'white beard' look at my age. I suppose that when you consider all I've been through, it's not surprising, but it came as a shock.

»

5 November

17.55.03 GMT

To: All Constellations

Up and about early this morning, determined to do something about my hair today. Cide told me about a 'shop' which specialises in doing men's and women's hair and I got Nuala to book me in at 11.30 a.m. this morning.

I didn't know what to expect when I arrived (my briefing manual has very little on this sort of thing), and was pointed to a chair by a very pretty young man who then spent about five minutes running his hands and a comb through my hair and groaning to himself. I asked him what the problem was and he said something like 'Are you 'avin' a laff?' In the end he suggested – well, he TOLD me – that the best thing would be to go quite short, with some spikes and a highlight here and there. I had no idea what he was talking about, so just shut up and let him get on with it.

Can you believe it? I was there for TWO HOURS. When he'd finished and he showed me the all-round view in the reflector I nearly had a fit. You simply would not recognise me. I'll confess, though, that after the initial shock had worn off, I quite like my new look. Anyway, that's all for now – it's nearly six o'clock in the evening and I am due to meet Cide in the bar then. Apparently this date is an annual festival and he has invited me to the inn's firework display, which is part of the celebrations. I've just got to put some 'gel' on this hair, and I'm ready to go. I wonder what they'll make of my new look.

»

6 November

11.23.42 GMT

To: All Constellations

I was the hit of the party! Surprisingly, I have got to know most of the hotel staff – or, at least, they know me by sight – and a lot of them were there. They all liked my new look. It's a pity that Nuala was one of the few absentees – I would have liked to show off to her.

The main topic of conversation – both at the festival and in the media at the moment – concerns the designate king of this country, a prince called Charles. Opinions about him seem very mixed. Over a few vessels of the Boddingtons early on in the evening, Cide told me his view about Charles. That view (summarised) was that he, the prince, was as much use as 'a barrel of cold piss'. (That's another one of his expressive sayings.) Now, I've thought about this a lot and I cannot think of any uses for such a barrel, so I assume his opinion is negative, and that does seem to be reflective of many people's view of this monarch-in-waiting. As to his princess (who I saw on television with him), she doesn't look like any princess I've come across before. In fact, if you get her from a particular angle, she looks a bit like *Sheshe* – my old (favourite) camel from way back.

The festival was a bit of a let down. We didn't leave the bar until about 10.00 p.m. and when we got outside the fireworks had all finished. This didn't seem to bother the lads too much, so we went back inside and had some more of the Boddingtons. I had learned my lesson, though – this time I avoided the *kebab*.

»

7 November

08.45.23 GMT

To: All Constellations

More about this prince. It's a bit complicated, and I cannot think of a similar model with any of you. His mother is the Queen (i.e. a reigning monarch) but she doesn't decide anything – that's all done by a kind of senate. Nevertheless, the Queen and her family – and in particular this prince – are constantly written about in the journals and shown on TV. The prince is clearly waiting for his mother to die and seems to just wander about the place telling people what he thinks, without anybody paying him the slightest bit of attention. There is much more for me to learn and understand about the power structure here because there do seem to be many anomalies. Here's an example. This prince was married, and he had a mistress. Now, he's not the first in the universe and he won't be the last – and I bet a few of you are reddening a bit while reading this – but here's the weird bit: his wife was *very* attractive, while his mistress (as noted) looked like a camel. Surely that's the wrong way around, isn't it? I mean, what's the point? Bear with me, I'll find out more.

»

8 November

11.20.34 GMT

To: All Constellations

Yesterday brought another strange expression from Cide. We were planning for him to give me my first golf lesson, but when he got in he said he felt quite poorly. Apparently, he had caught something that they call a 'cold', and one of the symptoms, as he quaintly described it, was that his 'nose was running like a glass-blower's arse'.

It took me a while to figure this one out. I understand the principles involved in glass-blowing, and that it puts pressure on other parts of your body. I had assumed this would be via the eyes or nose – but when I tried to simulate the action back in the privacy of my room I realised that leakage from the rectum might be possible as a result of the extreme internal pressures created. This is a fascinating language and I am learning more every day.

This 'cold' thing is very common, by the way. Around this time of year, apparently, everybody gets one – and begins to take off a pre-agreed amount of 'sickies' (i.e. days off work), which augment the holiday allowances. The genesis of this can be traced back about fifty years when this country's government, under the guidance of someone called Beveridge and another called Bevan, started to provide doctors and medicines free for all the population. It was precisely at that moment they discovered that everybody in the country was ill.

»

9 November

09.35.28 GMT

To: All Constellations

I've received a message from the Corner Office – that I have to undertake my first project. But first let me tell you about golf. I had my delayed lesson yesterday, and for quite a while I had no idea what all the fuss was about. Now, I am known as having quite good ball–hand–eye coordination, but I confess that when Cide first put one of the thin steel bats in my hand I had great difficulty even hitting the small white ball they use. I swished and I swashed, causing Cide much mirth, but couldn't get the ball to go any distance or in the right direction. And then suddenly, without any apparent reason, I connected and the ball flew for MILES (it seemed) in the general direction in which I was pointing. Cide gave me a big clap, and I was mesmerised. I tried it again, and it seemed that the magic had disappeared as fast as it came – but then whammo, another one. By the time we finished, I was hitting quite a few good ones off the practice 'tee', and I was feeling a strange sensation. I couldn't wait to get back to his little shop, and – much to his delight – spent about £1300 on some steel bats (called 'clubs', I'm told) and all sorts of stuff he told me I had to have.

»

10 November

11.23.11 GMT

To: All Constellations

I am in serious trouble with the Corner Office. I had hardly pressed the 'send' button on yesterday's bulletin, when my BLa started vibrating. Apparently, the spending of more than one thousand pounds on golf equipment is not considered mission-critical by you-know-who, and I got a serious dressing down. It seems that this expenditure, coming on top of me having my hair highlighted, sent Somebody who shall be Nameless into a bit of a paddy – a real hissy-fit. The language was not as expressive as some I've been getting used to in this location, but I got the message. I am to start NOW – not this afternoon, not tomorrow, but NOW – in planning my first project, with a view to implementing it within days NOT WEEKS.

I am to visit Granada, in a country called Spain, and examine in detail the Great Palace of Alhambra. While I am there I am also to soak in as much as I can about one of the Great Issues facing this planet: the conflict between Islam and Christianity. The Palace represents the last (and possibly greatest) outpost of Islam in Europe and (apparently) echoes with the sounds of the historic conflicts between these two belief systems. These conflicts are now as fierce as ever, and the fundamentalists on both sides seem as wide apart as ever. If I am to achieve my goals, it is critical that I get to understand why this has happened and how the conflict manifests itself today. From my early planning I see that there are golf courses in nearby Malaga, so it's not all gloom.

»

11 November

12.13.34 GMT

To: All Constellations

I have done some initial planning for my project, which will entail me flying in one of these aeroplanes that have become so common on this planet. It seems a very cumbersome way to get from A to B, and I'm not sure how I feel about it from a safety point of view. I will have to travel to a place called Luton, down in the south of this country (ironically, where I have 'come from'), where I will catch a plane to Malaga, and then travel by bus to Granada. They speak a different language there, so I am busy learning a few phrases in Spanish.

There is one practical point I need to factor in, which is that I will not be able to take the communications device I use for these bulletins with me. Apparently, there is a risk that it might be inspected by the government officials at the point(s) where I will cross international borders, and we cannot take the risk at this stage that it will be confiscated and examined. It is designed to look like a common portable (or 'laptop') personal computer, and we have branded it with the most common name used on the planet (Dell), but the risk is still judged to be not worth taking.

»

12 November

09.30.15 GMT

To: All Constellations

I can't believe this: I've got one of those 'cold' things. As you know, I've been in some tough situations in my 'life', but I've never had green slime coming out of my nose. I went out last night, just to sample more of life in a local tavern, and I didn't dry my hair properly after I had washed it. Today, I feel horrible, with this 'running' nose and many feverish symptoms. I'm staying in my room all day – I just don't feel like going out.

I will take advantage of my 'forced' confinement to look more into the music culture of the planet. It is very important to almost everybody, although no two people seem to like the same kind of thing. My communication device – the one that looks like a Dell laptop – is fitted with a software programme that has been made to look like something called *iTunes*, which is a popular way for people to record, store and access their favourite music. The only difference is that my *iTunes* has every piece of music ever recorded on earth on it. I have been given a list of what our research team thinks are the popular pieces with which I should be familiar, so I have an interesting day ahead.

»

13 November

11.56.01 GMT

To: All Constellations

Not a good day yesterday – and frankly I do not feel much better today. I spent yesterday in bed, feeling really sorry for myself. I had no appetite to eat or drink – and, strangely, I shivered for most of the time although the room was very warm.

I didn't really get far with the music plan. They have things called 'genres' down here, by which you categorise music, and I didn't really have any idea where to start. I decided, in the end, to try something called 'easy listening' as it seemed best suited to my mood and predicament, but it was just awful. The first piece was by somebody called Neil Sedaka. It made me want to scream to blot out the sound. Things went downhill from there as a long stream of 'entertainers' (WHAT a misnomer) warbled more songs of 'easy listening' that couldn't possibly have been more difficult to endure. After about an hour of being tortured by people with strange names (like Engelbert Humperdinck, Matt Munro, Fats Domino, the Singing Nun), I gave up. It was making me feel worse.

On this subject of music, there is some good news for me. I must understand and involve myself in it more – it is so important to the culture. My briefing manual tells me that I must go out and buy something called an 'iPod', which I can adapt and then transfer on to it the stuff I end up liking from this *iTunes* nightmare.

The day ended on a positive note – well, two positive notes actually. After a long time with it switched off, I tried some more music, and put it on 'random play'. Something quite astonishing came out, although I thought I'd done something which played the music at the wrong speed. As it transpired, it was a song sung by a man called Tom Waits, and after a couple of minutes I realised that this is how he MEANT it to sound. In two more minutes I was completely hooked. He sounded just like I feel.

The second piece of good news is that, at about 10.00 p.m., there was a knock on my door. It was Nuala, who was just finishing her time on the desk, and had heard from the bedroom-cleaning lady that I was ill. She kindly brought me some white tablets that she thought would help me recover. She only stayed a minute, but I felt as though I was well on the road to recovery after she'd gone – and that's without taking a tablet. Strange. I don't know whether I mentioned it, but she has wonderful green eyes.

»

14 November

09.45.23 GMT

To: All Constellations

Another bollocking from the Corner Office – this time to the effect that I am unlikely to be making much progress with my Five Key Goals if I am 'entertaining' a woman in my room at 'nearly midnight' and listening to Tom Waits. And I am not to even THINK about taking my golf clubs to Spain.

Sounds like somebody got out of bed on the wrong side this morning, but I have no time to ponder about confusing criticisms like this, I have a journey and project to plan. I have booked my plane tickets to Malaga, which is the nearest place to Granada where the plane lands, and I did this on a thing called the Internet. This is a very primitive data access and communicating system that has been up and running on earth for about fifteen years. We (the SCSC) all agreed we had to wait for this to be 'invented' before we attempted this mission, but, frankly, we hoped that it would have progressed (technically) a lot more than it has done by now. Still, I managed to book some flights and an inn in Spain for my project, and to make sure it was a risk-free process I used the office computer downstairs in the inn – which Nuala let me use when nobody else was about. Cide had already shown me how to access information on his computer in the golf shop. What happens is that there is a tiny space on the screen, which is called a Google, or something, and you just write in what you want. He is funny. To show me how it works he just typed in the words 'I need a shag' – you would not believe what came up on the screen.

»

15 November

11.25.03 GMT

To: All Constellations

I have been getting a lot of queries from you, and I will use today's bulletin to answer two questions that seem to be causing a lot of you some bother.

First question: 'Why Granada, and the Great Palace at Alhambra, for my project visit?' The first thing to point out is that this was a difficult choice, with quite a number of options discussed. There was some pragmatism – this is my first 'journey', so it's testing out a number of practical things around transport and travel in a low-key, low-risk sort of way. The Palace, however, is a valid subject for my first mission. Tracking the media, it is clear now that the clash of Islam and Christian democracy is STILL at the centre of much of the planet's frictions – there is just a change of cast and locations from the ones we know so well. Over the past one hundred earth years, two of the four the prime systems of government on earth (democracy, communism, theology and totalitarianism) have been all but eradicated – namely, communism and totalitarianism. The two that are left are all but re-creating the Crusades, and it is not hard to find the 'equivalent' cast members making a re-appearance (i.e. Pope Urban and his warlord Earl Godfrey seemed alive and well in the persons of George W. Bush and Tony Blair, and Saladin seems reincarnate in Osama Bin Laden). There are superficial differences in that democracy does not fight under the sign of the Cross (officially anyway), and theology does not fight under the flag of a single nation – but is as much of a unified *jihad* as it was three-quarters of a millennium ago. All this needs thinking about, as I will have to work near the front of this conflict, and a good place to reflect and understand more about it is thought to be the 'high tide' point of Islam in Europe – the Alhambra. So that's where I'm off in a few days

The second question that seems to be bugging you is about Norman Clarke (see November 4th bulletin). Where did he spring from? Who is he? Is he staying at the same inn? These and other (similar) questions indicate that I have left a lot of you confused. He is not a real person (in the context I referred to him at least) – it is just that his name is written on the small machine that I used to trim my beard. I think this is because he invented it – but I'm not sure. What matters is that this is called 'branding' – which many of you will recognise as the old practice of burning your initials on a goat's hind-quarters. It's the same thing in principle, but has moved on immensely over the past centuries. Every thing you buy – even an 'invisible' service – has a brand name attached to it, and this is important because, according to the marketing department (which reports into the SCSC), if I am to achieve my medium- to long-term goals, I will have to become a 'brand'. What an odd thought.

»

16 November

09.55.25 GMT

To: All Constellations

I have been invited to accompany Cide for a night out on Saturday (the day after tomorrow). The logistics seem odd because he said we'll be going 'Up 't' pub' when parts of the road are clearly downhill, but that's just typical of the anomalies I have to sort out every day in these, the early weeks of my mission. Apparently, I will be meeting a few 'older' people, including Cide's granddad – which will be good for me. I have always thought that a meeting of a tribe's elders is a good place to get background information on attitudes and culture, and I am looking forward to a good old debate on stuff.

One incident that caught me off guard a bit happened this morning. I mentioned to Nuala that I would be going out for a drink with Cide and this group of elders, and her response was (and I quote): 'Christ, you're not going out with that pissy old bunch are you?' As you can imagine, the blood drained from my face when I heard the first part of that response, but it was (thankfully) a false alarm. It is a harmless expression, used as a vague sort of expletive. And there was me thinking the game was up. On that subject, I think we can say I've survived the first few weeks – always the most difficult – without raising too many suspicions. I'm getting more and more at ease with the ways of talking and behaving around here. Fairly soon, I think we can move on from this 'base camp'.

»

17 November

13.25.03 GMT

To: All Constellations

Here's another oddity about this place – the kind of thing that you simply cannot cover in a briefing document. It's the kind of tiny thing I face day by day. It's the kind of thing that simply does not make sense – but it is obviously so ingrained in day-to-day life that if you express surprise when you see it, it can cause folk to look at you in a weird way. I was in the inn's drinks bar at mid-day and Cide came in. He is one of those who indulges in a very popular habit here called 'smoking cigarettes' – whereby the leaves of a plant are dried and rolled up in paper, and you then set fire to them and inhale the fumes. I noticed that, when Cide took out his little box containing these 'cigarettes' so as to remove one and set fire to it (and I'm not making this up), it says on the front something like (this may not be entirely accurate; I was reading it upside down) 'This activity will kill you'. Now, unless you are a martyr, it would seem to me that the avoidance of killing yourself is a prime motivator – but everybody (it seems) cheerfully ignores this warning on cigarette parcels, particularly if they are drinking the Boddingtons. If any of you have similar examples that will help me better understand this sort of behaviour and thinking, please let me have them.

»

18 November

09.24.07 GMT

To: All Constellations

Oh, this is funny. I just picked up in the media today – both television and journals – that people of the same gender are now allowed to form a legal relationship, rather like marriage. A lot of the media are in uproar about this, and I must make sure I bring this subject up tonight in the pub with the tribal elders. I remember when we had this debate in the Corner Office – and Somebody (Who shall be Nameless but Who was in a bad mood that day) issued the edict that, although PHYSICALLY there would be two sexes, in reality there would be three – with an indeterminate one in the middle. The joke was, of course, that we wouldn't tell anybody that there were three, and we could be entertained as they tried to sort it out. Oh, how we laughed – and it's all come to pass. I'm pleased to report it's caused consternation on this planet ever since.

Nuala gave me a big grin at breakfast today, and advised me to have a lot of mashed potato before I go out tonight. She seems a wise lady, so I will do so although I do not understand why I would need to do this.

»

20 November

11.25.34 GMT

To: All Constellations

I apologise. I missed a bulletin yesterday, and it was due to an entirely self-inflicted wound. I had what they call a hangover – which is the after-effect of too much alcohol. It occurred to me, during the evening, that I was setting some kind of personal record – so I started jotting down, on a little table mat that you put your beer on, all the drink that passed my lips. I started with the Boddingtons, and I recorded eight large (pint) vessels. The elders then carried on with the same drink, but as I was feeling a bit bloated, on Cide's advice, I switched to something called 'vodka', and a drink made up of three measures of that mixed with something out of a tin, which was called 'Red Bull'. I had three of those (although my records start to get a bit illegible at this stage). I remember I'd had some food before coming out, but later on I began to feel a bit hungry – so I ate a pickled egg and a jar (?) of something or somethings. I'll tell you about them later. It gets a bit vague after that, but I remember Cide's grandfather (more about him in a bit) announcing that he would have a nightcap of something called a 'Jamesons', so I had one of them (a large one apparently). Actually I had five of them as there is a tradition around here that you must buy your drinks in 'rounds' so, if there are five of you, you cannot drink in multiples of less than five. At least, Cide told me I had five – and he told me that somewhat admiringly. I have to rely on him because my records simply disappear under some sort of stain on my 'beer mat' around this time – and I have absolutely no recollection of the latter stages of the evening, apart from being sick (twice).

I spent yesterday in bed, unable to move. Cide knocked on my door about 2.30 p.m. and I managed to get to it and open it. He could hardly stop laughing, particularly – and this is SO embarrassing but I am committed to recording this mission honestly and in full – as it became apparent that I had urinated in my clothes cupboard during the night. I thought this was terrible and that I might be arrested by the police, but he pushed me back in the bed and (amid much laughter) he and Nuala cleaned everything up for me.

Such embarrassment. I don't know how I can face them again. Anyway, now you know – that's how I missed a day. You know what? I thought I was over it when I started this bulletin, but the memories have made me feel ill again, and I need to go back and lie down.
I'll finish this tomorrow.

»

21 November

09.57.23 GMT

To: All Constellations

No I won't. I am REALLY annoyed. Somebody – one of you – has accessed my communications. It has to be so – no one on this planet has the knowledge to do it. I opened my screen this morning and there among the messages was a source I didn't recognise. Somewhat nervously, I opened the message – to get what? 'An invitation to a course of treatment to enlarge my penis', that's what. How dare you, whoever you are? As if this mission isn't difficult enough, I get some clever dick not only making fun of my penis size, but cluttering up my communicating device with idiotic junk. I'm signing off, right now – and I'm going to use my BLa to get somebody from the SCSC to look into this.

»

22 November

08.23.45 GMT

To: All Constellations

Ooops! Apologies. Apparently, we have underestimated some earth-people. There are a very limited number of anally retentive people here who can penetrate almost any networked communications system, and they do so – sometimes just to prove they can, sometimes for money. Some of them invent things called viruses, which tunnel into your system and wreck it – but the majority seem to want to sell penis-enlargement treatments. My briefing manual has been useless in helping me understand this – just what is the deal here? Have they all got tiny penises on this planet? Now I've written that, I'm not sure what the plural of 'penis' is – it might be penii. Don't know; don't care. But I have been ordered to apologise for my rant at my Constellation Mailing List members. You were unfairly accused – the culprit is down here.

Who ordered me to apologise? I'll give you two guesses. Anyway, apparently, I need to go out and buy anti-virus and anti-SPAM software before I use this again for confidential stuff. If I get one that works for an ordinary earth-based system, apparently the gang in the Technical Centre will be able to adapt it from there.

»

24 November

09.34.56 GMT

To: All Constellations

Got it! The software came in a box with a picture of a Panda on it. (You know, one of those big Chinese bears – the ones we thought about transferring to another planet.) We should now be all clear and screened. I lost a day yesterday as it took me some time to identify and acquire what I wanted – but I found it eventually, and the technical part was loaded onto a small disc. It took us a bit to adapt it. Actually, it took the 'techies' a bit to adapt it – I just sat down this end with my BLa earphones in and pressed the keys and buttons they asked me to. One interesting by-product is that we now know who transmits all this stuff on earth – we know their identities and their source. Somebody in the SCSC suggested we should 'anonymously' make this available to the authorities on the planet as it seems to be causing such a problem, but my wise counsel prevailed – I might be able to use this information, these people and this process later. If people will listen to messages about enlarging their penises (?), they might listen to anything. I'll give it the rest of the day to de-bug it, then we can get on with the important stuff.

»

25 November

11.56.23 GMT

To: All Constellations

Right, I'm back to normal running. We were covering the events of the night out with the elders before I got sidetracked with my illness and my communications malfunction. A word about the characters first. As you know, I have got to know Cide quite well over the past few weeks. I'm not saying we are friends, but he may well be a key relationship in helping me achieve my half-year goals. He is younger than me – about thirty. As you already know, he runs a golf shop and manages the arena where they play golf. A point of interest here – it is a strange arena, not at all like the ones I think you are familiar with. It goes on for miles, and there are no areas for spectators. I haven't had a game yet, but I will do so when I come back from Spain and tell you how it works.

Back to Cide. He is a local man, having been born and bred in this part of the planet. He was actually born in a big metropolis called Manchester, which is about twenty-five miles away, but his family moved here when he was about six years old. This is one reason why I am cultivating his friendship – I must start my mission in a small way, and get to know a small community and their ways, and he seems to know everybody and how everything works.

It's important you get a picture, so let me describe him. He's not tall – about 1.75 metres. He seems to spend a lot of his available money on himself – he has a big variety of clothes and his hairstyle (and colour) changes frequently. He is not fat, but has a bit of a protruding belly, which he squeezes into trousers that are meant for a smaller size. If he wears short sleeves he reveals a tattoo (which is a permanent skin decoration). The tattoo consists of four letters – CTID – which, he tells me, stand for 'City Till I Die'. This is a reference to the soccer tribe he supports (which he has promised to take me to see) called Manchester City. There is a sad story behind his love of this tribe. His father supported them, and it was he who introduced Cide to them. But his father deserted the family when Cide was six years old. He has never seen, or heard of, his father since. He and his mother then came back to this area to live with her parents, and his grandfather effectively became his father. It is his grandfather who he drinks with regularly, and who was part of the fun on Saturday night.

To complete the picture – perhaps a bit more detail than you need – Cide (currently) has dark brown hair, with some lighter bits in it, which are like mine and come from the same place. Sometimes his face goes a bit orange, but that is just after his visit to the 'tanning shop' – where you buy some time under an artificial sun or you get sprayed with a fake sun-tan coloured stain (can you believe that?). His face is open and friendly, with his jaw-line now losing its youthful sharpness. His face only occasionally shows signs of the sadness he must feel about his missing father. Sometimes I feel I can see it around his eyes.

Let me pause there. I'll tell you about the night out when I write tomorrow – I promise – but I feel you should digest this character before we introduce more of the cast. He tries to be simple, but I suspect he is quite complex. He laughs a lot, and makes other people laugh – but I suspect he is quietly sad when he goes off his own self-made stage. He is the life and soul of any gathering that includes him, but I suspect he enjoys his occasional solitude. I feel he will have a part to play in my journey.

»

26 November

09.36.23 GMT

To: All Constellations

Cide and I walked into Whalley to meet the other three guys we were going to join for a 'few' drinks. It takes about half an hour for me, a bit less for Cide who was already dressed and ready to go when I knocked on his door. On the way in, he told me who we were going to meet.

The most important was his grandfather, mentioned above. He's apparently simply known as Sid, or 'Lord'. The latter is short for Lord Whalley, and does not reflect the fact that he was titled or aristocratic, but rather his habit of sitting in the same spot in the small (tap) room of the local pub for about forty years and 'lording' it over everyone. Apparently he had once yelled at a new bar-tender for service, and the guy (not knowing the essential who's-who of the tap room) had replied, in an equally loud voice, that he would get round to serving the Lord of all He Surveys as and when he fucking could. He (the bar-tender) didn't last long – but the nickname did. Apart from that, and the fact that he was eighty-two years old and had spent his life working for the regional railway company before he retired at the age of sixty-five, the only pre-briefing I got was that I shouldn't be offended by anything he said. He liked meeting new people, but liked to test them early on – and if they turned out to be a bit 'precious' he'd just ditch them.

In the last few paces before getting to the pub, Cide gave me a thumbnail sketch about the other two. One of them was Dave, although everybody called him 'Skins' because he had been a drummer (percussionist) in a popular 'group' some forty years ago. Cide wasn't sure, but thought Dave was about sixty, which was about five years younger than the other guy we were to meet. He was named Rhys, and whereas the other two were both locals, this man was distinguished by the fact that he was from Wales, which is a separate nation although it is attached to the same island land mass and is less than one hundred miles from here. He was also retired, having been a policeman – and had come up to this area to live with his married daughter after being widowed.

It was a sparse briefing, but I recognised the three of them just as soon as we entered the pub. They were all wiry guys, with two of them illustrating what you shouldn't do when you lose your hair on top – Rhys having grown a 'pony-tail' and Dave having let it grow long at the back and over his ears, almost to his shoulders. Sid had met the problem head on by cropping his hair all over to what must have been a 'number one' on his Norman Clarke. Sid didn't stand up as we went over, but the other two did. He greeted me with (what Cide told me later) was a quite friendly opening burst: 'You must be Tom. Cide's been telling us you're a good lad, 'cept in a few things where you don't know your arse from your elbow. Here 'yar – sit thee down. I'll get 'em in.'

Actually, it occurs to me that if you are going to get the best from me reflecting the evening and its contents, I should record more of the conversation. The actual words used give much more 'life' to the contents we covered – and the attitudes and prevailing culture. It's a good time to pause so I can try to remember it verbatim.

»

27 November

09.56.23 GMT

To: All Constellations

Picking up where I left off – I was confused by the accusation that I didn't know my 'arse from my elbow'. My briefing manual had made all this quite clear and I was not only quite certain I knew the difference, but I could also point it out on a diagram if required. I decided just to let it ride – wisely, as it turned out. It was not the first time I was to be confused during the course of the evening.

I volunteered to help Sid carry the 'round' of drinks back from the bar for the five of us. As we both reached the bar, he surprised me by ordering SIX 'pints-a-bitter'. I reminded him that there were only five of us, and he gave me a really odd look. 'Have you any idea' he said 'how long it takes to pull six pints of the Bodds? I'll sup one while we're waiting.' And he did. Made sense.

These guys have been friends for years, and I'm telling you this because they ended up yelling at (and insulting) each other. I was fascinated because these were men who had witnessed three generations of this planet, and I felt their views and reflections would be important to my understanding of the big issues. I'll try and remember their exact words on some of them:

Football (also known as soccer) is a big thing in these parts, with almost everybody having a tribal affiliation with one 'team' or another. The players, results and gossip form a big part of most (male) conversations – and these guys were no different, with the exception of Rhys, the guy from Wales. His point (made loudly) was that another game – called rugby – was a real man's game, and that (I think I have this correct) football was played by a bunch of 'bejewelled, braided, moisturised chutney-ferrets'. His game was played by real men, and the supporters were civilised – respecting the opposition and never wrecking the grounds they played in or the surrounding communities. Skins' response was that that was because the Welsh were all 'dysfunctional, parasitic, joyless, whingeing twats'. This went on and on, and it was difficult to remember how friendly these three guys were. I understood most of it, and my slang overrider software has helped me with the rest, but neither I nor my program can come up with anything for 'chutney-ferret'. Can anybody throw light on this one?

From sport the conversation went on to cover some of the planet's conflict issues, and again, if only to remind myself, I must stress the friendship of these men. Indeed, half way through the attack on the Welsh, in fact right in between 'parasitic' and 'joyless' – which, to me, would have been deeply insulting had I been of Welsh origin – Skins paused to confirm his beer order to Rhys, who then disappeared to the bar and left him ranting to an empty chair. (Sid was temporarily talking to someone else.)

We bridged from sport to other issues via comments on the recent death and proposed statue of the soccer star George Best (who I'd heard of in the news earlier). Sid was really up for this one. The footballer, who had drunk himself to death, had been awarded a state funeral in

Northern Ireland, which is another affiliated nation, like Wales, just a couple of hundred miles away. This was, apparently, in Sid's view, 'total bollocks'. He didn't seem to take a deep breath but he must have done because he suddenly let fly:

'Greatest player ever? Total, total bollocks. Wasn't even best player in't team, Law was. An' as for all this weepin' and moanin' and fillin' every fookin' paper and TV screen with it, that's all bollocks as well. An' what's all this crap about puttin' shrines everywhere? Drive up every road and there's a mess of old flowers on it somewhere where some pillock's been knocked off his bike. Fook me, we got bombed to fook in't war and next morning we 'ad to get kids to school. Went through all that without puttin' fookin' flowers all over't pavement. An' this son of his, that pillock, he were never on't scene till Bestie threw a six and what sort of name is fookin' Callum anyway? He did nowt for Ireland, which is a shit-heap anyway, so what's all this hero bollocks? Jesus, give us another Boddies. It's all because of fookin' America this. I can't stand this cryin' in public, that's not what we are about. Fook them and this bollocks about "closure" an' everythin'.'

In all fairness, after this particular piece of oratory, the others were silent for a few seconds. It was as though a master had spoken, and the occasion needed a few moments of reverence. I followed most of it (I had been aware of the controversy in all the media) although a couple of things threw me. Two-thirds of the way through, I thought it was a personal command to me, so I started to stand up to get another round – but it wasn't my turn and I realised I had nearly tripped up again. And it was only afterwards that I found out that 'throw a six' is a local expression meaning to die. Interestingly, its origin is from games where you have to throw a six on a die to BEGIN playing, so it would seem to signal the start of something rather than the end – which is a train of thought I must follow up. Could be useful.

After that the evening became a bit fuzzy. Sid's reference to the 'bombing' was from what they call down here the Second World War, but which we know as the latter part of the 1914–45 Intra-Planetary Conflict. (Remember? There was no real gap between the First and Second 'World' Wars.)

We got on to the modern conflict between (it seems to me) democracy and theology – where there had been a recent bombing in the capital city (London). In this group, the enemy was described (by Rhys – but with the support of the others) as 'them bastards'. This is grammatically incorrect (it should be *those* bastards), but I let it ride. The preferred option as to what to do about it seemed confused, but that may have been the beer affecting them as it was (by now) surely affecting me. Their strategy seemed to range between an unusual approach of just leaving 'the fookers' alone to 'pray their bollocks off all day and treat their women like shit' to (what would seem to me) a contradictory policy of 'bomb every one of the twats into a black sticky paste.'

I do not remember much more. At a late stage, Sid came back with his round of drinks, and gave us all the small glass jar (see above) that contained (so he said) something called 'cockles'. It was only when I was well into them that I realised they were shellfish, and should therefore have been refused by me in accordance with my dietary constraints (as I had refused some things called 'pork scratchings' earlier). It was too late. They looked like nothing I had ever seen before, and extremely unappetising, but I dared not risk seeming to be 'odd man out' so I ate them. I knew something was wrong with me fairly quickly after that, and Sid noticed it too. The last words I remember from the evening were his to me. Grinning, he told me not to forget to put the bog paper in the fridge overnight.

»

28 November

10.48.45 GMT

To: All Constellations

That was a more than a week ago, and I'm only just fully recovered. Nuala and Cide still regard what happened to me as a source of much hilarity (which is a quite different position from that taken by Somebody in the Corner Office). My position is simple: it is only by mixing with ordinary people – particularly those who prove to be accessible, talkative and experienced – that I will find out the issues concerning this society and the positions taken. Only then can I make progress without risk. I will certainly seek more audiences with Sid, Skins and Rhys – although I will cut down on the alcohol and avoid the shellfish next time.

»

29 November

10.23.56 GMT

To: All Constellations

You are not going to believe this. In each of the rooms in the inn, there is a small machine – in the room where the water comes out of the faucet in the ceiling – which weighs you. I know from my pre-mission medical that I was 1.83 metres tall and weighed 83.8 kilograms when I set out. It is only two earth-months ago but I have put weight on. And not just a little bit either – I am nearly FIVE KILOS heavier. I was struggling to zip up my trousers this morning and couldn't figure out why, although I presumed they'd shrunk. I suddenly thought that I should check my weight on this machine, and there it was – the truth. This has never happened to me before. I let the SCSC know early this morning, as it might be of significance, and they said they'd get back to me. They didn't sound best pleased at the news.

Meanwhile, I need to nip out and buy some more trousers. My waist size says 34 inches on the pair I have – I think I'd better up it an inch or two.

»

30 November

11.34.35 GMT

To: All Constellations

Interestingly, Nuala had noticed my weight gain, but had been too polite to mention it. When I told her what had happened to my weight number she smiled and told me it often happened to people who came 'up north' and stayed for a bit. She thought my custard slices were much to blame, but I only have two or three a day. She also told me that the Boddingtons doesn't help either, and that I should chuck a few vodka and slim-line tonics in the mix. She is a very helpful lady. I'm not sure I told you but her eyes are a lovely green.

The SCSC came back to me directly on this weight thing. They are very concerned, and it was accompanied by a VERY pointed BLa message from the Corner Office about the need for discipline. Apparently my 'image' will be very important on my mission, and it will be critical that I stay quite lean – which has never been a problem in the past. Anyway, the SCSC have put a task-force together and will be coming out with a diet and exercise sheet for me to follow. They are also considering getting me to start this smoking thing – apparently (somehow) it helps you stay thin. I just don't know what's happening here – this is new and troubling.

This diet thing is going to have to wait till I get back. I got some new trousers, and some items I have been advised that I will need to travel. I'm all set to leave for Spain tomorrow. I get a railway train down to a place called Milton Keynes, and then a bus to Luton, which is the place the aeroplane goes from. I'm staying overnight at an inn by the airport and then I fly out very early the day after tomorrow to Malaga with someone or something called Monarch. I'll be gone about a week, and – as I have already noted – I will NOT be taking this communications device in case it is examined and seen to be odd by the authorities. We hope to have this sorted in time for any future visits, and I will, of course, be taking my BLa – mine is indistinguishable from the normal earth model.

DECEMBER

»

9 December

09.34.27 GMT

To: All Constellations

Back at last – late last night, in fact. I had paid for the room while I was away (which raised a few eyebrows, and I need to make sure I think through a plausible reason why I would do that – and quickly now I'm back).

I'm not going to dwell too much on the travelling. In the context of history, the distance of my journey was interesting in that it seemed to hold up the old Central Office theory about 'comfortable travel' distances in a day. In 1800 it was 24 miles, in 1900 it was 120 miles and now it's about 600 miles. On the actual day of my flight, I covered a bit more than that, but it seems about right. Whether the SCSC projections come true (3,000 miles in a day in the earth-year 2100, and 15,000 in 2200) is a matter of extreme doubt in my mind – but who would have thought 600 miles was 'do-able' on this planet two hundred years ago? Score one for the back-room boys.

Very quick summary: I got a train from another nearby metropolis (Preston) and travelled south to Milton Keynes. This was uneventful, although I had to sit near a man who spent much of the time shouting into a small communication device sticking out of his ear. I found it quite annoying and intrusive, apart from the two times when I found it quite funny – once when we went under a bridge and he realised the other person wasn't there, and then when (I think) his battery ran out.

That journey took a couple of hours, then I caught a bus to the airport at a place called Luton, where I stayed the night at an inn (actually called the Holiday Inn). I had an evening free as the plane did not depart until early the following morning, so I decided not to waste it. I got a 'taxi' (a driver with a car who you pay to take you where you want to go – you know the principle, you've all got these in different guises) to the metropolis centre. It was VERY SIMILAR to Burnley, and I reflected on something I remember Skins saying during our night out – that anybody wanting to make a fortune in Burnley could start a company called White Taxis. But I don't think Skins likes a lot of people, let alone those who look and sound different to him. Anyway, there were very few of what I have come to recognise as 'native' English faces. I had a meal at an Indian restaurant (another nation on my 'to visit' list), or, at least I had two mouthfuls of the meal. I didn't believe the first mouthful, so I had another. I thought I was trying to eat flowing lava.

Early next morning, I went to the airport to catch my plane – which would transport me through the air to Spain. Because of the nature of modern conflict, where aeroplanes can be turned into weapons in the wrong hands, I had to answer some questions that obviously were designed to spot whether I was going to do this. I was confused. Surely, if I was going to do this, I wouldn't tell them so. When I had my ticket validated they gave me a card with my seat number on, and I then had to wait an hour or so for the plane to be ready. It was a nice waiting area, with many shops – but I only bought a cup of coffee, which cost me THREE TIMES what it costs in Whalley.

The plane taking off was a bit frightening, but nobody seemed to bother. Soon after we were in the air, one of the ladies came and asked me when I wanted my champagne – which confused me. She then asked to see my ticket and, sure enough, when I booked the ticket on the computer (I used the one on the inn's reception office), I had mistakenly ticked the 'quarter bottle of champagne' offer – in fact, I had not only ticked it, I had ordered eight such quarter-bottles. I smiled and made myself very popular by giving it out to those passengers around me. I was going to catch up with my pre-reading (*The Ascent of Man* – still not read), but I got out my new iPod and found somebody called Rod Stewart singing The Great American Songbook and I fell fast asleep after a couple of them.

Before I get a bollocking from You-Know-Who on falling behind with my pre-reading, just let me say that I WILL do it. It's just that *The Ascent of Man* sounds terribly like the one I had to read before the start of the mission – that thing by Stephen Hawking. Everybody in the SCSC knew it by heart of course, but I couldn't figure it out at all – in fact I found it unreadable. I tried to get into it about seven or eight times, but never got beyond the second chapter. Either, as Sid would say, I don't know my arse from my elbow, or Hawking doesn't.

The arrival in Spain went smoothly enough. I had pre-booked an inn in the centre of Malaga, and the plan was to spend a day or two there, getting a feel for this new nation (new to me, that is) and its culture, before getting transport to the Alhambra. Remember – there are two reasons for me being here: to get a sense of the seminal issues in the Great Christian Democracy versus Islamic Theocracy Pissing Contest (that was Rhys's description by the way) AND to explore the possibilities of Spain as a Plan B Location in case England doesn't turn out right (see previous description of the Five Key Goals).

I got a public bus into the city centre, and found my inn without much difficulty. It was called the *Hotel Don Curro*. Most inns appear to be called hotels and this one seemed ideal for my purposes. My first walk around the metropolis centre revealed it to be entirely different to Burnley. The natives of Spain have a very light colouring to their skin, and in the streets of the centre they looked slim, prosperous and sophisticated. The opposite, in fact, of the vast majority of people I have come across in Whalley on all three counts. I found a café called *Gorki,* and when I looked at the menu card, I had a delightful surprise. I don't know what I had been expecting – the usual Burnley variations on pie and chips, I think – but there it was: *rabo de toro*. One of my all-time favourites – the tail of the bull cooked slowly in red grape wine. I cannot tell you how happy I felt, sat outside the café in the gentle evening sun (remember, this is still a northern 'winter') and washing it down with a glass of wine. I read and translated as much as I could of the menu for future reference, and noted another favourite, *canejo*, bringing back memories of those wild rabbits we used to catch and cook. I'll be back tomorrow.

The hotel proved comfortable, although I had a broken night. I had read about *flamenco* dancing when I was putting this trip together, and I think somebody was practising it in the room above me all night.

The next day I concentrated on planning the journey to Alhambra – finding the bus station, reserving a ticket to nearby Granada, and sorting out a supply of local money. I had been well briefed on this. There is a different unit of currency here, and I needed to test if my virtual currency cards worked here. All went smoothly – great job guys! I also had to book my ticket for the Alhambra, which for some reason you have to buy in advance from the BBVA bank. This enabled me to choose a time for the visit, so I firmed up my plan to travel to Granada the next day in the morning, visit the palace in the afternoon – and then return to Malaga in the evening.

In the afternoon, I allowed myself a sentimental visit to the bullfight arena – the *Plaza de Toros.* Now THIS is what I call an arena. I found the Spanish language strangely familiar, and there are nothing like the dialectic and vernacular oddities I find in my Whalley base with Cide and his bunch. In the evening I made a bit of a mistake, deciding to pop into a *bodega* before I went for my *canejo*. The first of these had wine in barrels, but it is only after I had had a few glasses – normally no problem – that I realised that it was *fortified* wine. I hadn't realised how powerful it was until, during my meal, a minstrel came round the tables and started to sing. It took a while, but then I recognised it as one of Rod Stewart's Great American Songbook, from my iPod, so I joined in with the bit I remembered. He (the minstrel) got a bit 'precious' about that (as Cide would say). If I say so myself, I have a pleasing light tenor voice, but he seemed particularly unhappy at my contribution, and stomped off. I slept well that night.

The next morning I felt a bit delicate on the bus as we began the climb up the foothills of the glorious *Sierra Nevada*. I was seated next to a man of about my own age, with long, dark hair framing his friendly, tanned face. When I say 'tanned' I do not mean with the orangey colour that Cide has when he comes back from the tanning salon – this is much more natural. It wasn't long before we were talking – with him showing a fair command of English. We were heading for the same place, but for slightly different reasons. He was going, rather oddly for a European Catholic I thought, to visit one of the great buildings of Islam to celebrate his own religion – or, at least, the 'great day' in 1492 when 150,000 of the Catholic Emperor Ferdinand's troops forced the surrender of the last Sultan of the Nasrid dynasty.

As we were heading for the same place, we got to chatting – and he apologised for seeming a bit on edge. This was because smoking was banned on the bus, and a couple of hours without a cigarette always made him a bit tetchy. His name was Xabi Cachaldora, and I noted he pronounced the 'x' at the start of his first name as 'sh' – which, rather ironically, is the old Arabic way. It was only when we arrived at our destination, and we both stood up to leave the bus, when I realised how tall (and skinny) my new companion was – he must have been almost two metres high.

We still had two buses to catch – the last one from Granada centre up the steep hill to the palace compound. Xabi had no ticket for the actual entrance to the palace, relying on the late time of the year to have diluted the normally frantic tourist traffic. In the end we had to wait half an hour or so, but then we entered the grounds together.

From the outside the complex looks to be a simple, brutal fortress. It is only when you are inside, and then see the inside of some of the buildings, that you realise that you are in the presence of a vision. It was the Koran's written description of Paradise that inspired the structure and style of the buildings. It was not hard to make the link.

There will be few of you on this mailing list who don't know the basic facts about these buildings and their history. For those of you who neither know nor care, let me give you the essential 'facts', as it is important in my mission and, therefore, *some* background is helpful:

There are no statues or figurative paintings in the place as Islam forbids either. It was in the Hall of Ambassadors that Columbus presented his plans to cross to the Atlantic to the new Catholic monarchs in 1492. In the Hall of the Abencerrages, the last Sultan, Boabdil, invited thirty-nine members of the Abencerrage family to dinner – and then had them all slaughtered after he had discovered one of them was having an affair with his favourite concubine, Zorayda. It was, in fact, the struggle for the affections of Zorayda which weakened the unity of the Muslims and led to the fall of Granada. The cunning of the conquering Fernando, noticing and using this weakness, inspired Machiavelli. The Duke of Wellington later found the place dilapidated, and made his base there during the Peninsular War.

I hope you found that helpful – it was just to set the scene for my visit and report.

But now let me tell you the truth. NONE OF THE ABOVE IS LIKELY TO BE CORRECT!! They are typical of the myths and legends surrounding this place, and the rubbish you read in the guidebooks. It was only by digesting the real facts – clearly defined and laid down in my briefing manual – that enabled me to see and think objectively during my visit.

Xabi, of course, was one-eyed. He was there to reflect the triumph of his world, as it was and hopefully will be again. There were no smoking restrictions in the grounds, and my tall, stringy friend was happy to spend most of his time looking out over the walls, particularly in the old fortified military zone (the Alcazaba), imagining (I expect) the sight of 150,000 Catholic soldiers ready to drop in.

I was happier letting my mind wonder about what was lost. The culture, the art, the music, the way of life. The Greeks never invented the arch, and the space within their roofed buildings was limited by the width of a structural beam – but here you could see the glorious benefits of the arch in architecture, maybe never bettered before or since. Nor has the use of water – for its sight, utility and sound – ever come together as well in one location. Here, all around me, was the core of one of the Big Issues I must understand – *why, when the best of the different worlds is so positive, do circumstances (then and now) bring out the worst?*

Another thought occurred to me. This was a long way from Whalley – in EVERY respect. For the first time I began to have some doubts about our chosen location, but maybe the 'downside' of Lancashire itself IS the main reason I'm there. *Maybe I am meant to do my best work in a shit-hole*. Maybe getting fat, eating pies, drinking the Boddingtons, constantly whingeing and living amongst twenty nationalities and five crap football teams is part of my challenge. I have much to think about.

Xabi changed his plans and joined me on my journey back from Granada to Malaga. He was much lighter in spirit on the way back – and I found out that his life had more in common with Whalley than I had first thought. He, too, was football crazy, for his local tribe team Malaga, who play in the Spanish leagues. He liked to go out and have some drinks at night, although he didn't like beer. He was also like Cide inasmuch as he spent all his available money on buying things for himself and enjoying life. He worked for a (building) construction company, which had full order books on account of the explosion in development along the coast (a lot of which was being bought by British people apparently).

We agreed to go out for a meal together that evening and, although he was due to start work very early the next day (as is the custom in the building industry over here), he surprised me by suggesting we did not meet until 9.00 p.m. In fact, we didn't eat our meal until it was past 11.00 p.m., which was very late for my newly acquired habits, but it was worth waiting for. I had *sopa de ajo* (garlic soup with an egg in it), some small fish (*sardinas*) and some hard sheep's curd cheese (*queso manchego*) to finish. Delightful. In all honesty, I could have been back you-know-where. The only problem arose when he introduced me to a drink called *sangria*. I had got de-hydrated in the day, and was quite thirsty – and took this for a simple fruit drink. I had a lot of it, which surprised Xabi. Apparently, it also surprised me, as I was sick again on the way back to the hotel, although not terribly. Luckily Xabi had left me by then and missed my embarrassment. The good news is that I have my new friend's name and address, and he told me that he was coming to England in a month or two so we promised to meet up.

I decided to stay for a few more days in Malaga. I got some earache from the Corner Office via my BLa, but there were a couple of things I wanted to experience which I felt would help me gain a wider understanding of the planet and its people. Besides, there was a bullfight on the Sunday.

Basically, you can stuff your football – and all the other games I have witnessed on the television so far. I am a fan of the *corrida*. It is not for the squeamish, and more than one member of the SCSC pointed out that my attraction to it might not prove a fit with the persona I need to portray for my mission. They really are concerned about my image, much more so than previously, but I assured them I would stay out of trouble and it can remain a secret. Interestingly, I got no complaints about me doing this from the Corner Office – and I suspect I know why. He's a fan too.

At the *venta de taquillas* I managed to get a ticket in the *sombra* (shade), and spent a most enjoyable couple of hours watching six bulls slide off their mortal coil, helped by assorted sharp poles, knives and swords. My favourite bit is when the horse-mounted *picadores* come in to stab the bull's neck to weaken its muscles, forcing it to lower its head. The horses are padded and blindfolded, but one or two always get gored – which is both magnificent and not very nice.
I was sitting next to a tourist from (I think) Germany who expressed surprise that the horses remain silent through the ordeal. I don't think he knew that their vocal cords are cut before they come into the ring. After two hours of mostly clean kills, with one of the matadors getting the ultimate reward (both the ears and the tail of his kill), I was as exhausted as though I had been a part of the event – which, in a way, I was. Such spectacle; such drama. I thought back to Burnley against Sheffield Wednesday, the football game I had seen on the TV a while back where nobody died and no goals were scored, and found no comparison.

Malaga had another subject for me. It was the birthplace of Pablo Picasso, whose 'art' has generally left me frustrated despite all the research and positive briefing I have had about him and it by the SCSC. There is one glorious, devastating exception – his painting entitled *Guernica*.
My visit so far has concentrated on the historic clash between Christianity and Islam, but Malaga has also sinister echoes for Judaism. It was here that the first 'runs' were made by Hitler's 'borrowed' bombers, before they moved to, and wiped

out, Guernica – the events so dramatically remembered by Picasso. It is in this painting that I found my spiritual affinity with the horse in the *corrida.* In the painting, the bull (Franco) wins, and the magnificent horse (the people) dies. It was here in Malaga that the concept of *Blitzkrieg* saw its terrible genesis. It is a possibility, therefore, that it was here that ideas of the Third Reich and the Final Solution for the Jewish race started their ominous move from the drawing board. Just before I left England, I saw a strange lady on the television. She was called Edna Everage (I think), and I can't remember much about it – except the audience thought her HUGELY funny and I couldn't understand what they were laughing at. What I do remember was that she used the word 'spooky' a lot, and that's the word that keeps coming back to me when I sit and reflect in this metropolis. Spooky.

I enjoyed my visit, I have a new friend – but my visit has uncovered much more than that. Much of the planet's issues have become so much more alive for me here. Spooky indeed.

In all honesty – and I am committed to being honest in these chronicles – I did delay my return journey to England for a day (maybe two) longer than was absolutely essential. To my surprise, English language papers were available on the same day in Malaga, and when I was reading them, I checked out the weather in the north of England. I usually did this over my morning *café con leche,* sitting outside in the sunshine. I kept reading that, back in England, the rain was 'coming down in stair-rods', to quote Cide, and I couldn't work up much enthusiasm for the return. The day before yesterday, however, I got both barrels from the Corner Office.

I travelled back yesterday, and was able to get back to Whalley without an overnight stay. The trip – exactly the reverse but without the airport hotel – went off without incident. What was strange was that, when I got on the plane, the lady, whose job was to keep walking up and down the inside of the aircraft, insisted on telling me (and everybody else) how to fasten my seat belt again. This did seem odd as (a) it's VERY simple and (b) she'd told me on the way out. She also explained that, if we crashed into the water, I must put on a strange piece of clothing (which she demonstrated). I have seen young women in Burnley wearing similar vest-type things, which expose their stomachs (which seems odd as it is usually very cold there). These water vests were a bit like those, but apparently this 'tank-top' would help me float in the sea. It also has a whistle. I saw a sport called water polo on television while I was in Spain, and they used a whistle a lot – but I can't see why we would want to play that if we crashed in the sea.

»

10 December

09.56.23 GMT

To: All Constellations

Is nobody on this mailing list paying any attention to what's going on here? I clearly told you of my plans, but got back to a backlog of twenty-seven messages from a whole range of you. Some are just ridiculous ('Are you still alive?'). Others – the more sensible ones – I will get round to answering as soon as possible.

I have a busy day ahead, but let me tell you about a strange thing before I sign off. I was quite honest about my feelings in Spain. I loved it – the climate, the people, the culture, the food, the drink and the dead bulls. Frankly, and I'm being ruthlessly honest here, I was mentally working on some reasons that could justify me aborting Plan A in England and switching rapidly to Plan B in Spain. Then, when I got back, I felt strangely at home. When I got down to breakfast on my first morning back, it was almost as though *raba de toro* had never existed. I took one look at the breakfast buffet and helped myself to three sausages, two pieces of bacon, two heaped spoons of baked beans, two fried eggs, two pieces of black pudding, two grilled tomatoes and three slices of fried bread. Afterwards, I walked (quite slowly) into the reception area, and received a very friendly greeting from Nuala. I don't know whether I have told you this, but her eyes are a very attractive shade of green.

I extended my stay at the inn until the end of December (when a new Earth-year starts) – but I must begin thinking about getting some accommodation of my own that will be more suitable for my needs.

While I was talking to Nuala to extend my rental, she mentioned something called Christmas, which is coming up in a couple of weeks. Apparently it is a national festival and public holiday, and she told me that she would be going home to stay with her parents for a couple of days. They live in somewhere called Norn Iron. I'll find out more about that, and this Christmas thing, and let you know.

»

11 December

08.23.12 GMT

To: All Constellations

I must be stupid. It's not Norn Iron where Nuala's parents live, it's *Northern Ireland*. It's just how they pronounce it. Cide had a laugh when he explained that to me, but he also gave me a bit of a weird look. It was as though he was thinking that I must have come from another planet not to know this kind of thing. It was a mistake, but no harm done (I think). I made a note to myself to be more careful – but I do need to get out and amongst people, so it's a risk I have to take.

Incidentally, in my attempt to map the Big Issues of the planet, I reported on the impending disaster of bird flu. Something seems to have happened while I was away in Spain. I don't know whether it came and went, or they have solved it, but I can find no mention of it anywhere.

I made a second mistake on top of the Norn Iron thing, and it's rather important. It's also one I should not have made. It's not Christmas, although that is how they spell it. It's Christ-mas, with the 'i' pronounced as in 'bit' not as in 'mind'. Yes, exactly.

This is an event, or series of events, whereby the Christian population of the world celebrate the birth of Christ – but I don't understand why. They are almost two months out from the correct date during the earth-cycle year, and the whole thing to me looks like a load of trumped up bollocks. (This is an expression I got from Cide, who uses the term 'bollocks' frequently to describe anything that has negative associations in his mind – except when he calls something the 'dog's bollocks', which means it is VERY GOOD. This, I know, is confusing, but knowing these things will, I think, come in useful.)

Back to this Christ-mas thing. Frankly, my briefing on all of this was sketchy considering how important it might prove to be in my mission. There's a whole lot of stuff going on down here that makes no sense. Apart from the Birthday being wrong, there is something called the Lord's Prayer (appendix 12c in the briefing manual for those who want a full version). Half of that is bollocks as well. What's with this 'trespass' thing? It's mentioned twice in what is supposed to be THE seminal essay of the religion. Did I miss something? Exactly when was 'trespass' a big deal? Did I sleep through it? Here's another one – the 'Birth' YEAR. It is clearly reported as happening when Herod was alive, but he died in what is recorded as 4BC.

By copying this to the SCSC members, I am asking to be put straight on these issues.

»

12 December

11.30.34 GMT

To: All Constellations

Had a lie-in this morning. I was not particularly tired, but I had a feeling my responses from assorted bodies and offices might not be totally to my liking. I was so right.

On the mistakes re the Birthday and the importance of trespassing, the SCSC has surfed its monopoly of wisdom and come up with two answers. They are both the same. Essentially they are telling me that that's the way it is down here, and that they (the SCSC) cannot be held responsible for 'factual erosion' over time and that I (the Main Man) should just accept it and get on with the mission. I have a feeling that they wanted to add 'and stop picking fly shit out of pepper', but their collective *gravitas* precluded such a move. (The 'picking fly shit from pepper' saying is another one of Cide's, and it means to waste time on trivial, useless pursuits.)

There was no such *gravitas* on the part of the Corner Office. Ooh, I got a stinger. It was thinly disguised by a series of questions ('**How** long have you been here? **Exactly** what has been achieved against the FKGs? And so on). So much for all that 'empowerment' we talked about (and agreed, or so I thought).

I am in a bad mood as a result, so you can ALL piss off, and I don't care what the slang overrider does with that, OR what the Corner Office thinks. I'm signing off.

»

13 December

10.03.40 GMT

To: All Constellations

All's well again! Got a nice message on the BLa late last night. Apologies blah, blah, blah – shouldn't put too much strain on me – blah, blah, blah – do recognise the responsibilities I carry – blah, blah, blah – understand that progress will be slow – blah, blah, blah – learn from our mistakes – blah, blah, blah – better right than fast etc. etc. etc.

I feel a frank exchange of views has taken place, and it has helped clear the air. I feel good.

This Christmas thing is a BIG event. I went to the shops yesterday for the first time since I got back from Spain, and they have all decorated themselves. It seems to be a festival of tiny lights, with millions of them hanging from everything – including some people's dwellings. Everywhere you go, there is music being played through loudspeakers – and it's the same three or four tunes. I was only exposed to it for a couple of hours, but I was sick of them by the end that. When I got back, I tried to find them on my iPod in case they came up on 'random play'. Does anybody know what a 'manger' is? And why would anybody be 'away' in it? Honestly, this language is making my mission so difficult. There's a guy singing on and on about a 'White Christmas'. What's with the 'white'? Anybody know? I don't remember Bethlehem being white. Is this a 'racial' thing?

»

14 December

07.45.23 GMT

To: All Constellations

Following on from yesterday's bulletin, 'white' refers to something called snow. It falls out of the sky, and everything gets covered in it. It's cold and wet. And some guy's dreaming of it.

I saw Skins again yesterday. I'd just popped into the bar area at lunchtime and he was having a glass of the Boddingtons after a game of golf. (I still haven't had a proper game, and I must organise this with Cide.) Anyway, I got to know Skins a bit better. He has a bit of a limp, and he told me that this came from his childhood when he fell victim to a disease called polio. As luck would have it (or would not have it in his case) this disease was all but eradicated just after he caught it. Of course, when I'm in conversation with anybody like this, there's much I don't understand, so I just have to nod my head a lot – and then hope that I can put sense to it afterwards. For example, Skins was born just after the war ended (1946) and called himself a 'Boomer' – which I think refers to an explosion in birth rates during this period. In the mid-1960s, as he left his teenage years, the country was, apparently, undergoing a social revolution. There were two aspects to this that affected Skins – the first one being about sex. This was the time when sexual freedom became the rule rather than the exception for Boomers, greatly assisted by the advent of effective, cheap and available birth control. Well, that's what the world believed in general, but it had some notable exceptions according to Skins. In his words, the 'sexual revolution' started out in London, and then set off in a northerly direction – rather like the 'red clouds' you see on a TV weather map of the Atlantic Ocean when a hurricane is crossing it. All the Boomers in Burnley area were looking forward to it arriving – but, according to Skins, quite unbelievably, right at the last minute, it swerved and missed Burnley. There he was, ready 'to shag for England', and nothing happened. According to Skins, you were lucky to get a bit of 'upstairs outside' in Burnley until the very late 1960s. That is, apparently, a local slang term for the placing of a (man's) hand on top of the (several) layers of clothes covering a (woman's) breast, and falls many degrees short of genital penetration.

He fared better in another exciting aspect of the 1960s. He joined a group of musicians, as many of his peers did at this time. They were all led by a group of four musicians from the coastal metropolis of Liverpool, who started the revolution with a so-called 'Mersey Sound', which was followed by similar groups all over the western world with their own 'sounds'. Skins played percussion (drums) in a four-piece group, which called itself the 'Four Leadbellies' and which offered the world the 'Whalley Sound'. Apparently, they were successful, releasing a piece of recorded music called 'Cotton Love', which reached number 27 in the weekly league tables that tracked such activity in 1966. The Four Leadbellies STILL perform for live audiences, although Skins is the only member of the original line-up still in the group, and they regularly get a booking or two each Christmas. He told me this with his voice lowered – because he is without employment at the minute, he is receiving a weekly handout from the government, and shouldn't be earning anything else. When I asked him how long 'at the minute' had lasted, he told me that he had been jobless since 1987. I think this is nearer ten million minutes, but say nothing. His group would be playing at the Golf Club's annual party in a week or so. I agreed to pop in to give them a cheer (he told me that Sid, Rhys and Cide would also be there which will be fun), but I cannot help thinking that this skinny, limping, balding man, who has a fascinating sense of humour, but who openly dislikes anybody who is not of his own tribe, cannot be at the vanguard of popular entertainment.

»

15 December

10.05.34 GMT

To: All Constellations

This month is the last one of the earth's calendar year-cycle. As such, a lot of people take stock of their lives and make resolutions to do things differently (or, occasionally, do some different things) in the New Year ahead. I will do the same. I will reflect progress against my Five Key Goals and start some 'Action Plans' to help them. I will sort out more details at the time, but in principle I know some of them now.

As already noted, I need to find myself more appropriate accommodation, I need to acquire a car (one of the personal transporter things) and I need to plan my next trip or visit.

The need for new accommodation is not just about finding somewhere more suited to being a base for my work, but will move me out of the public eye. I can tell my lifestyle is starting to raise eyebrows a bit – as it seems all I do is spend money rather than do anything to bring it in. When I paid for my lunch the day before yesterday, Cide asked me if I was living on a 'Fat Bastard Company' loan. This is a reference to satellite TV, which I do not have access to in my room (another good reason for moving). Amongst the adverts on the numerous satellite channels are many for loan companies which specialise in lending money to people who seem down on their luck – maybe they have got themselves in debt, or been convicted of a crime, or expensively divorced. These loan companies seem to target these people, who are always interviewed in the adverts, and they are always sat on settees, and they are always (it seems) what Cide calls 'fat bastards'. Hence the name. When the New Year comes I need to do something that is SEEN to either generate money or sensibly explain my lifestyle.

»

16 December

11.20.32 GMT

To: All Constellations

There are many celebration parties planned for the period between now and the change of year. The hotel is fully booked every night – both in the restaurant and the function room. I have been invited to the Golf Club party by Cide, which will be on 23 December, and (apparently) the pub in Whalley has a late-night party planned for the evening before the actual day of the Birth celebration. With the staff being very busy, Nuala will be working almost non-stop throughout the period, but she told me she has managed to get some time off over the Christmas period, so she is having a 'do' at her apartment. I understand she shares this with some other tenants.

Even in this time of celebration the conflict between religions seems ever-present. Although very few of the English actually go to church, and there is a constitutional divide between church and state, the 'native' population seem to get very worked up if anybody tries to stop them being quasi-Christians for just under three weeks. This involves them (as I see it) getting drunk even more than is normal and buying a fir tree to put INSIDE their houses. They then decorate this tree, and the house, inside and occasionally outside, with hundreds of tiny lights. Groups of (retail) businesses often pool money and decorate whole streets in the same way. Individual (local) government and business buildings have also been decorated this way for as long as anyone can remember.

»

17 December

10.03.45 GMT

To: All Constellations

This Christmas thing is much bigger than I originally thought. Pretty much all serious business activities have already been suspended, with the notable exceptions of selling goods and partying. The religious issues that are raised are but one aspect of a much wider set of concerns which affect this country, and which I must understand if I am to make progress.

There is a section of the population who believe they are English nationals, whatever that means. The reality is that the nation is officially called the United Kingdom, and is, in fact, known throughout much of the world as Britain. These 'English' feel increasingly beleaguered. Their brother and sister countries (Wales, Scotland and Norn Iron) are moving away. Their old Empire has gone. They see themselves being sucked into a European super-nation, where they would have but a small part to play. They profess a 'special relationship' with America, but increasingly realise that that is a way to increase alienation with much of the rest of the world while the benefits of the relationship become harder to calculate. Worst of all, in their eyes, they see 'their' country being invaded by immigrants who bring their own non-English customs and cultures – and who, irritatingly, want to keep them.

The last issue is at the core of much modern conflict. Things may be changing in the rest of the world, but that doesn't mean they have to change here in (such as) Lancashire. After all, they were the original inhabitants of the island, weren't they? Fundamental to this attitude is the belief that they were the aboriginals of this land.

Not according to my briefing manual they weren't. The Britons and Romans preceded the English. Throughout this formative period of history, there wasn't an Englishman in sight unless you crossed over to Northern Germany and headed down to the home of the Angles in Schleswig-Holstein.

All this deep uncertainty about who they are as a nation surfaces at a time like Christmas. Only a minuscule percentage of the population are actually practising Christians, while the Islamic faith goes from strength to strength with the immigrant population. As a result, when some Town Hall official somewhere suggested that, while the Holiday should still be celebrated, it should become a secular occasion, this proposal (and many like it) provided a cue for outrage in the media – and an endless series of rants by (such as) Sid and the guys. They immediately decided they would 'defend' Christmas – a strategy which involves the tactics of drinking more for a longer period, spending money they don't have on things they don't need, doing the exact reverse of fasting and buying more and more lights to put outside their houses. Yup, that'll show 'em that English Christianity means business.

I will watch developments over the next one or two weeks closely. I feel it will reveal things that are important to my mission.

»

18 December

09.24.34 GMT

To: All Constellations

Nuala is not happy. After promising her all year that she could have some time off at Christmas, the management of the hotel have changed their minds and told her she must work, but that she can have some time off at the turn of the New Year. Apparently her 'union' (a body that collectively 'represents' workers interests) can't help her on this occasion, and she is very upset. In fact, when I bump into her at breakfast she is still crying. I find myself really upset for her – those eyes should be sparkling, not blinking back tears. The cloud has a silver lining though. She will have time to go back to her family in Norn Iron, in a part called Antrim, and join them for the New Year celebrations.

I had an interesting experience last night, which may throw some more light on the religion/culture clash that is in the air around this Christmas period. I decided to get a taxi home from Burnley, where I had been doing some shopping. The traffic was heavy, and the journey took longer than normal. I got into conversation with the taxi driver. His name was 'Bash' – short for Basharat – with his family name being Hussein. His parents are from Pakistan, near the Kashmir border (and many of his relatives still live there) – but he had lived here all his life and now had two children of his own. He was a devout Muslim. He was a bulky man, with hair cut impossibly short at the sides. He seemed friendly – so I (very carefully) broached some of the issues I have noted about the conflicts around Christmas. He laughed – and was genuinely amused. He told me that no Muslim he knew had any problems with the idea of Christmas, and, in fact, welcomed the holiday. In Bash's case it was a very good time for business, so he thought the whole thing was a great idea, and as far as he was concerned the Town Halls had no need to be too sensitive about upsetting members of the Islam faith. But then he went all serious on me. He slowed the cab down as we were coming down a crowded street. He pointed out several people who were clearly drunk and several females who, despite the cold, were VERY scantily dressed. In his eyes, THOSE were the actions that upset Muslims – and it was those that they couldn't come to terms with.

I got his mobile telephone number. You are supposed to call the taxi company and they decide which taxi you get, but he said I should try to call him direct next time. I like Bash, and he gave me a lot to think about.

»

19 December

11.34.23 GMT

To: All Constellations

You are not going to believe this. We are well into the 'party' season, with the hotel now packed every lunch time and every night – and guess what? My 'diet sheet' has arrived from the SCSC. I've had a quick look at it, and it sounds a nightmare. It includes a programme they've called EXERCISE whereby I have to tire myself out doing things like running. Have you seen my feet?

They are very determined I lose this weight I've put on. I checked this morning and it has got slightly worse – just over 89 kilograms. If and when I start appearing on TV, that apparently deceives the eye by making whoever is on screen seem much heavier than he or she really is. In fact I may have to lose more weight than I have put on to combat this. They really are concerned about this 'image' thing – although I have scored some points with my new-style beard and haircut.

I decide I'll start the diet on the first day of the New Year. Frankly, it's not a good time to even think about it now. Being a resident at the hotel, I get 'sucked' in to a lot of the parties and I've found I can pretty much eat for free each day if I'm careful. I went to a 'buffet' lunch yesterday, and I found out something interesting about sandwiches. The normal tradition around here is that sandwiches are BIG, but at this party they were small and cut up into triangles. I asked the lady who was serving them why they had done this, as it seemed such an unnecessary process to keep going back for another one. She told me that sandwiches always taste better if they are cut in triangles – particularly small ones, with the crusts removed. She didn't know why, but they just did. It was confusing, but I think she is right.

»

20 December

11.03.05 GMT

To: All Constellations

There's a problem coming up. At some stage I am going to have to talk about my background – where I come from, who my parents were, where I went to school and so on. I spent a lot of time on this with the SCSC, and we have put together a plausible script, with all the necessary back-up documents and details. It was expected that, as I gather pace and profile, a lot of people would start digging into my background and that my story would have to be robust enough to withstand the most penetrative analysis – but it was not expected that I would have to use it this early in the mission.

For those who want full details, my artificial 'family' history is outlined in full in appendix 17 of the briefing manual. In brutal summary (for those who can't be bothered to look it up), I was orphaned virtually at birth, which explains the lack of parents or close family. An exhaustive piece of research found a young married couple who died in a car crash, in Bedford, in 1972, and the story we have 'superimposed' on that is that the young wife was pregnant and I survived. There followed a childhood in assorted government care establishments, and we have rewritten and altered the paper-trail so that when it touched real people, those people are now themselves dead or untraceable.

One aspect of this Christmas thing, however, is that families get together, often travelling to get the job done. If you fly solo, it raises eyebrows – and the fact I was planning to stay in the hotel on my own throughout Christmas was causing me unwelcome attention, albeit of the sympathetic kind. There was no way I could carry this off without explaining some of my background, and, after I had told Cide and Nuala the main points, all of a sudden I found myself invited to several Christmas day 'family' lunches. Cide is the most insistent, as his granddad and grandma (Sid, who we've met, and his wife Betty, who we haven't) come along to be with him and his 'mam'. I've agreed, but if I can find a way out of it I will. I suspect this kind of thing is very traditional, and my lack of knowledge about these things might point a few questions at me. Besides, both Sid and Cide sometimes talk in a language that my most sophisticated slang-overriders cannot translate. Here's another example. A couple of nights ago, we were having a quiet glass of the 'Boddies' when he suddenly announced that he had to nip out to 'lay a cable'. I have that right, I know, because I wrote it down. I had no idea – absolutely none – of what that meant, and spent the rest of the evening, long after he had gone, wondering what it was. Had he really left a drink half finished for five minutes to go and do some electrical work? It turns out – and I have to thank some research guy in the SCSC for this, who dug it up from some VERY remote slang program – that it is a metaphor for excreting.

»

21 December

09.21.45 GMT

To: All Constellations

I am getting into the swing of this Christmas thing, and looking forward to my 'proper party', the Golf Club one, the one I have been invited to, on the 23rd.

Apparently, it is the custom that you buy your family and close friends a small present to open on Christmas Day, and I decide that I will buy Nuala something, along with Cide and the members of his family as it looks like I will be attending their lunch celebration on the day itself. I ask Cide about Nuala, and if he had any ideas as to what she might like as a present. He gave me a bit of a strange look, and suggested I got her some 'sexy keks'. When I looked blank, he kind of raised his eyeballs in his head in mock exasperation – and then explained that these were intimate undergarments, and, with a bit of luck, if you gave them as a present to an attractive woman, it might not be the last you see of them. I was HUGELY embarrassed. I know nothing about women's underclothes, and feel it is no business of mine. I decide to buy her some chocolates as I think I know her favourite.

»

22 December

16.50.45 GMT

To: All Constellations

I'm late with my bulletin today as I wrote up my list of presents for the people I have targeted, and went shopping to get them. I called Bash in his taxi, and he took me into Burnley and agreed to pick me up after a couple of hours. He was, apparently, still worried about his family back in northern Pakistan. There had been a big earthquake a while back, and although they had all survived – remarkably without any injuries – life was very hard as they were having to fight another winter still without support or services. He had sent them as much money as he could afford, but it wasn't a great help – there was nothing to spend it on.

His taxi cab was interesting. On the ledge in front of the wheel he uses to steer there was a small altar, and sitting next to it a little television. Or so I thought. It seems the little television was actually a complex navigational system. Built into the instrument fascia underneath was a device for playing music discs. Next to that was his meter for charging people (which seemed to be broken whenever I was in the taxi – it was always 'just' going for repair). Next to the meter was a phone system, which linked him to his headquarters. Next to that was his own (portable) phone system on which he took bookings that SHOULD have been made through the company, but where he made them directly. This was linked by something called BlueTooth, which involved some wiring being wrapped around, and then stuck in his ear. Complicated business driving a taxi.

I am getting used to the winter here – although I don't mind admitting that in the first few weeks I suffered. It was particularly difficult coming back from Spain, where I laid to rest my initial thoughts that the whole planet was staring at the first big Ice Age for ten millennia. Back in Lancashire, I stay inside as much as possible to avoid the cold – doing my reading and researching. On this subject you may please note I am up to Essay Nine in the *Ascent of Man*, and have passed that tricky bit on the Theory of Relativity. That's the one where, if you remember, we calculated that only seven people on the planet understood it (and, if you want my view, not many more at the SCSC offices did either). If you are confused with its title (as you may have your own version – this thing's pretty constant through the constellations) it's the one that says if you have a spinning disc (like they have to record music on down here), then the edge of the disc is younger than the centre. Or it may be the other way round.

Where was I? Oh, yes. Presents. In the end I got a nice box of sweet chocolates (called Thorntons) for Nuala. For Cide, I got some of the balls he uses for golf. I knew the brand name because he was always moaning about the price – they were called Titleist Pro V1, and I got him six. He suggested I got Sid a disc which records film (called a DVD) because they had just bought him a machine to play them on – and he thought something called *Dad's Army* would be good. His mum always liked a good read – so he suggested I buy one which looked like an adventure in history, but actually had a bit of 'heavy breathing' stuff in it. He further explained this concept as a bit of 'rumpy-pumpy'. He then further explained it as a 'bit of slap and tickle'. When I STILL looked blank he told me to get one with some veiled shagging in it. I knew that word. But the lady in the bookstore seemed a bit nonplussed when I asked for it. Still, I got one. I've forgotten the name as she wrapped it up for me in decorative paper.

A lovely surprise later in the evening. I got a phone call from Xabi in Spain. There were two reasons for the call – apart from just seeing if I was OK. The first was that one of the English soccer clubs (I forget which) was about to buy a player from his team (Malaga) when something called the 'transfer window' opened. This I don't understand, although I am getting more and more knowledgeable in the aspects of the game that fill all the media. Buildings have windows, so I assume a transfer window is some player-market/bazaar-type centre where players are traded through a window. I like Xabi, and hope to develop our friendship – so I pretended to be interested – although I just got more and more confused by this 'buy a player' idea. My briefing manual indicates that slavery has been abolished in these islands for centuries. Anyway, it seems this player is very good (whoever he was, I've forgotten), and the team he will be bought for (whichever it was, I've forgotten that as well) will be very lucky.

The second thing he had to say was of much more interest. There is a chance he will be visiting England in the New Year sometime – possibly early spring – and he wondered whether we could meet up and spend some time together as he knew very little about the place. I kept the obvious response – that makes two of us – to myself, wished him well and told him I would be delighted to see him again.

This brings me to a wider subject – which is the progress I'm making against my Five Key Goals. You are aware I've had a bit of what Cide would call a 'pissing contest' with the Occupier of the Corner Office on this, but that that's gone quiet. I do sense, however, a growing sense of frustration from the WHOLE back-up team as to my progress on the big targets. I am however, more than satisfied with my progress as this has to be done in my style in my time. What I will do for all of you is to take stock in the New Year and do a formal Interim Report on the status and outlook for the mission and, in particular, the FKGs. All I would say at this stage is that we have had two goes at this, and both times we've ended up in what Cide calls a 'tits-up' situation (that is, a failure). Keep your powder dry, guys. I'm OK.

»

23 December

12.45.03 GMT

To: All Constellations

I'm so excited. Today's the day for MY party – well, it's actually the Golf Club's yearly celebration. Cide tells me that they have a 'disc jockey' and a 'turn'. I have no idea what either of those things are, so I will have to tell you tomorrow. Nuala is working, but says she will call in after her work is finished to say hello to everybody – as the hotel and the golf course are part of the same business, she knows most of the people involved. Cide is really pleased about this – as he says we need to get more 'crumpet' to come. I'm latching on to a lot of this stuff now, and realise quickly that this is another world for female. There are few actual female playing members at the club, and although some wives accompany some of the men, Cide's concern is that there won't be enough 'spare'.

Although Cide is the Club Professional, it is actually the Club Secretary who is organising the event. My briefing manual had informed me that 'secretaries' were female, but this secretary is a little fat man from a place called Birmingham. I am beginning to realise that, although this island is small, the people speak quite differently in different parts of it. I have not visited Birmingham, but if they sound like this secretary, I will give it a miss. I'm not sure I agree with Cide, who says that when people from Birmingham talk, their faces look like they've just kissed Yoko Ono (Help? What's one of those?), but it does look and sound awful.

It sounds as though it will be a late night tonight, so I'm going to have a sleep this afternoon. I will have to pick out the clothes I wear quite carefully. I expect that, with all the prize-giving and a 'turn', I will need to be smart. I'll sign off now and let you know how it went on.

»

24 December

15.45.34 GMT

To: All Constellations

Bit late today. I had thought that the party might involve a lot of the Boddingtons, so decided to plan my evening carefully. I didn't arrive until quite late and then deliberately kept my drink intake low. It's not that I don't like the Boddingtons, but I've had quite a lot recently and I suspect there is quite a lot to come over the days ahead. I was also aware of some facts I remembered from my diet sheet, notably that the Boddingtons (and its peers) is 'public enemy number 1'. I also wanted to look objectively at how the community behaved in what is, after all, a traditional religious festival. All that went well (more in a minute) but I didn't get to bed until 4.30 a.m., hence the late bulletin.

Well, where do I begin? I got the dress code wrong for a start. I chose a nice dark suit (as I've previously explained, this is a matching top and bottom outer layer of clothing). I'd seen a few 'business meetings' at the hotel, and noticed that the men often wore one of these twin garments, and seemed to hold themselves in some esteem as a result. As a result, when I was in another of these enormous undercover markets recently (this one called Tesco), I saw such a suit and bought it. It is called Cherokee, and I thought I looked very smart in it – and ideally dressed for such an auspicious occasion. That was until I walked in the room, and was greeted by Cide, who was wearing a black short-sleeved cotton round neck vest kind of thing, on which someone had printed: 'Merry Christmas. Now piss off'

For your information, I found out that a disc jockey is somebody who operates a desk on a stage, from which music comes out over loudspeakers to fill the room. I think he spoke English, but it was almost impossible to tell. He thought himself very funny, continually saying things and then laughing for long periods. The music was (generally) very noisy and by the time I got there dancing had already started. Unfortunately, the Four Leadbellies had finished their act and I didn't get to see Skins do his bit, but I'm sure there will be another time. Whatever they did, it had not left much of a buzz about the place.

Through research, I have found that you can learn a lot about a community from their communal dancing, and I studied it closely. I don't know, however, just what to tell you about this place and its rituals. No two people did the same steps or body movements. As part of my briefing I have studied the planet's diseases, and at one stage I saw a man exhibit the symptoms associated with extremely advanced Parkinson's Disease on the bit of floor reserved for dancing. Facing him was a woman who ignored him completely, and who kept her handbag pinned between her ankles, on the floor, all through the dance. At other times, when the disc jockey played slow music, they turned the room lights low and I saw hands doing things that hands shouldn't do in public. All very confusing.

I also found out what a 'turn' is. It is a man who stands on stage and tells stories. This man was the son of a famous footballer and he just kept mentioning names that obviously meant a lot to the people present, and then swearing almost every other word. When this man was on, I was sat at a table with Sid, Cide, Rhys and Skins – and they were helpless with laughter most of the time. At times Skins (who was the man who had recently evidenced Parkinson's) was literally crying with laughter but I swear that all I heard the man on the stage say was: 'Emlyn Hughes – what a wanker.' It didn't seem a funny joke to me, but I'll do a bit more background reading and see if I can find out what was making everybody laugh.

In all honesty, nothing much happened. Sid ranted about the government; Rhys ranted about anything that wasn't Welsh; Skins ranted about somebody called Robbie Williams; and Cide took us through his recent 'two-over-par' game of golf, ball by ball – and then something happened just after midnight that has thrown me completely.

I mentioned earlier that the men outnumbered the women at this event, and for most of the latter part of the evening we sat as a group around a table some way away from the dancing. Occasionally Skins would get up and have another dance with some woman, but generally groups sat at their own tables and didn't communicate with each other. The awards were given out for the Golf Club members, with Cide winning the Longest Recorded Drive – which is nothing to do with a journey, but the distance he hit one of his balls. Then, during one of the slow music pieces, somebody tapped my shoulder, and when I looked around it was a young woman who I didn't recognise, but who had something about her that reminded me of someone else. Two things then happened simultaneously that . . . well, that made me feel like an idiot. I suddenly realised what was familiar about her. It was her eyes, they were the eyes that belonged to Nuala. At the same time, Cide looked up and welcomed this new arrival: 'Watcha, Noo, how's it goin'?' (Noo was his friendly name for Nuala.)

I was used to seeing Nuala in a dark outer jacket and skirt, with a white shirt. Her work shoes were flat and sort of clunky. She normally wore her hair kind of combed backwards and stuck there. All that had changed. Had it ever.

Her hair – a kind of fairish colour but with some copper in it – was shoulder length, and swished like a curtain occasionally hiding part of her face. Her face was painted beautifully, no part of it more so than her lips, which were a stunning kind of red-wine colour. But it was her clothes that really caught my attention – or rather, quite frankly, her lack of them. Those green eyes were complemented by a TINY sort of vest in much the same colour. Her dark skirt – if that's what it was – ended between upper and mid thigh, with most of it covered by a wide belt with an enormous silver buckle. She was standing and I was sitting, but the gap in height between us still seemed odd. It was explained when I looked down. Her shoes ended in points sharper than my pencil, and balanced themselves (and her) uneasily on spiky heels that added what must have been three or four inches to her height.

I am not naïve, and I have been briefed (and warned) well about sex and sexual attraction, and the dangers it might have for my image and mission. I have steeled myself (again) to ignore temptations, diversions and those annoying groin-throbs. But I couldn't ignore this, particularly as, when I stood up to welcome her, she bent down to put her drink on the table in front of me. The front of her vest shirt kind of billowed out, and I saw one of her raspberry-like nipples – which were not protected by any underclothes whatsoever. I was mesmerised, and it took a few moments to realise that she was shouting (over the noise of the music). It seems she was shouting at me: 'C'mon, Mr Mystery. I've been waiting for this. Let's dance.'

With that she grabbed my hand and we pushed through to the dancing bit. The music was slow and as soon as she had wrapped her arms around and nestled her head by one of my shoulders, I figured out EXACTLY and without ANY briefing what to do with my arms and legs. Basically, it was easy. All my limbs seemed to know exactly what to do, all on their own. Then, as the music was coming to an end, she looked up. She smiled. The room seemed very dark all of a sudden. Then, without saying anything, she put her lips on mine. That would have been bad enough, but suddenly, I felt my teeth being forced apart, AND SHE PUT HER TONGUE IN MY MOUTH. WAAAAGH.

Honestly, I didn't know what to do – but luckily the music ended quickly, and with a cheerful laugh she grabbed my hand and led me off the dancing bit of floor. I noticed her glass was empty so I volunteered to buy her another one – something called a Breezer, I think, but you will appreciate that my mind was elsewhere. I excused myself and went to the lavatory, and stayed locked in one of the little rooms for an hour while I collected my thoughts. When I came out, the party room was still full and noisy, and I realised I would have to pass it to get to my room, so I went the other way. Outside. It was just above freezing. I waited there until the very last person had gone, and the very last light was off, and then sneaked in as quietly as possible. It was 4.30 a.m.

when I finally got to my room, checked the inside of my mouth in the mirror to see if there was any damage, and jumped into bed, fully clothed. I was very troubled, but try as I might I could not sleep. I closed my eyes – tightly – but all I could see was a collage of eyes and hair and lips and raspberries and tongues. All I could feel was softness. It was some time before I realised I had my arms around my pillow.

»

25 December

13.34.45 GMT

To: All Constellations

Today, the Christian world celebrates, and I should be having a traditional festive lunch with Cide and his family. I am not. I am locked in my room, for two reasons. The first one is that I know that Nuala is on duty today, and there is no way I can get out without the risk of meeting her. The second reason is that I am shivering and have a body temperature of 101 degrees. I do not know what caused that, although I am suspicious of my mouth. I check it every thirty minutes or so in the mirror, but it seems OK. Perhaps it was being out in the cold and damp for three hours last night. I do not think my Cherokee suit was meant for such conditions.

About noon, there is a knock on my door – despite the fact that I have the little whatsit that says 'Do not disturb' on the handle outside. I ignore it, and bury myself deep in the bed clothes. I am shivering and sweating and when I close my eyes all I can see are giant lips. Whoever it is goes away. A giant tongue-like presence seems to be taking over my whole insides. I must sleep now.

»

26 December

09.32.45 GMT

To: All Constellations

We are snowed in. Overnight this longed-for weather condition happened, missing Christmas Day by just a few hours. I am not well enough to go out (or eat, which will be good for my weight), but I see what's happened on the TV, and when I open my curtains everything is white. The white golf course stretches away over the hills, and everything looks so peaceful.

There is no peace with me, of course. I have had plenty of time to consider this setback and feel I must redraw my plans. Obviously, what happened between me and Nuala is some sort of mating ritual. I am not sure of either the next steps or the consequences of the first one, but it is clear in my mind that anything more would be disastrous. One thing is obvious – early in the New Year I must accelerate my efforts to find more appropriate accommodation.

I also need to devise a plan for my next meeting with Nuala. I cannot stay in this room for ever, but I do know she is going home to Norn Iron for the New Year – so she will be gone in a couple of days. If I lay low, I may be able to avoid her, or at least avoid being one-to-one with her before she leaves, and I MAY be able to find somewhere new to live before she's back. Sounds like a plan. But it's strange how I shiver when I remember that kiss – and the memory seems to warm me when I'm cold and cool me when I'm hot.

»

27 December

11.03.45 GMT

To: All Constellations

Another low-profile day. Watched TV in my room, gradually recovering from my fever. The in-room TV facility has been extended to include some satellite channels, and I spend much of the day watching adverts for (a) furniture, which, apparently, everybody either wants or needs to buy in the week after Christmas, and (b) the Fat Bastard Loan Companies. I break that monotony by getting up to Essay Number Ten in the *Ascent of Man*, but it's all that bollocks about atoms, molecules, bases, proteins, amino acids – stuff that I never understood when I was briefed on it before I arrived. Then I have a terrible thought – did she leave her amino acid in my mouth?

All I ate during the day were seven of the small oranges that were given me as a present (by Bash, the taxi-man), and I drank about two gallons of tap water. It occurs to me that all this is very good for my soon-to-be-on-the-horizon diet and de-tox programme, and I am delighted to note that I have lost two kilos since Christmas Eve.

»

28 December

16.25.43 GMT

To: All Constellations

I got out really early this morning, hoping to get through reception before Nuala came on shift. Unfortunately, we bumped into each other, and I was just about to launch into my rehearsed speech about her not being upset and that we must stay calm when she let out a joyous mini-shriek, shouted to no-one in particular that on the third day Tommy had risen again, kissed me (on the forehead this time) and then danced off with some sort of jig-movements to her place behind the desk. I was stunned. Risen again? What was all that about? Where did that come from?

I had booked Bash to take me into town. I needed to get some information on different accommodation. I needed to start thinking about buying one of these car things. I needed to start planning my next visit/project. I needed some food, and some bits of clothing. My Cherokee suit had not responded well to a night outside in the damp.

All these things were suppose to be on my mind as I sat in the taxi, but all I could think about was a pair of green eyes that were laughing when I expected them to be tearful. I began to feel a whole lot better, and I gave Bash £25 to send to family in Pakistan who were still in a mess. This gesture seemed to astonish him. As he explained, most of time he had a hard time getting any tips at all, and for somebody to do this was unheard of. He then turned the tables and surprised me – by telling me that his mother made the best curry 'outside Pakistan' and she would make one for me. It would not be like the crap that was available in the Indian restaurants, though – which he reckoned the proprietors all got from a common vat which was situated in the hills just above Darwen. No, his mother's was the real thing. It's funny. Apart from the fact that he says 'innit' at the end of almost every sentence, I now understand Bash's English better than Nuala's, Cide's or any of the others I met regularly.

If I thought the place was busy before Christmas, I was wrong. There seemed to be a million people in the shops and markets, and I have just got back now – well, after 4.00 in the afternoon. I have a lot of literature to read. The good news is that while I was in Boots (which is another covered bazaar-type shop), I spotted something called Oral B mouthwash. I bought three for the price of two.

»

29 December

09.45.23 GMT

To: All Constellations

Am almost back to being myself this morning. I feel suddenly unafraid of Nuala – in fact quite the opposite – and am quite disappointed to find she has had to go out when I go down to try my first spot of breakfast for a few days.

I have been in direct touch with the SCSC overnight, debating whether my new accommodation should be something I have to myself or something where I share a facility with others. It's a simple trade-off. Alone, I take no risks of exposing the nature of my being, or my journey, via a simple mistake in some unguarded conversation. The downside, however, is that I miss the opportunity to understand a handful of people as deeply as you can when you live alongside them. Time is moving on, and in weeks rather than months I will have to be establishing relationships, because without relationships I will not secure the type of support I will need.

We decide to narrow the search down to two of each kind – and then weigh up the specifics of each individual case. During my toing and froing with the SCSC I try to glean if there has been any 'comment' passed about what happened with Nuala from the Corner Office. 'No Comment', apparently, and the consensus was that the Old Man was in a good mood. In fact, yesterday, he walked around the SCSC offices and wished everybody a 'Happy New Earth Year Cycle' with a smile on his face.

»

29 December

10.34.21 GMT

To: All Constellations

Every surface in my room is covered in paper as I try to pull together my Interim Report (for the SCSC and you guys), and I try to find a new car, new accommodation and a new country to visit. Strangely, I find it hard to concentrate – which is usually one of my strong points. Nuala has left to get a plane to Belfast, and there is a strange face behind the desk. She is pleasant enough, but I start to feel flat and the feeling stays with me – in fact gets worse – during the day.

There is nothing to watch on the TV of any substance – there just do not seem to be any issues of global importance going on at the minute, so how I'm supposed to get my head around them for my report I just do not know. I watched a TV show last night which was billed as 'The 50 Greatest Comedy Shows Of All Time As Voted BY YOU' – but I barely laughed throughout all three hours of it. One of them featured somebody called Joe Pasquale (or something like that) and I don't think I would have laughed if he'd stayed on TV all night.

»

30 December

12.23.56 GMT

To: All Constellations

I have been invited to (yet another) party tomorrow evening – another festival, it seems; this time it takes place around midnight as the Old Year disappears and the New One arrives. Oh, I don't know. I'll see. I'm still strangely flat, and don't know why – I'm feeling physically fit again, though.

I'll be busy today and tomorrow with paperwork. It's no good trying to DO anything about my car, trip or accommodation – the whole country seems to be shopping.

Weighed again – stayed the same this time. Finished my little oranges.

»

31 December

23.45.34 GMT

To: All Constellations

What a miserable day. I decided not to go to Skins' party. It's nearly midnight, and I can't wait for the new day, the new dawn, the NEW YEAR. I hope it gives me the energy and the incentive to get off my arse and get stuff moving. Today I have been useless – lying about on my bed feeling sorry for myself. I feel depressed at my mission – from this vantage point it just looks overwhelming and impossible. I feel lonely, stuck here among a nation that could win any inter-planetary whingeing contest. Drink and shop and whinge and rant and borrow – that's all they seem to do. There is no sensible debate. Every position on every issue is too much for one camp, not enough for the other. In reality, I have no friends. The SCSC aren't friends, I'm just a voyager to them. The people I've met here aren't friends – they are with their FRIENDS now, while I'm playing Billy No-Mates on my bed. (That's another Cide expression by the way – self-explanatory, I think.)

I'm writing this in real time now, with the New Year transition moment approaching. I've switched the TV off as it was featuring some madman running about between his piano and a bunch of badly dressed (presumably) celebrities. I'll try the iPod – and put it on 'random.'

See? See what I mean? Just WHAT is that? Hang on, it'll tell me on the little window on the front. It sounds like some guy is having his testicles wrapped in barbed wire. Here it is: somebody called Michael Bolton. That is all I need.

I'm going to bed. I hope a new ME awakes in the morning or we are in trouble. In the meantime, when I close my eyes, I know whose face I will see. Can't wait.

JANUARY

»

1 January

19.45.23 GMT

To: All Constellations

Big surprise! I'm miles away from the hotel.

When I woke up this morning I knew I needed a mini-new beginning. I needed to get rid of that whining self-pitying mess that had gone to bed the night before, and I greeted the new day with new energy and determination.

My first task, over the next few days is to bring you up to date on the status and outlook for my FKGs and I decided that the hotel wasn't going to be the right place to do that. Apart from that, Nuala's due back either today or tomorrow.

My briefing manual has given details of the capital city of this country, and mentioned that it has a fantastic library facility. It sounded like the ideal place to provide the peace and quiet needed for me to focus – not to mention any research stuff I might need. So, today, I made the two-hundred-mile train journey to London (note: you may know it as Trinovant, its first recorded name) and then made my way to my new temporary base, the Marriott Hotel. I booked this by telephone, and was lucky to get a room at such short notice, but it is ridiculously expensive. Good job we print the money.

I'm tired after the day's travel, but looking forward to getting a good start tomorrow.

»

2 January

11.45.34 GMT

To: All Constellations

Bad start. I got a taxi to the library, despite an odd look from the taxi driver. This turned out to be because the library was closed, which he could have told me before we set out, but he chose not to. This is a bit complicated so you might want to make a few notes here. New Year's Day (January 1st) is a national holiday, but if it falls on a Sunday, that can't work because Sunday is a holiday anyway – unless it isn't (for example, for the millions of people who work in shops and restaurants and trains and golf clubs). But if you work in a place like a library, *you substitute the next day for the holiday you would have had if you weren't having one already on the Sunday.* I think I've got that right.

Anyway, not to worry, I'm booked in for the week and I can do some preparation in the hotel's 'business centre', which is very well equipped and is where I'm sitting now. The delay will also give me time to look and listen as I walk about the capital, which, at first glance, seems MUCH bigger than Whalley and maybe even bigger than Burnley.

Although I was tired, I took a short walk last night. I reached a main thoroughfare named Oxford Street, which was absolutely packed with pedestrians, even though it was cold and wet. There was so much to see, and at the end there is a big *piazza* with some kind of monument in it. I turned north there and suddenly all the shop and restaurant signs were in Arabic. I was a bit wary after my experience in the Indian restaurant in Luton, where I tried to eat molten lava, but I tried out a small café and had a delicious supper of mutton and flat bread.

I feel good, although a bit lonely in this bustling metropolis. I'm ready to get off to a flying start tomorrow.

»

3 January

12.56.23 GMT

To: All Constellations

This library is neat. The facilities here are such that I can adapt my devices to go directly to the mailing list. At least, I think I can – we'll find out when I hit the 'send' key. It's lunchtime now, and I've had a good morning. Most of it has been spent trying to get my thoughts in order. I'm going to take one of the FKGs a day, so let me see if I can pull those thoughts together on the first one – ***relationships***.

First, let me clarify a couple of things. From the outset we realised that the first six months are NOT going to see me all lined up and ready to go with a group in place. Relationships take time – and if you make a mistake it can hole the mission below the waterline (as we have found out on two separate occasions already). For sure, the eventual journey will need a bunch of people to share my burden and add different skills to the mix, but by the end of the first six months it is NOT a Key Goal to have these in place and 'joined and committed'. In fact, although there will be a handful of people identified and with whom I will have maturing relationships, it is unlikely that they will even be aware of what's ahead of them.

I also want to point out that this mission will be different. The plan is NOT to 'recruit' a dozen or so 'monomaniacs with a mission'. Zealots will be no good this time. I will be seeking to put together a team of people with wide-ranging backgrounds – including their 'modern' religious ideas. This time we must not divide; we must gather and include.

So far, I think the most promising prospect is Xabi, back in Spain. I'm not really sure why, but we did seem to hit it off and I think he is looking for something to give meaning to his life – something beyond the fortunes of Malaga in the Spanish soccer league. We plan to meet again in a couple of months, and I really intend to work on him at that time.

Cide is another possibility. He seems very superficial. He lives day to day and seems to care little about others or about what is going to come next in his life. BUT, if I could engage him, he would be a powerful magnet for the millions of other young people who appear to think the same way.

Bash also offers potential. Quite simply, if I could lock him into the collective mission, it would enable us to reach an audience that is both massive and alienated. There are millions of people in the world of Islam who, I'm sure, would welcome an initiative attempting to bring the world together rather than divide it violently. I will develop this further.

I do not hold out much hope for my three wise men – Sid, Rhys and Skins. They are funny, and sometimes good company, but appalling at the same time. I will not abandon them, or the hope that they (or one of them) might play a part, but the likelihood of them celebrating the necessary diversity of my group is low.

What of Nuala? Indeed, what of the idea of a woman in the Team? As to the latter, I agree with the SCSC that it is an absolute 'must' this time. Female emancipation is widespread in many nations, and it is unlikely that any initiative will make progress without me harnessing their support and addressing their issues with a role model in a front/centre team position. Could Nuala do it? She is the only one of my blossoming relationships to have touched the back of my throat with her tongue, and this may be clouding my judgement. I am both scared and invigorated by the thought of our next meeting. But she potentially could represent a whole gender, and her religious background (a Norn Iron Catholic) and thoroughly modern outlook on life could be invaluable.

More to be done, but I think we can record a solid start on this Key Goal.

»

4 January

17.35.32 GMT

To: All Constellations

As you'll see by the time of this bulletin – I've had a bit of a setback. I'm delaying the report on the second Key Goal until tomorrow as I never made it to the library today. But the good news is that I might have another fertile relationship in the making.

I was wandering about last night, looking for something to eat, when I came across an Italian restaurant called *Botticelli*. It seemed very popular – which is a good sign – so I had my evening meal there. It turned out that it was its first night under a new owner, and it was chaos. The owner, who was also the main waiter, was a hawk-nosed man with a pony tail, and was getting into a bigger panic as the evening wore on. When he got around to taking my order, I told him to relax as far as I was concerned. There were a lot of Americans in the place who were complaining about slow service, so I told him to deal with me last – I was in no hurry. He seemed very grateful, but it meant that I was virtually the last person in the place when I finished. At that stage he came up to me with a bottle of clear liquid, sat down at my table and offered me a drink 'on the house' to thank me for being so considerate. He pointed to the remains of my meal – some veal – and asked me if it had been OK. I told him, honestly, that it had been a bit tough, but that there was no real problem. Oh, yes there was, he told me – and disappeared into the kitchen. He then reappeared with an electronic hand drill, and proceeded to drill holes in the remaining meat. He then pronounced it 'officially' tough, and told me that I would not be paying for it. The whole act just caught me off-guard, and I just laughed out loud – which seemed to please him. He then sat down and poured me a glass of the clear liquid. At first I thought it was water, which didn't seem very generous – but one sip quickly told me I was wrong. It was something called *grappa*, and an hour or so later we had finished the bottle. I could barely find my way back to my hotel, and this morning I had NO wish to sit and write a report, so I stayed in bed and watched CNN.

All I remember is that my new friend is from Argentina and he speaks Spanish. I do not know (or at least I do not remember him telling me) why he had opened an Italian restaurant, but I will find out. I will go back tonight or tomorrow. This relationship is worth cultivating – he would bring a whole new continent and outlook to the Team.

»

6 January

13.38.15 GMT

To: All Constellations

Yes, I missed a day. Another one. I'm back in the library, having decided not to go back to the Spanish/Italian/ Argentine restaurant at all so far because I need to keep a clear head for this. I've spent all yesterday and this morning putting my thoughts together on the subject of ***location*** – and whether England is the right place to base myself.

I have reported on my agreed position with the SCSC about not basing myself in America. It is true that it is now the only 'superpower' on earth, and can command vast audiences and resources. It is also true that I must visit at some stage. And it is also true that I might end up there. But it is not right now.

I have had comments from a number of mailing list members suggesting that Jerusalem might be appropriate. Let me address this head on. I can think of nowhere LESS appropriate to begin my journey. Yes, it is the epicentre of three religions, but it is also the epicentre of the conflict of their fundamentals and fundamentalists. There is no room for inclusiveness, no room for compromise and no room for jaw-jaw ... every initiative is too much for one side, not enough for another ... if you do not believe, you are a heretic ... if you believe in something else, then you should not exist ... part of my belief is that I must destroy your belief. If I got any foothold in THAT circus, at THIS stage, I would add to the problem not the solution.

Spain is a possibility. Many of the issues of the planet are reflected there, but it is generally peaceful. It is also sunny, has GREAT food and no death penalty. It's worth bearing in mind.

From my research and thinking so far, however, I'm thinking that Ireland could be a good choice as a Plan B location. It is divided by bigotry, but seems to be slowly blinking at a brighter future. From my research, it has one very important element: namely that, over the years, the world seems to have taken to its heart an extraordinary number of Irish 'wordsmiths' – poets, writers, lyricists and orators. I can imagine you frowning from here as to the relevance of that – but if I called them 'messengers', you might pick up on my meaning. I've spent all morning reading and listening to this stuff, and nine parts out of ten is full of crap – but, buried in the self-pity and whining, are some powerful messages, and the world seems prepared to listen.

Let me give you two examples. There are two popular Irish singers, one called Bono and the other called Bob Geldof. I have listened to their music on my special iPod. One is a very ordinary singer in a very good band; the other cannot sing at all. Remember when your camel kneels down too fast and you catch your testicles on the horn of your saddle? Well, the other one looks and sounds as though he has done that. However, they both have a secular message, and both have raised enormous amounts of 'aid' (through a process in which the poor people in rich countries give money to the rich people in poor countries). They are uncouth and arrogant, but they can command worldwide audiences. All the key figures on earth listen to them (in the case of Geldof, usually via a slang overrider). There's something in this model that I need to understand and harness.

I'm going back to see my new restaurateur friend tonight. Last night, I was wandering about again, and found a place that looked very popular so I tried it. It was called KFC (any ideas anybody?), and it was awful. It was supposed to be a chicken-based menu, but I didn't recognise the piece(s) that were given to me, and I began to worry about bird flu again. I'm not making this up – the group on the table next to me had their food served in a bucket. Ugh! Think what we used to do in buckets.

»

8 January

14.24.28 GMT

To: All Constellations

Same again – missed yesterday. However, this is not a bad pattern. It gives me a day to gather my thoughts on one particular subject – but also some time to explore this (capital) metropolis. It's some place.

I went back to my new friend's restaurant the night before last. His given name is José (which you might expect) but his family name is Tomaceski (which you wouldn't). He was born in Argentina, but of a Polish immigrant family. He married an English woman, and they came to live here about five years ago. They have since parted, but remain business partners in the restaurant, which they have just opened with her family's backing. It was much calmer than on opening night, and I had a delightful *risotto al vongole.* I headed out before the grappa bottle emerged, but I managed a couple of chats with him, and would be very interested in following up this relationship. I'll be back there again before I return to Whalley.

Today, my Interim Report subject is my planned ***modus operandi***. Obviously some of the Key Goals are not mutually exclusive (it would be odd if they were), and this one has ripple effects in a number of others – which also ripple back into it. The Old Model, which was to reach the people through a single belief system, will not get the job done. There are now too many of them, and they are too well entrenched. As you know, most of the key ones have elements that are right, but also contain howling – and I mean howling – errors. To pick one would simply declare huge tracts of the planet's population unreachable. No, the message has got to be original and timely, and the vehicle has to be new and inclusive. The Geldof model is interesting – indeed, it is somewhat spooky that he looks a bit like I used to look before I had my hair done. The key is to get the right team in place, and then get myself in front of people with my new, original and timely message and take it from there. I know I'll have to start small – and I'm thinking of the 'turn' we had at the Golf Club Christmas party. That might be a sort of 'entry point' for my first six months.

»

9 January

07.56.22 GMT

To: All Constellations

Yes, yes – I know you weren't expecting this today, but something weird happened last night. I had a light (early) supper at the hotel, and was just going out for a walk when I started chatting to the woman at the reception desk. She's pretty, but her eyes are just ordinary. I don't know what colour they are, but they are certainly not green. Anyway, she suggested that, as the weather was poor, I should go to the pictures. Apparently (and this is NOT pointing blame at my briefing team, who did not tell me about this – it's not possible to cover everything), a popular form of entertainment is to go to a building and watch moving pictures on a screen that isn't a television alongside dozens of other people. She told me about a picture that was showing locally – on what they called 'classic night' – which was called *King Kong*. I found the place and (after a bit of difficulty) found the room it was being shown in.

I watched these so-called 'pictures' for a while and, frankly, didn't see what all the fuss was about – it was like the TV but bigger. However, I had bought a box of chocolates (sorry about the diet; will start next week) and had just opened them to eat the first one when something happened that you will NOT BELIEVE. All of a sudden, there, right in front of me – real as you like – were HUGE beasts that the SCSC had convinced me had disappeared sixty million years ago. Never mind slang overrider – what the fuck is that all about? Never mind what the fuck – what the FUCKING fuck is that all about? THOSE MONSTERS HAVE NOT GONE. They're still here, right here on earth. Pictures of them were there, right in front of me. Bastards. You've never seen anything so big and frightening. Amazingly, there were two young boys in the seats near me, and they didn't seem bothered at all. I ate all my chocolates in under a minute and then fled from the cinema. I did not sleep at all. You'll not hear from me again today. I have some thinking to do.

»

11 January

12.45.35 GMT

To: All Constellations

I lost virtually a whole day as a result of those 'pictures', and I need to think very carefully about where I head to on this mission now. If those guys in SCSC are holding back stuff like that on me, what else is there that I might 'bump' into?

Nonetheless, I'm back on track with the mission now, and have had a good day – nearly a day and a half – pulling my thoughts together on what is perhaps the biggest of the Key Goals. It is to get an understanding of the ***Big Issues*** facing the people of the planet, and to figure out the implications for what we need to achieve.

This is so, so difficult. I am almost drowning in media coverage of the 'issues' of the day. It's like trying to sip water out of a fire-hose (another saying of Cide's). Brash headlines scream out that something or someone or other is of earth-threatening significance – and then the next day the story's disappeared. There are whole channels devoted throughout every hour of every day to 'news' and its analysis. There are programmes on 'issues' – and half way through them I forget the issue and find myself thinking about something else. Here's an example: yesterday there was a programme on every relevant issue of terrorist bombing. I watched it with interest, with my notepad handy. They then brought in somebody to the TV studio to pass comment. This person was introduced as the Head of Terrorist Studies at (I think) St. Andrews University –

a prestigious seat of learning I assume. I forgot about the bombing and became entranced by this man. What was this job? When did he identify this as his vocation? How did he qualify? What was on the curriculum? What does his wife think he does when he sets out each morning? Does he teach practical terrorism as well as theoretical? All I know is that if I was a terrorist, I would kill this man immediately. And my message to the world when I did that? Of course, if I can kill the Head of your Terrorist Studies . . .

This is a MASSIVE filtering job because the important element is not to identify the issues, *but how I use them to make progress.* Some issues turn out to be symptoms rather than a disease, but I'm aiming at listing the four that I think will offer me the most fertile ground. Here are the first two:

- There is an enormous amount of attention being given to the 'abuse' of the planet and the allocation and use of its resources. There are two very well-developed schools of scientific thought on the earth's climate – one that believes it is warming up, and the other that believes it is cooling down. Both provide hard evidence to prove their case. As a result, the broad population ignore it. People keep on chopping down trees and driving cars; their cattle keep farting. In addition, the allocation of oil, water and other resources that are available naturally (including land) is beginning to be a Big Time Overt Issue – as against the covert reasoning behind many of the planet's past conflicts.

- The Internet is out of control. Totally. What has been a wonderful breakthrough in the sourcing and using of information for the planet has also proved a lottery win for sexual predators, bomb makers, organised criminals, stalkers, bullies, fraudsters, blackmailers, 'spammers', anal-retentive virus creators, copyright pirates and penis-enlargement kit vendors. In fifteen years, the planet has built up an extraordinary reliance on the World Wide Web, and its attendant information system structures. As a result, it has built an equally extraordinary vulnerability to its potential abuse. In the next ten years, the downsides of the Internet will dramatically overtake the good news – most of which has been banked already.

Right, there's the first two of the four key issues facing the planet. I guess you are expecting an in-depth analysis of all the issues I identify, but you can forget it for those two. Why? Quite simple: the only point in identifying these issues is to make a judgement on whether they may provide opportunities for my mission. In my view, which is backed by the SCSC, they don't. But, the next two are very different when viewed from this angle:

- There is a sense of 'loss' engulfing the planet. Everybody on the planet has more stuff – whether you are a mega-rich media magnate ordering another yacht or a tribe of remote nomads who have acquired a hand-cranked radio. Families of two have three lavatories in the house. Wardrobes are stuffed with clothes that have barely been worn and will never be worn again. Stuff, stuff, stuff – but with it comes a sense that a price has been paid. Some miss the 'old' ways and the 'old' family structures and boundaries. Some miss the old values of respect, deference and discipline. In my research this morning I read that, in India, wealth creation has come at the cost of no longer caring for a family's elderly. Cultural and ethnic heritages are being diluted and then abandoned all over the world. It is this universal 'sense of loss' – which manifests itself in a billion million different ways – that offers me real opportunities

■ There is also a sense of 'alienation' felt by the common people. Increasingly the world is ruled by governments or huge organisations that are thinly disguised kleptocracies. Personal greed, power-group vanity and vested interest groups hold sway over the majority of the broad policy decisions that affect ordinary people living ordinary lives. As a result they are alienated from their leaders, whether they are political, organisational or corporate. But this alienation, this time around, has NOT bred revolution. It has bred APATHY – principally because, if you unite and force changes, you just get more of the same in power. By my calculation, about 95% of the earth's population no longer gives a shit about anything outside their own immediate social and financial hinterland.

THESE are the two areas – the almost universal senses of *loss* and *alienation* – where I can, and will, work. But I will need a car (amongst other things), and I have seen one on the roads called a BMW Mini – which looks absolutely brilliant.

I have one more Key Goal to report on, but I may head back 'up north' tomorrow and work on it while I am on the train. I am excited by the work I have done here – and feel the need to start some things moving. I will call in tonight and say my goodbyes to José.

»

13 January

08.23.34 GMT

To: All Constellations

Fairly uneventful travel up to Whalley yesterday – I'm getting the hang of moving about this country. Met up with José the night before and we polished off a few *grappas* when *Botticellis* closed – and this looks to be a very promising relationship. He is good fun, with the driest sense of humour. As a restaurateur, he only really dislikes three things – all Americans, all children and groups of more than four women. The first demand to be served a three course meal in thirty minutes, the second leave the place looking like downtown Baghdad (which becomes even worse if they are American AND children) and the third group won't tip and demand individual bills. Other than that he seems to like everybody, although by my calculation his 'dislikes' would seem to add up to half the planet. As I have already mentioned, he is separated from his wife, although they remain business partners – and he suggested that, when I came down next, we should have a night out together chasing the ladies. That's something I don't need, but I will keep in touch.

I got back quite late last night, and was quite relieved to see Nuala was off-shift. Cide was in the bar, however, and he greeted me with what looked suspiciously like relief on his face. He asked me what I was doing tomorrow night – and when I told him that I had nothing planned he almost whooped with joy. Telling me that he had something planned for me that 'would make my eyes water' he suddenly rushed off jabbering into his mobile phone, leaving me mystified.

Right – on to ***religion***. If you've lost track here, this is the fifth of my Five Key Goals of the year – to identify the strengths and weaknesses of earth's major current religions, and the associated problems and opportunities these offer the mission. In summary, my Interim Report could read: 'Major religions: somewhere between five and a billion in number; Problems: insurmountable; Opportunities: not a lot'. I suspect you want a bit more.

Here's the kind of bollocks you get into when you open this door. There is a place (in what you might remember as Gaul) called Lourdes. No, you won't have heard of that, and nor should you. However, it is a location that has been defined as 'Special Place' by one of the Big Religions, with a reputation for miraculously curing ailments of all kinds. I used the London Library facilities to look into this further, and here's what I found. People have been travelling to Lourdes for about 150 earth years. Each year about 80,000 'pilgrims' make the trip. [Where's my calculator – here it is – (pause) – that's twelve million visits.] Now then, records indicate that, over that time, there have been sixty 'miracle cures' – which is a 0.0005% success rate. That does not include a wheelchair-bound man who died when he was lowered into the water, but whose wheelchair was reputed to have come out with *new tyres on it*. Further analysis of the sixty 'miracles' reveals that it was somewhere between possible and probable that these illnesses would have could have cured themselves naturally. But still they believe, and still they come – and there's my problem.

Judaism, Christianity and Islam, though themselves riven with differing interpretations and sub-beliefs, now form the

Big Three. There follows any number of additional regions you could wish to name, with all of them having two properties in common: (a) once you hang your hat on one of them you never change and (b) you are encouraged to become more fundamental and extreme in your beliefs. For my mission it is, therefore (and rather surprisingly), a no-go area. I must find something that binds not divides. My work will be in the universal senses of 'loss' and 'alienation'.

I must go now as I have a busy day. There is a car sales place just outside Whalley, and I have just read in the local paper that they have a BMW Mini for sale, and I fancy it.

»

14 January

15.25.12 GMT

To: All Constellations

Got it! The Mini, that is. One task completed – but it was NOT without incident. I had been thoroughly briefed on cars and the owning of them before I came, including about 50 hours in the simulator to make sure I could drive. So, when I went up to the salesman and he suggested a trial drive, I was confident there would be no problem. It was a beautiful thing to behold – I can only describe it as Canary Yellow, and it looked lovely in the pale watery, wintry, sunshine as we approached it for my drive. Then he opened the door and I almost had a heart attack. *The steering wheel was on the wrong side*. Then, when we (rather bumpily) got on to the road *the other cars were on the wrong side*. Somebody on the briefing and research teams, and I will mention no names, had not done their homework.

I survived, and managed to get through the paperwork – which I only finished this morning by finalising taxes and something called insurance. I now own a car.

I got back to the hotel about lunchtime, and saw Nuala again – who seemed to have forgotten everything that happened. Surely not. She greeted me with a cheery wave and (I assume) pretended to be busy, but surely there must be a turmoil raging inside her. She has touched my tonsils, and there can be no going back. As Cide would say 'Once you have squeezed THAT toothpaste out of the tube, you can't get it back in.'

Talking of Cide, he's remained mysterious about this evening. As he rushed off, he just said he'd pick me up in his car about 8.00 p.m. and that it would make sense if I was 'prepared'.

»

15 January

12.45.23 GMT

To: All Constellations

I can hardly believe what happened and I can hardly believe I am writing this. Here's what I can recall about last night. For some time Cide has been trying to get a 'date' with a local woman called Terri (short for Theresa). It seems there was enthusiasm for the idea from her side as well. There was a barrier, however, which was Terri's lifelong friend Debs (short for Deborah), who would have been left alone if Cide and Terri had started 'going out' together. Are you following this? The solution was obvious

– find somebody who could 'occupy' Debs while they did their thing. Which was why Cide greeted me like an identical twin he had not seen for sixty years when I got back from London.

This was explained to me as we went in the car to a local restaurant – although it was sold to me much more on the basis of my attractive nature, (the as-yet-unmet) Debs' delightful character and my perceived needs to get a life.

What a disaster. Debs turned out to be hiding her character inside a body that was too big for it. She turned up wearing one of these vest things that exposed her stomach. Whereas when Nuala did that, the effect was, well, disconcerting, with Debs the effect was, well, nauseating. Really. This was particularly so when she was sitting, as her stomach considerably overhung her skirt – an effect that was worsened by the fact that she had a ring in her navel. Her shoulders also overhung her sleeves, and her chins (three) overhung her scarf-like thing around her neck. She had obviously made an effort and her (very dark) hair kind of stood up and looked as if it had been glued in place, which it had been. Her heavily made up face was an odd colour, which I later found out that Cide called Clearasil Orange, and the effect was completed by a red slash of a mouth. Still, she was friendly enough.

Cide dominated the table in his usual confident way. I made a note of how he ordered his meal:

'Right, pal. I want the Barnsley Chop. And I want it well done. And when I say well done, that is what I mean. I want it cremated. I only want to be able to recognise it as a Barnsley chop from its dental records. OK?'

The waiter grimaced a bit but our lady friends seemed to love it.

When we had finished our meal, and were getting to the end of our coffee, our conversation seemed to slow down and become a bit strained. Suddenly, Debs sort of leaned conspiratorially across the table, affording me a view of a gap between her enormous breasts that you could lose a goat down, and uncovered the plot:

'I know. Why don't Cide and Terri head off to that Club they want to go to – and Tommy and me will just get a cab home.'

I had barely enough time to say anything before those two were up and away, with a cheerful cry from Cide as he went out:

'Cheers you two – bill's been paid – it's my treat tonight. Now, don't do anything I wouldn't do.'

This (paying the bill) seemed very generous, but, as Debs explained, Cide was on top form as his soccer team, Manchester City, had just recorded a victory. Apparently, this doesn't happen very often, and causes the supporters of Manchester City to head for oblivion during the next few evenings.

However, being stranded (good word) with Debs was not what I wanted. After those two left she slid around the banquette seats, like some sort of walrus with a slightly smaller moustache, until she was up close and next to me. It needed some quick thinking, but you don't get to where I've got to in my lives without being able to do that occasionally – so I called Bash in his taxi. I managed to shield my mobile phone and mutter into it for him to organise TWO taxis at the same time, and then closed my phone down and prepared to grit it out.

Bash arrived just as she was outlining her plan:

'How bout we call in at the offie and get some Jacob's Creek out of the fridge? Then we can go back to my place for a nightcap.'

I did not know (and still don't as yet) what an 'offie' was; nor did I know (and ditto) what a Jacobs Creek was. But the message was getting clear. She had eaten (at least) four baguettes of garlic bread during the evening, and as she leant closer to 'whisper' in my ear I was overcome by waves of foul breath winds. Her final words of this terrifying passage were:

'Guess what? I hate taking my own stockings off.'

At that moment, Bash rescued me – or, at least, the speaker system in the restaurant did as it announced that the taxis were here for Mr. Ramsbottom. Debs looked quizzically at me as we got our coats, but I said we'd probably misheard. When we got outside Bash was wonderful, catching on immediately. I pretended there must have been a mistake, but – with a deep sigh – said that it might be for the better this time as I felt I was coming down with a cold. It would be wrong to say I ushered Debs into her cab, but I 'helped' her into the back seat in a way that saw her ended up sprawling all over it. Her legs were in the air and the contents of her handbag sprinkled all over the seat and floor. If I ever had any doubts as to whether I was doing the right thing, they faded with my last sight of her. As I closed the door it became obvious that she was not wearing underclothes. I will never eat a Barnsley chop again.

I paid her fare to her home, and waved politely as she left – promising that 'next time' I would be feeling better. Then I collapsed in the back of Bash's cab, and escaped. Our journey back to the hotel was silent but for his barely audible laughter. I had escaped.

»

16 January

12.34.12 GMT

To: All Constellations

I've had a long message on my BLa this morning. It was the Corner Office calling. It was mainly to respond to my Interim Report and progress against my Key Goals, but it did also contain a few comments – and some welcome advice – on the problems I seem to be having with women crossing my path. It was private, and I intend to keep it that way – but I will circulate some of the general thoughts it contained. Sex, and the drives and activities that accompany it, have been ever present on this planet. But they have never been so overt and without boundaries. In my previous visits, if I did not wish to be involved or deflected – as was the case – then so be it. But not now. I would have to factor the Planet's new freedoms and attitudes into my work, and I may well have to become involved to gain the necessary insight. Hmmm.

As to my Interim Reports, I got nothing but a ringing endorsement for my analysis and approach. That's a first.

I was a bit worried about meeting Cide yesterday, but there was no problem. I told him that me and Debs had agreed to meet again and he seemed well pleased – then told me the gory details about his night with Terri. I have already mentioned that he supports a soccer team called Manchester City and that they had just had a win. Terri, too, is a fan of the same team and they celebrated well into the night after they had left us. So well, in fact, that the sexual union which had been plotted by Cide didn't come to pass. They both, apparently, reached Cide's bedroom, and were in the process of preparing for the 'great act' when, according to Cide, he suddenly did the 'one-legged trouser dance' across the bedroom, crashed into his HiFi and fell asleep on the floor surrounded by broken CDs. Terri, fortunately, did not witness this as, exhausted by the efforts of trying to undo her bra, she had already fallen asleep head-down in the pillow. When they woke the next day, they agreed they would postpone the 'great day' until they felt better.

»

17 January

14.56.12 GMT

To: All Constellations

I drove the new car today – all the way into Burnley!

I have decided that I will have an initial visit to Ireland, and I wanted to find out something about the place before I decide which part to visit, so I've bought a pile of books (and some music discs – CDs) to help me decide. I'm off to lose myself in them now.

»

18 January

10.45.32 GMT

To: All Constellations

A bit late, I know, but I decided to start my diet programme today. My weight is not really improving (87 kilos this morning) and I am realising that this – like the 'sex' thing – is something that I will simply not be able to ignore this time. I've read and understood my guiding sheets, and I've got to drink two litres of water every day. TWO LITRES – I'll be pissing like a racing camel. This morning I had just a bowl of a breakfast cereal called Special K and some fruit juice and then I went into the hotel's 'Fitness Centre' (referred to in short as 'the gym'). It was suggested I ran for 5,000 metres, and they have these things that you stand on in the gym which suddenly start moving under your feet until you have to run to stand still. You set it at a pace you can manage, and then watch the dials as they tell you how far you have run, what calories you have used, how long you have been running and so on. They even have a little TV on the instrument screen so you can watch news of sporting activities. Anyway, I set off.

FIVE THOUSAND METRES. Do you know how far that is? WITH MY FEET? I can't do that. I set off at a rate of twelve kilometres per hour, but was exhausted after about eighty metres. Then I went down to 10 kph; then to 8.5 kph; and then in steady downward increments to 5.0 kph for the bulk of the journey. The embarrassing thing was that on the running machine next to me was a sprightly woman who was clearly older than me but who was running faster and for a longer period.

Two hours later, my legs refused to work properly. I am going to bed now to read more about Ireland. I will not be playing any more of their music. I'm feeling bad enough as it is.

»

19 January

10.43.12 GMT

To: All Constellations

Some good news and some bad news about this diet and exercise programme. I did not read my sheets properly. I am supposed to WORK UP TO five kilometres, not start off with it on the first day. Which is good news because the bad news is that I can barely walk. The backs of my legs, and my ankles, and the balls of my feet are all either swollen or in agony or both. Of course, the other thing that didn't help me is that I now realise that you should have proper shoes to run with, and I only had my normal shoes – a pair that carry the name of Dr. Martens, which Cide had recommended. No wonder the little old lady laughed on the next running machine. I must drive to a sports shop today and get some appropriate footwear.

While I'm out, I will also follow up on a small house that is available for rent. From the description in the newspaper it will suit my purposes ideally. It is fully furnished, and has satellite TV available, and a special place specifically for parking my car.

For the moment I seem to have got away with the escape from Debs – Cide has mentioned nothing and, in fact, seems in a good mood about everything. He's trying to get me to play my first 'round' (?) of golf, but I need to get on with some other stuff – notably organising my next project trip.

Before I leave the subject of Debs (for ever, I hope), I've had a couple of messages from you expressing concern at the fact I lied – both to her and to Cide about the outcome (and meeting her again). The main gist was that there were, in fact, quite a few lies – and that they seem to come easily. Is this compatible (I'm asked) with the integrity and requirements of my mission?

Look, that was then, this is now. I am finding unplanned complications and challenges everywhere. While I'm flying solo, I'm having to get through on my own wits and resources. Nobody, I repeat NOBODY, is more aware than me about the need for spiritual purity, but it is more important at this stage that I survive and establish a solid base position. If I get in a jam that threatens the success of the mission, then pragmatism rules and I'll lie if I have to in order to get out. But I'll be honest with you guys.

»

20 January

09.45.34 GMT

To: All Constellations

I've seen the house I want. It's small for this country – really just two rooms on the ground floor and two rooms up the stairs. I can rent it furnished, which provides everything I need apart from luxuries like satellite TV – but, as we are under-budget so far, I can splash out on a few cool things. I have signed up for a six-month rental, and paid an additional one month's rent as a deposit. Today I have to fix up supplies of electricity, gas, telephone and local taxes. The Sky TV man is coming in a few days. With luck, I can move in at the start of February – which will leave me time to acquire the additional stuff I need (bed sheets and towels and so on). My address (doesn't that sound grand!) will be Number Eleven, Hodder Street. Whalley.

Apparently the house was originally built in 1890 – more than a century ago – to house factory workers for the local cotton mill. The cotton trade was eventually lost to India during and after the Great Intra-Planetary Conflict (1914–45). What seems rather surprising is that, when the work disappeared to India, the Indians started to come here to live. I have much to learn about this planet, and I feel a visit to India is a must.

»

21 January

17.45.32 GMT

To: All Constellations

Tomorrow is Sunday, and I have been invited out to Sunday lunch – by Nuala of all people! I told her about my new house yesterday when I gave notice of leaving the hotel – and she seemed quite bemused. Then I told her I was planning to visit Ireland and she told me that we MUST meet up together so she could tell me where to go and where not to go. Her parents live right up in the north – a place called Antrim – and she said she could give me some great tips about the whole place. When she suggested we have Sunday lunch together, I must have appeared a bit reticent because she started smiling – which soon gave way to her lovely infectious laugh.

'You're a wee bit of a shy boy wit' de ladies, aren't you, now, Tom.'

'Well, not really. It's just . . .'

'Aaahh, c'mon now. I know I know. But I'm not goin' to bite your bloody hid off. I get bored on Sundays. I've only got a small flat and once I've finished me paper and done the weekly wash, it's a long auld haul through to the Antiques Road Show. There's a pub near us that does Sunday dinner for a fiver, an' I can tell you all about Derry an' where to find the last feckin' proper frying pan in use in the UK.'

'Well, if you are sure . . .'

'Sure I'm sure. It should be youse askin' me, but if I wait for that, the hole in me arse will close up. I'm just talkin' 'bout a meal out, but if it'll help yas I won't mind if you shove the Yellow Pages down the front of your jeans. OK?'

'OK.'

About eighty percent of the conversation was lost on me. How can the hole in your arse close up? What are Yellow Pages? But I agreed and – in fairness – I am fair looking forward to it. I should get some really useful information on Ireland.

»

22 January

18.24.56 GMT

To: All Constellations

What an interesting and rewarding day. It started badly – I still am full of aches and pains from my ill advised 5,000 metres 'run' – and I am particularly concerned about my feet. Obviously they carry 'baggage' – but they shouldn't look like this, even after a traumatic bit of exercise. Parts of my right ankle and toe joint are red and swollen and painful – I can barely get my shoe on. I will have to watch this.

Let me report on my lunch. I do like Nuala, she is such a mix of a lot of positives. She is a hard working example of modern womanhood, and a fair representative of what I believe is one of the biggest single societal changes since my last visit. She is funny, bright, and thoroughly modern. She can be rude (very rude) and irreverent, or polite and official – sometimes all at the same time. She has a strong Norn Iron accent, and is neither proud nor embarrassed by it. She can give off sexual signals or 'plain Jane' signals. The planet has dealt her a hand of cards and she plays it as she wants to, how she wants to and when she wants to. If I can steer clear of the obvious pitfalls, she could be a key member of the Team.

It will not be a surprise to you that the positioning of her tongue in my mouth left me somewhat shocked. What is astonishing is that it seems to have had no effect on her. It is as though it was a routine part of a barely extraordinary evening. I am slowly coming to terms with that – although it took the first half hour of our lunch together to get me to feel at ease. We then had a lovely lunch, driving in her car to a restaurant called the Tickled Trout. After our chat, I changed my plans for the Irish visit.

I am still planning to go as soon as I am settled in my new house. What changed is that I am no longer planning to make Dublin the focus of my visit. I had been reading up about Ireland, and bought several books by Tim Pat Coogan and Brendan Behan. The Coogan ones have been reduced to a role to help me get into bed with my sore foot (they provide a handy step up as they are so thick). Behan is different, and I have fallen in love with his work and memory – principally through an old book I found in a second-hand bookshop, which contains some short essays he wrote for the *Irish Times* newspaper in the 1950s. They are absolutely magical, and go some way to explaining this weird fascination the rest of the world have for this odd-ball country and its dysfunctional spokesmen. There are lessons here for me in using language as rhetoric.

When I explained that the aim of my visit was to do some 'research' for a project I was doing on modern religious issues, Nuala's response was immediate. I should start in Norn Iron. I should land in Belfast, hire a car and follow the coast around through Antrim (where her parents live) to Derry – the epicentre of all the issues. Only then, if I felt I needed more, should I cross the border and head down to Galway, giving Dublin a wide berth. Dublin, in her words, was 'full of thirty-somethings wearing Rupert scarves, lunching in Wagmama and going home for a wank 'cos the value of their tiny apartment had just gone up another zillion Euros'.

It sounds like a plan. I will go early next month.

»

23 January

11.27.34 GMT

To: All Constellations

Right foot still bad. I'm going to have to see somebody about it – the SCSC are looking into my options. Meanwhile I am almost desk-bound – doing all the stuff involved in me moving into my house next week. The Sky TV engineer is booked to come during the morning of the 1st February. Already this morning I have FINALLY sorted out the supply of electricity and gas (both from the same supplier), the telephone and water. I also sorted out my local taxes.

The water supply system, or rather the water 'disposal' system, is amazing. As I think I have already explained, you can pass your solids into the toilet – a little white bowl that you sit on – and then, afterwards, you just press a handle and it just gets 'washed' away. I don't know where it goes (or how) but it's brilliant – none of that digging a hole stuff. And there's no smell, unless it's a really bad dump – in which case you can get a little tin of stuff from ASDA which has a spray fixed on it. Two sprays and the room smells like a pine forest – or, at least, that's what it says on the tin. I wouldn't know, but it's better than what it replaces.

The good news is that all that research and briefing paid off – all this house moving thing was done without a problem concerning my identity, credit rating, virtual and real money supply. I'm now all but a real person.

»

24 January

12.45.23 GMT

To: All Constellations

My foot is in absolute AGONY this morning. I cannot get a shoe on, so am confined to my room – and, as though that wasn't bad enough, I got a bombshell from the SCSC. At least, that's what it said at the bottom of the communication. I suspect, however, the Corner Office is behind this.

The gist of it was this: they have conducted their own interim review of progress and are not happy. They have 'brainstormed' and come up with an idea that is designed to help me make progress. They stress this is a 'positive' development and in 'no way' reflects a 'value judgement' of any kind about the way I am tackling the mission.

Here's the jewel they've come up with. After I have got settled into my new base and done the Irish visit, I should consider employing a PR 'consultant'. PR, apparently, stands for Public Relations. Nothing big and fancy, but somebody who (possibly) runs a single person business, who is 'hungry' for success – and who could help me establish the 'profile' they feel I need to start getting some 'traction' (their word) on the mission. As if I didn't have enough problems trying to understand the bloody English they speak down here in England, they have to trail out a bag-full of bollock-speak.

The message is clear, though, and it is that I am perceived to be splashing about in the shallow end. They are researching suitable PR agents, and will give me a name or two when I'm back from Ireland.

»

25 January

10.34.27 GMT

To: All Constellations

Can't move. Something's got to be done. I can't wait for this Grand Pooh-Bah medic that the SCSC are fixing up for me. I need help now – my foot's on fire.

I asked Nuala if she knew of somewhere I could go or someone I could see to get help. She told me that the local Medical Centre would see me – all I had to do was to tell them I was from Bedford but working up here and give them my National Insurance Number and they'd see me.

I've phoned them and got an appointment for tomorrow at 11.45 a.m. – but then I got the bad news. All that brilliant briefing and research and they've forgotten or omitted my National Insurance Number, so they'll be working overtime overnight to fix me up with one, along with (I hope) sorting out the paper-trail behind it.

»

26 January

12.56.23 GMT

To: All Constellations

I have a problem. I limped to the car and just managed to drive myself to the Medical Centre in time for my appointment. I went in to see a doctor, and he turned out to be from India, and he was very polite and helpful. With some difficulty I managed to get my shoe and sock off, and I'm sure I saw a faint smile come over his face when he saw my foot. Obviously, he was fascinated by those 'other' marks, but he needed only a VERY short look at my ankle and the ball of my foot to diagnose the problem:

'What we have here, Mr Ramsbottom, is a case of gout. Not just an ordinary case of gout, but one you might call a case of gout with a vengeance.'

'It's what?'

'Gout.'

'Gout?'

'Yes.'

'Gout. What the . . .what's that? Where did it come from? What do I do about it?'

'It happens because you are creating uric acid inside your system, and I suspect you are doing that in great quantities and of industrial strength.'

'If that's the cause of this pain, I must be creating uric acid like a racing camel pissing. What can you do?'

'I will give you some tablets – they will quickly reduce the inflammation. Meanwhile, while that's getting better, we will take some blood samples and see if it's a big or small, or temporary or permanent problem. Then we will fix it properly.'

Apparently, men of my age, if they don't eat and drink properly, and they have had some problems with their feet or joints (and haven't I just?) are prone to this thing – so I suppose I'll be getting more diet sheets from the SCSC.

Anyway, I stopped off at a chemist's shop on the way back and picked up my pills. I've just had two – so I'll let you know how I get on.

»

27 January

08.15.34 GMT

To: All Constellations

Blessed, blessed relief. Oh, the relief. The pain and swelling began to go last night. Cide laughed when I told him what I'd got – but he did tell me that Sid used to get it and, as a result, had come up with an interesting theory. He calls it his 'Theory of Piles'. Some things are SO painful – and he names the theory after one such symptom, piles, which are miniature red-hot coconuts (his description) on the rim of your anus – that they are almost worth experiencing *for the relief when they've gone*. I am just wondering if the Theory of Piles could have any wide ramifications in society, and maybe for my mission.

All I know is that it has all left me exhausted, so I'm going to catch up on some sleep today.

»

28 January

11.34.23 GMT

To: All Constellations

As might have been expected, lots of panic-mode stuff from the SCSC – and a real up-and-downer of an argument to follow. They STILL want me to have a thorough medical examination because they are worried about my overall health for the mission ahead. They were also not overly impressed with either the diagnoses or solutions of my Indian Doctor, but I defended him stoutly. We need to wait (about a week) for the results of my blood tests, and then let's see. If that wasn't bad enough, I got three pages of diet advice for addressing the out-of-range production of uric acid in the body. Add that lot onto the first lot of diet sheets I got and I'll starve to death.

The one thing I have agreed to is to up my water intake to two and a half litres, so my current activities are hindered by having to stop for a slash every half hour.

I am starting to get all my things together for the move. I have acquired a lot – from a standing start – and it's going to take a couple of trips in my car to get it all over to Hodder Street.

»

29 January

10.45.23 GMT

To: All Constellations

Busy day, but luckily my foot is improving. The SCSC are really concerned about this gout thing inasmuch as it's not a 'cool' or stylish illness. It may (in other words) be bad for my image. I have instructions to call it an arthritic problem – caused by past traumas to my feet. That's one way of putting it.

Gout, apparently, will not play well with the media if (or, rather, when) my mission gathers momentum.

On that subject, I have challenged them about this PR thing. My issue is that I cannot retain professional help like that principally because it will be impossible for me to provide a sensible brief. The whole point here is that I am starting from scratch, and I have done nothing for them to try to get into the media. The SCSC's response is that you don't need that in the current climate in this particular country – that, with appropriate help, *you can become famous just for being famous*. I might have to accept that the initial exposure may not seem a step in the longer term direction I want, but with the right budget I can get some very helpful wind in my sails.

»

30 January

16.23.24 BST

To: All Constellations

After I finished my packing last night I popped into the pub in Whalley and had a few of the Boddingtons with Sid – who was in there on his own. I think I have found a way of condensing all the complex issues facing (a) the planet in general and (b) this country in particular. If you haven't got a filtering or condensing device of some kind you can be absolutely overwhelmed with dozens of papers and news channels. I think I've found one in Sid.

I made the mistake of flippantly saying 'Hi Sid. What's pissing you off, then?' as a sort of silly 'hello' when I sat down with my beer. It was as though the floodgates had opened:

'What's pissing me off? WHAT'S PISSING ME OFF? I'll tell you what's pissing me off . . .'

And off he went. Without pausing for breath he covered all the major and minor things than are currently annoying him – which ranged from that 'Corrupt Turd' running the United Nations to footballers wearing gloves. I just need to tee him up like that every couple of weeks and I'm right at the heart of what's important down here. I'll try to remember the next one and report it back to you as close to verbatim as I can.

»

31 January

14.34.21 GMT

To: All Constellations

Last day in the hotel, and I feel quite wistful. I've just had lunch in the bar and said goodbye to everyone. Just as I was leaving, Nuala appeared and gave me a potted plant – a cactus of all things. It's a LONG time since I've seen one of those. She gave it to me as a 'house-warming' present, and right there, right then she gave me a little kiss to accompany it. It was nothing like the first, just a brushing of my cheek. She does have lovely eyes – as I think I may have told you.

All set to move tomorrow – and my Irish trip is planned for the 4th of February. I can't wait for both. I feel we are making real progress now.

FEBRUARY

»

1 February

17.24.32 GMT

To: All Constellations

That was an exhausting day. I had no idea I had accumulated so much in such a short time. It's amazing how many things I have acquired that I deemed – at the time of acquisition – as essential to the mission. As part of my drive to improve my health (and image) I bought a juice-making machine, which I have yet to use, although I have several pounds of apples, carrots and some things called kiwi fruits just ready to be juiced. Actually, they are looking very tired by now, and several need throwing away.

It took two trips in my car and one in Bash's taxi to get all my stuff to my new place, and most of it is still in cardboard boxes.

The highlight of the day – and one of the reasons I haven't unpacked yet – was the visit of the Sky TV 'engineer'. When he left (for the first time), I stopped everything and sat down and recorded as much as I could remember of the conversation we had. I am including it here to give you some idea of how this planet makes the simple things very complicated. It started when I answered the door after the bell rang for the first ever ring under my occupancy.

'Morning Mr Ramsbottom. Sky TV installation.'

'Oh, great – right on time.'

'All part of the service.'

'Do you want some tea of coffee while you do whatever it is you have to?'

'That'd be great. Coffee if you have it. Milk and two sugars. I'll just be having a look at your set and the layout of the house.'

It took me about five minutes to get a couple of coffees made – most of it used up hunting for two mugs to put it in. When they were ready I found him by the front door.

'Bit of a problem here, sir.'

'What's that then? TV not right? They assured me it would be . . .'

'Nah. It's the dish. It needs somebody to go up a ladder to do the installation, and I don't do that.'

'You don't do WHAT? I thought you were the installation engineer.'

'That's right sir. But the free installation package doesn't allow me to go up a ladder.'

'But you've got a ladder on top of your van.'

'Ah. Yes. But that's not for this kind of job sir.'

'But every one I've seen is high up on the front of a house or on the chimney.'

'That's right sir. I think the best place here will be high on the front of the house, left side.'

'You mean like every other house in the terrace?'

'That's right sir.'

'But you won't do it?'

'I can't sir. You need a high-level installation engineer.'

'But, I repeat, you've got a ladder on top of your van.'

'I can only use that for authorised jobs and this isn't one.'

'That's just bloody ridiculous.'

'There's no need to use language like that, sir.'

'OK, OK. It's not your fault. OK, what do I do now? How do I get somebody to come and do the installation?'

'Oh, I can organise that for you sir – but there will be a charge.'

'Ah. I see. OK, I'm hung out to dry. I get the message. Can you book this guy for me? When can it happen?'

'Oh, it can be done today sir. Anytime after four o'clock.'

'And I suppose you know of such an engineer.'

'Oh, yes, sir.'

'Who is it? Do I have to phone him?'

'No, sir. No need. It would be me, sir – and you don't need to phone me. We can fix the appointment now.'

'How do you mean?'

'I'll come back and do it for you sir.'

'You mean YOU are the high-level engineer as well?'

'That's right, sir – except that I'm sub-contracted in that role, whereas I'm on a different sub-contract in this role.'

'What will it cost?'

'Eighty pounds sir.'

'I'll see you at four.'

This is an almost faultless scam – beautifully thought through and carried out. Sometimes you just have to admire a master craftsman at work – and pay up. He came back at four o'clock and the job was done in forty minutes. I have Sky TV. I need it as I must assimilate all aspects of modern culture as part of my mission, and I've also got all the sports channels.

»

2 February

11.45.27 GMT

To: All Constellations

Late up this morning – largely as a result of watching TV until the early hours. I have learned how to play interactive Poker, which seems to be an astonishingly fast-growing element of modern life, and I found the Babecast Channel. The latter is also immensely popular among young people, particularly males, but I need to study it a bit more before I report back to you on its content.

I am having a bit of an up and downer (Cide's slang for an argument) with the SCSC about this PR thing. They have gone ahead and researched and BOOKED ME AN APPOINTMENT with a London-based agency – and I'm not happy about the process or the content of this approach. Direct intervention like this puts me and the mission at risk – and, despite the assurances they gave me about doing it all by 'untraceable e-mail', I am unhappy about this major departure from the rules we all agreed. I suspect the Corner Office is behind this, and it's a thinly veiled comment on my perceived lack of progress.

What it forces me to do, of course, is to start putting my charter together. I need to provide this PR lady (it is a 'her') with something she can work with. Frankly, every day makes me less sure of my ground on this. Maybe the trip to Ireland will help.

»

3 February

09.45.23 GMT

To: All Constellations

I am getting nowhere with my diet and general health problems. To tell the truth, I haven't been that disciplined in keeping to my eating and exercise programmes, and I am finding this aspect of 'modern' life both strange and uncomfortable. The idea that whole communities are suffering life-threatening health problems through having too much to eat is something that none of us foresaw as an issue. I've never thought about my weight before. I've always been tall and rather skinny and, although I have never had a BMI (body mass index) calculated before, I am sure that, if it had have been worked out in the past, it would have been 'within range'.

I am getting a sympathetic hearing from the SCSC on this but they are determined that my health and weight should get back on track. Hence, they have researched and made ANOTHER appointment for me – this time at a specialist hospital. It's near London (at a place called Harpenden), and I'm booked to go on the day after my PR appointment so I can do the both of them on one trip. The two appointments are on the 16th and 17th of this month.

Tomorrow I travel to Ireland. I have a short visit planned, and Nuala has helped me put an itinerary together – including a place to stay on my first night, which she has booked for me. It's near her home town – right in the north, in the County of Antrim. I have a lot to do today to get ready. Tomorrow I have to drive to the metropolis called Liverpool, and from there I fly to Belfast. I have arranged to hire a car there, and from then I'm on my own.

»

4 February

20.34.18 GMT

To: All Constellations

That was a long day. The flight was uneventful – except for the fact that everybody associated with the airline was wearing orange. There has been a lot of controversy on the planet recently about an American prisoner-of-war camp in Cuba where all the prisoners wear orange overalls and it was hard to get these images out of my mind while we were flying. The only other item of interest from the journey was that it took ten minutes longer to queue for my rented car than it did to fly from Liverpool to Belfast.

My aim was to head out of Belfast as quickly as possible and find my way over to the east coast. Although Belfast is the capital city of Northern Ireland, I have identified, with Nuala's help, the city of Derry as having more relevance for my needs. From the parts I saw of Belfast, I don't think I missed much. In fact I was not impressed with anything or anywhere until I suddenly hit upon a sleepy little coastal haven called Cushendun. It was pretty deserted on this grey, cold winter's day but I needed a break (mainly for a pee). I got out of the car and had a walk around. In five minutes I found myself on the small 'sheltered' beach and my mind began ticking over.

Why am I here? This land has a special set of issues – issues that are of prime relevance to my mission. Apart from being an early outpost of the Christian religion, this island now epitomises how INTERNAL divisions can split a movement or a belief system. The main religions have all got such divisions – Judaism and Zionism, Shiia and Sunni Muslims (which started within thirty years of the death of the prophet) and, here, Catholics and Protestants. If I am to unite people, I must understand their divides. The wind howling in from the North Channel began the mental cleansing I will need.

Back in the car, I carried on around the Antrim coast, passing the stunning Glens of Antrim. After a couple more hours, I reached my day's destination – the friend of Nuala who lives on an exposed stretch of the northern coast called Whitepark Bay. I'm here now, having just met Brian and been shown to my room.

He welcomed me with a glass of something called Bushmills – a distilled spirit drink that comes from a place hardly five miles away. I didn't know what to expect so I just raised my glass as a token of new friendship and downed the drink in one. For a moment there I thought my chest had caught fire, but gradually it softened to a warm, inner glow. That's some kind of drink.

Incidentally, as you have probably worked out, we have fixed the technical glitches that meant I could not communicate during my last trip (to Spain). I'm sending this from my bedroom, which Brian's wife has adorned with many oriental (I think) pictures and statues. I gather she travels a lot, and in fact she's away now.

Brian does not provide an evening meal. He suggests I drive into Bushmills town where there are several restaurants. I'll see – I'm tired after a long day and not particularly hungry. I also need to save some room for my breakfast tomorrow. In Nuala's words, 'Brian has the "last great frying pan" in the western world – and performs magic with it.' It is, apparently, a dying art. We shall see.

»

5 February

10.23.45 GMT

To: All Constellations

I am back in my room, having just finished breakfast. I am replete – not just in the physical sense (which I could get just by raiding the breakfast buffet at the hotel back in Whalley) but in a spiritual sense as well. Let me explain.

Part of the 'sense of loss' felt by many in this nation – and which I have already referred to as an opportunity for my mission – is a perceived longing for things and processes of the past. The irony is that both the things and the processes are (largely) still available but (a) nobody can be bothered acquiring or doing either and (b) the new ways are (generally) more effective and efficient. There is no finer example than the frying pan.

The frying pan that I met this morning – and I feel I should relate to it on human terms – is a monster. I have seen many frying pans – in fact I bought one during a raid on the kitchen department of ASDA before moving in to my new home. The one I bought was clean, small with maybe – MAYBE – enough room for two eggs. It is 'non-stick' which is self explanatory. It is dishwasher proof and a light silvery colour on the outside and a sort of gun-metal grey on the non-stick bit. I intend to throw it away when I get back.

Brian's frying pan was a thing of beauty. It was huge, iron and black. It had been previously owned by his mother. It was legendary in the region. Brian's father had been a bomber pilot in the 1940s and, like many other ex-servicemen, became a middle level manager after the war. He ended up running a team of salesmen and quite regularly would hold his sales meetings at his own house. His wife, armed only with the frying pan, would feed the team. In would go an acre or two of bacon, many yards of sausage and black pudding, a stone or two of tomatoes, half a hundredweight of field mushrooms picked that very morning and enough eggs (fresh enough to still have chicken-shit on the shells) to bring a rhino to its knees. Out would come lunch for eight hungry men – accompanied only by endless freshly baked soda-bread and enough tea to float a barge.

The pan, passed on as part of his parents' minute estate, is Brain's prized possession. He would not soil it with anything other than local butter, and produced me the solo version of the team breakfast – with the added delicacy of a triangle of local potato cake.

This kind of pan has all but vanished from the nation's kitchen cabinets. Nothing – but NOTHING – now lasts fifty years, improving all the time. It is big and cumbersome and wholly inappropriate for the muesli and cranberry juice breakfast needs of a society that has the same affinity for the word 'fry' as it does for the words 'venereal' and 'disease'. But there is something here for me. There's a recent world that has been lost and few SEEM to mourn its passing. However, I believe there are few who, if faced with the art of breakfast I faced this morning, wouldn't fill their boots and smile all day. It's that gap I have to fill – but on more important subjects than breakfast.

I'm leaving now, heading for Derry – but will visit the coast near Giant's Causeway to walk off the kilos I have put on since I woke up.

»

6 February

08.23.15 GMT

To: All Constellations

I arrived in Derry late last night, as my 'walk' around Giant's Causeway took me way longer than planned. The reason for that is simple: at this time of the year, and with the weather being miserable, I had the place virtually to myself. I took the long walk along the cliff tops and approached the Causeway from the remote east. I was cold and wet, but I was soon in love. It is impossible not to be inspired by the majesty of the cliffs and the scale of everything – and the whole experience helped clear many of my muddy thoughts about the next steps of my mission.

P.S. The causeway itself is bollocks. Silly little thing.

I have booked myself in for two nights at a cheap 'bed and breakfast' inn, in an old three-storey terraced house right in the heart of Derry. The bad news is that it has Sky TV in the room – and I lost £43.18 playing on-line poker. But it is very important that I understand this cultural phenomenon, so I will keep playing despite some heavy and discouraging hints from the Corner Office. I suspect I'm seeing some early signs of discomfort with the budget.

Today I am going to walk the city walls. Along with Jerusalem, this is the modern planetary capital of doctrinal division. I need to understand how this works.

»

7 February

09.45.23 GMT

To: All Constellations

I am packed and ready to leave. This has been a depressing visit.

There has been much optimism over the past few years about the so-called Peace Process, which threatens to bring an end to the centuries-old violence and divisions that have blighted this small island off Britain's west coast. Many are encouraged by the reduction in overt violence and terrorist-style activity, and the fancy words about democratic solutions.

I'm not – and I've only been here a day.

The walk around the city walls is memorable. It takes about an hour if you keep a normal walking pace – or about three hours if you frequently pause and reflect as I did.

The violence and division associated with the city are still wholly evident. The ugly barrier that divides Loyalists from Republicans, and/or Protestants from Catholics is still (thoughtfully) in place, albeit with holes in it so people can cross (physically) from one side to the other in pursuit of some form of normality. You can, as it were, walk under the wire, but you can smell the dogma like dog shit just below the surface.

From where I started it was a half an hour before the red, white and blue Loyalists' houses became evident as I looked out over the inner-city wall. Twenty minutes later, having passed through the hole in the wire and the 'dormant' military station, I looked out over the Republican Bogside, with the city-facing walls of the houses adorned with murals of hate. The climate all around is one of confrontation and mistrust. Non-believers are deemed heretics. Republicans and Loyalists alike mouth a position that you'd trust as far as you could throw Canada. Behind the scenes organised crime and sectarianism governs daily lives.

Here's the problem I face – which is (in my judgement and backing up the research of the SCSC) that any substantive proposed movement to close the gap is always too much for one side and not enough for the other. These trenches are dug too deep. I have no personal route forward for my mission that can be built on uniting one religion, let alone combining any two or more.

I spent last evening in a bar. I have no idea whether it was a Loyalist or Republican – or neither or both. That's the scary part: it's under the surface to the outsider – about one-eighth of an inch under the surface. But you can smell it. And it's ready to roll at a moment's notice.

On top of that, I lost again at on-line poker (£23.28), and my breakfast was shite. Not a potato cake in the house. It'll be a while before I'm back in Derry.

I have a lot of travelling immediately ahead – I'm heading for Donegal and into the Republic. I'm then going down the coast to Connemara and Galway, then making my way to Dublin. I'll be using the time to ponder, so I may be off line for a couple of days. But you can always reach my BLa.

»

9 February

18.35.23 GMT

To: All Constellations

I have reached Galway. The long drive was good – if only inasmuch as it cleared my mood of whining self-pity after visiting Derry. I am not as pessimistic as I was – there must be room for me to manoeuvre within all these societal and religious pissing contests – and I guess if it was easy then (a) somebody would have figured it out and (b) there would be no need for me – and all the resources of the SCSC – to be focused on sorting it.

It is a tribute to the ditzy nature of much of this island that you leave Northern Ireland to head into the Irish Republic by actually heading north. I hugged the coast into Donegal, where the stunning mountains and coastline were poxed only by the large and increasing population of executive homes being built. Then the long drive through Sligo and into Mayo, where I stayed overnight at an inn owned by a Frenchman who arrived twenty years ago to write a book and just stayed on. The book never got written.

From there I made my way down to Connemara, and found myself driving across a vast expanse of Bogland that must be 'twinned' (as are many towns around this part of the planet) with a particularly rugged and unpopulated section of the moon. Whoever oversaw this project back in the Home Office used a lot of imagination.

I feel our choice of this land for a visit at this stage of my mission has been spot on. The Big Issues are nailed up there on the wall for all to see and for me to analyse – but there is time and space to reflect on them. The westerly winds clear your mind of all but your subject matter – and your thoughts can be as bright and clear as the air that you breathe.

That feeling finished about two hours ago as I hit the outskirts of Galway. I have just checked in to my inn (a place called Jurys, at the bottom of a very busy looking street). My plan is to head for Dublin tomorrow, but first I want to spend an evening in this, my first cosmopolitan call in the Republic.

»

10 February

11.23.45 GMT

To: All Constellations

Listen while I'm talking to you. This will need to be quick. I have to check out in half an hour and I haven't packed yet. The whole scenario is not helped by the fact that I have a head like a robber's dog.

They have a drink over here that is like a black-coloured Boddingtons. It is called Guinness. I have tasted it back in Whalley, and thought it unremarkable. It tastes different here.

Last night I wandered into the bar before my meal and, as every male in the place was drinking this stuff, I ordered one. In the corner were two scruffy Irishmen of indeterminate age, one armed with a guitar and one armed with some sort of hand-drum. They began singing in some sort of unison, about some sort of tragedy. The details are beyond me as I could barely understand their accents. The whole thing was not helped by the guitar not being in tune and the drum not being in time, but I know that the song's content was sad. I know this because they wailed the lyrics with their eyes closed.

I had another Guinness, and fairly soon something astonishing happened: I began to sing along with them. That I didn't know the words proved no handicap, particularly after I ordered another Guinness.

I had another Guinness, and ordered my food for the night. I cannot remember what I ordered, but I can remember one detail: it came with an accompaniment of THREE kinds of potato on one plate. Sorry, I need to correct that, my head is not working correctly this morning: it came with one kind of potato, but which was cooked in three different ways – boiled, roast and fried (chipped).

When the waitress brought me my meal, she mentioned that they had a special offer on wine – something coloured red from Bulgaria. It seemed a remarkable bargain, so I had a bottle, and – to the best of my memory – it certainly helped the potatoes go down a treat. Afterwards, I picked my way (carefully) back to the bar to hear the rest of the stuff from the two entertainers who, I am convinced, were composing the material and singing it at the same time. I found no difficulty in singing along, just quietly, to myself. I found a couple of Bushmills helped me keep pace with the composing.

Things get a bit foggy in my memory from then on – but (apparently) I was invited to an upstairs room for a 'poetry reading'. I remember climbing some stairs and paying out six euros, and then stumbling into a big room which was already jam-packed with people – sitting on any manner of seating. The only vacant seats were on an old settee – right in front of the 'stage' (which consisted of two upturned crates). I slumped into it, and was just nodding off when a young, pimply youth stood up and began to read out aloud from a sheaf of papers held dramatically in his hand. Whatever it was he was reading, I could tell it was serious stuff. His face looked as though his finger had just inadvertently poked through the toilet paper.

When he reached the end of his poem, there was an embarrassing silence. Nobody knew whether he had ended – or whether this was just a dramatic (short) pause. It was only after what seemed to me that an excruciating period had elapsed that someone started to clap, to be joined slowly by the rest of the crowd.

This happened again with his second poem. I could tell he was getting annoyed.

Suddenly another solo voice echoed around the room:

'Tell you what, pal, make it easy for yourself and all of us. When you get to within two lines of the final, final end of the poem, give us a signal. Then we can clap at the right time.'

I remember thinking at the time that it was strange. The voice did not have an Irish accent. It was only shortly afterwards, as I was being escorted from the premises, that I realised it had been mine.

Today, if I can find my car, I will drive to Dublin.

»

11 February

17.24.45 GMT

To: All Constellations

I arrived safely after a long, boring and (literally) cross-country drive yesterday – and booked in another Jurys Inn. I have read much about Dublin, and accept there is much to do and see for the ordinary visitor. But not for me – I had but one target in mind and I have spent much of the day there. A few blocks to the north of the infamous Post Office, in a quiet square of tall terraced buildings, is the Irish Literary Museum.

In the SCSC we talked much about my style 'needs', and the importance of 'performance' in today's media flooded world. We have spent days – weeks – on the need for 'impact' and the possible ways to get it. I stood alone, and still do as far as the SCSC are concerned – I cannot ignore the role and importance of the written word and the use of language.

This land was historically late using writing to record its history. It was a nation of storytellers – and that heritage comes through right into modern times. You see it today in the spotty bar poet and the scruffy musicians of Galway. That journey has been 'milestoned' by some of the great writers of any period and of any genre. I have spent the day soaking in their names, their background and their work. I have acquired twenty-three books to read – that I must somehow get back with me on the plane tomorrow.

There will be no poker tonight – and no Guinness either. I am in the land of the Master Wordsmiths, and I must not be deflected for a minute from listening and learning. There is something about these people and their use of language – and their ability to dump it on a paper page or breathe it out into the chilly island and then see it land, revered, in the furthest corners of the planet – that I must harness.

»

12 February

23.23.45 GMT

To: All Constellations

It is very late at night. I am back in my 'home' in Whalley, and very tired – but feel I must communicate.

When I finally got on the plane, I spent the journey reflecting on the past few days – but couldn't get rid of the notion that I had seen or heard something that I had not registered. It was only when I overheard the voices of a bunch of young people, most of them in their twenties, who were sat all around me, that it suddenly dawned. They were laughing and joking, talking about their jobs, their boyfriends and girlfriends, the movies they had seen, their mobile phones, their iPods and their holidays. Not once did they mention the violence, or the hatred or the divisions that gripped the land we were leaving – their land. And it was that simple. When I re-ran my journey through my mind, the poisonous vitriol had all come out of the mouths of the old folk. The youngsters had more important things to do and talk about. The kids in the South were not interested in a united Ireland – they'd got stuff to talk about that was far more important than that over their noodles in Wagamama. The kids in the North were not keen to put on a bowler hat and an orange sash – they would clash with their coordinated fashionable clothes.

The answer lies with the next generation. The divisions are unbridgeable with the old – so let's leave them to it and hope that they and the hatred die simultaneously. My target and my route must be through Youngtown.

»

13 February

13.25.45 GMT

To: All Constellations

Busy, busy morning. My washing almost ran on its own to the laundry machine. I had a lot of mail to open and catch up on – although it transpired that not one of the envelopes that almost blocked me from opening my front door was anything but either a sales pitch or some charity appeal. Still, I opened them all and I now have six new biros. I need to start preparing for my visits down south – but first I must tell you about a phone call I have just had.

It was from Nuala. Apparently she saw my car was back when she drove to work this morning – so she knew I was home. She asked me something quite strange – had I remembered it was Valentine's Day tomorrow?

This is where I am surprisingly vulnerable. It is stuff like this – that you can't research if you had a million years (let alone only 178) – that can throw you. If you admit ignorance you look suspicious – but if you bluff and it goes tits-up on you, you can actually risk the whole mission. I just muttered something unintelligible back down the phone – and I got a shriek of laughter back down the line.

'I knew it, I just knew it! I've gotcha between girlfriends haven't I?'

'Mutter. Mumble.'

'Well, here's the deal – and I won't take "no" for an answer. You and me are having a Valentine's supper tomorrow at my place. Just come in your jeans – and bring some red wine. See ya about eight.'

The phone went dead.

I'm not against seeing her again – far from it. But I have – had – no idea about this Valentine's thing. I looked it up on an information searching system called Google that they have on computers down here. It's actually a saint's day, and he's one of ours. And it's do with romance.

Shit.

»

14 February

19.25.23 GMT

To: All Constellations

Disappointing start to the day this morning. I have put on ANOTHER two kilos (now I'm back to 89 kg) and it is now becoming noticeable. Basically, my face is now glistening with fat – at least that's how it seems to me after what I've been used to. My trimmed beard and shorter (lighter coloured) hair seem to emphasise it. However I fancy it up, it is not good news for me, or my mission, and the guys in the SCSC are getting pretty pissed off now.

I tried a run this morning, out on the street outside my house. All I can report is that it was bitterly cold and that, over a distance of less than a mile, I managed an average speed that a sloth could manage after some heavy sexual activity. On top of that, my feet are still swollen and feel hot to the touch.

I've spent the rest of the day trying to get my thoughts sorted out and arrangements made for my visit to London. I will travel down tomorrow, and stay in the city. I've agreed to meet José when he closes his restaurant after lunch – about 3.00 p.m.

I must also get my ducks in a row (another Cide expression, which means getting things organised – and, no, I don't know why having your ducks in a row improves this aspect of life) for the PR meeting on the 16th. At the very least I need to start pulling all my thoughts together. The long(er) term plan will be to have a clear Charter on which to base my mission and appeal. I have started endless sheets of paper with this today but they've all ended up in the bin. Maybe my mind is being deflected by my supper meeting tonight (I'm all but ready to go out now). Whatever the cause is, it's stopping me making any kind of breakthrough.

Tomorrow may bring clearer thinking. Right now, I'm all dressed up and ready to go. I actually didn't have any 'jeans' to wear (as suggested by Nuala) so I nipped out today and got some – from a shop called Gap. I've twinned it with an old long-sleeved black T-shirt and a hooded top. If I may say so myself, with my hair glued in its new position, I look like the dog's bollocks. (You will remember that's a positive comparison – although I'm sure you share my confusion about how it became so.)

I've got a bottle of red wine – from somewhere called Shiraz (which sounds vaguely Arabian?) – although it occurs to me that it might not be a place.

I've got my guard up, but I'm looking forward to catching up with Noo again.

»

15 February

17.34.28 GMT

To: All Constellations

I'm back in my London hotel – the same Marriott. I've just left José, after the two of us had a very late and pleasant lunch. But first let me tell you about supper last night. It was fun and went well – but it was not without its surprises and dangers.

Let me start by telling you that Nuala looked delightful. I will NOT use the term 'dog's bollocks' because those that I have seen and remember do not do her justice. She wore a simple black dress that came disconcertingly low at the top and high at the bottom. Her hair was in the style I like, curtaining her face in a light coppery frame. It was all simple – stunningly set off by an emerald-coloured stone attached to a long leather shoelace-type thing around her neck. It was long enough that, when she assumed certain sitting positions (which she did – remember we were having supper) the stone all but disappeared down the shadowy valley where her breasts disappeared into her dress. I confess that I spent much of the evening tracking its progress as it went up and down.

All was going well. With being away from the hotel I had forgotten how her abrasive Norn Iron accent became mesmerising after a while, particularly in quiet one-on-one situations. We were well into the simple meal of pasta and salad she had prepared – and then, out of nowhere, things took a dangerous turn. Suddenly, putting her fork down, she sat back in the chair (which brought the stone into clear view) and looked me straight in the eye.

'Tommy. Can I ask you a question?'

'You surely can.'

'Will you be honest with me?'

Danger signals. Tracking the stone was suddenly forgotten. She got my full attention.

'Sure. Why not?'

'OK. Here goes. Just who the feck are you?'

My heart almost stopped beating. A million thoughts fought to get in the queue at the front of my mind. I spent a l-o-n-g ten seconds in a frozen position – and when I say frozen, it was as though somebody had shoved an index finger made from ice right up my rectum and then paused as if to say 'your move next'.

It was only when I saw she was smiling and heard she was still talking that I was able to adapt some humanoid characteristics again.

'You confuse me. I don't know where I stand with you, or – for that matter – where anybody does. I mean, you work but you've no job. You have money but don't seem to do anything for it. One moment you can seem a brain-box, and the next minute the most dumb things seems to confuse you. You have high-tech computers and suchlike, but I've seen you struggling with an electric plug. I gave you a little tongue-pie at Christmas and you nearly died of embarrassment, but you've just spent the last ten minutes looking at my tits with eyes like a golden retriever's balls. You travel to Spain in mid-winter to see some palace. You visit Ireland on your own just to drift around the place. What's it all about, Alfie?'

By my (later) calculation it took her about twenty-eight seconds to get through that last paragraph, during which time half of my mind was in 'receipt' mode while the other half was scrambling. I had formed at least the start of a reply, when she saved me, and the day, by letting me off the hook she'd stuck me on.

'It's OK. I'm only rambling. Don't answer any of that – it's just that you fascinate me. I spend a lot of my life fending off guys who just want to get inside my keks. They're

thugs or mugs and sometimes both. Sometimes it all goes pear-shaped and I fall in love wit' someone who gets past my guard. And then I fall out again. Wit' them, I go from where I can't live without them to a position where I want to feed their empty smiles and their penises and their boozy bad breath and their replica football shirts into me mam's old cast-iron mangle. I can make this movement within an hour. But with you I have two entirely new feelings. Part of me wants to attack you with my tennis racket, and part of me wants to suckle you to my right tit. Want some more pasta?'

I remained silent. I was confused. Who is Alfie? Why the right tit?

I stayed (mostly) that way (silent and confused) for the rest of the evening. Nuala carried on asking questions and then thoughtfully answering them for me – and it was only after an hour or so I recognised it as another manifestation of the Irish talent both to sing a lament at the same time you are composing it. It was not an ambush. There was no risk of exposure – for me or my mission. My heartbeat slowed, my jaw unfroze. My smile returned and by the end of the meal I was contributing the odd word or two. We parted like two old friends, with a hug that was about two seconds longer than the definition of platonic would allow. At the end I threw caution to the wind and, with my tongue firmly behind my lips I gave her a gentle kiss on the forehead. My reward was a lovely smile.

'You're a lovely guy Tommy. Somehow I just know we are going to stay in touch – but you just be careful. There's women around here who've got fannies like mousetraps for a guy like you.'

I think I have found someone who can come with me on the journey if I play my cards right.

My lunch with José was not so positive. It was enjoyable, but I could not get the conversation away from the Argentine football team, their new teenage sensation (who can, apparently, 'catch pigeons') and their plan to murder the English team the next time they meet. I know nothing of these tribal teams or the players – which leaves José bemused to say the least. I made a note that I would have to familiarise myself with this – there may be other conversations where my lack of awareness might be a more serious risk.

I like José, but I'm bored and tired after my journey, so we call it a day after a couple of hours. I also now know all about his idol – a man called Maradona – although I'm sure that this is the same man that Cide called a 'little fat fuck' just recently.

»

16 February

12.00.56 GMT

To: All Constellations

This will be quick because I'm in trouble. I've had my meeting with the PR lady and it took a bit longer than I thought, and I've only just got back to the Marriott. I'm supposed to have checked out by now but I've not yet packed my bag.

Quick summary of how the meeting went: IT WENT CRAPPILY.

The problems were largely my fault. I've made it plain to you – and about fifteen times to the SCSC – that I don't see how professional PR help has a role to play. In my view, I can't have somebody in my team who is paid. But the same response comes back time after time on my BLa: times have changed, blah, blah, blah; professional help with media training, blah, blah; getting the right exposure, blah. I still don't see it – and it showed in my contribution to the meeting. I was NOT well prepared. My 'Charter' could still be described as work-in-progress. It actually consists of a few notes scribbled on a napkin from when I had that three-potato feast in Galway. One of my key points has been obliterated with gravy and I've forgotten what it is.

The PR 'consultant' was called Corina Vialli – shortened to 'Cori' on her business card. Short and slender, I got the feeling she could punch way above her weight. Dressed in a black formal pants suit, set off with a high neck white silk blouse, she was all business. Her makeup was carefully understated apart from a crimson slash-mouth. Her hair completed the no-nonsense image – looking like it had been cut around the sides of a pudding basin that had been clamped on her head (a bit like that Caesar guy), but probably costing a week's wages for an ASDA check-out operator in Burnley. The picture was completed by the severe media-spectacles perched on her sculptured nose.

It didn't take long for her to abandon her 'the client is always right' initial positioning. All I could contribute was the fact that we had a well-resourced budget (which pleased her) but that I clearly had no formal briefing, or even an idea of what we wanted her to do (which didn't please her).

She interrupted one of my more shapeless verbal rambles.

'OK. Here's what I got. You have some kind of message – which is not yet fully defined – and you want to reach a

target audience with it – also undefined. A Big Audience, if I'm right. I've suggested, and you have rejected, a heavy-money-guns bombardment, which might get you appearances as a motivational speaker, or as a stand-up comedian, or as an evangelist of some kind, or as some sort of independent politician fighting the system. I've even suggested – and this would costalotta – trying to get you on a TV reality show, or at least one on the lower slopes of the genre, and you don't seem to know what one of those is. Look, I like you and I like your budget – but you gotta give me something to work with.'

'I appreciate your problem. I'm just going to need some more time – but this meeting has helped me understand what I have to do – so just send me a bill for it and we'll meet again when I'm in better shape.'

'OK – but you don't want to hang about. The market for ECs is massively – and I mean massively – cluttered and competitive at the minute and I don't expect it to ease any time soon.'

'What's an EC?'

'Oh, it's just a bit of shorthand we use. It stands for Empty Celebrity. It's a very busy market.'

That was then. This is now. Somebody has just banged on the door. I've got to vacate this room or I'll be charged for another night. I'm travelling to Luton this afternoon, and staying at that hotel by the airport – but only because I know it from my Spanish trip and it's just a half hour or so from the BUPA hospital at Harpenden where I get my check-up tomorrow. No, I don't know what BUPA stands for.

When I've done that, I intend to drive straight back up to Whalley – so it may be I'm off air until the day after tomorrow – which I make the 18th February on this calendar.

»

18 February

08.23.45 GMT

To: All Constellations

Empty Celebrities. Those two words have been echoing in my brain ever since Cori uttered them. They surely cannot reflect my goal. They cannot even shape my means to the end, my *modus operandi.* Since I heard the words, I have become much more conscious of media content – watching TV for two nights and buying a number of journals. Cori is so right – the screens and pages are chock-full and littered with Empty Celebrities – with nothing to do or say other than being drunk or drugged in public, or being at the right place at the right time to coincide with a camera, or making complete arseholes of themselves on a screen.

That cannot be my route. If I have to work with Cori, she has to find me a high road. I was so depressed that I asked the SCSC research guys to look up how the guy called Nelson Mandela got kick-started – because he is a potential role model that we all noticed during our researches. The answer came back that he kick-started his high road by spending nearly thirty years in an island prison. Bollocks to that. We must find another way. Something a bit quicker and lighter on the personal sacrifice bit.

Anyway – my health. This BUPA thing is impressive. First of all I was seen by a nurse, who did the basic measuring and weighing. I gave a blood sample and peed in a little cup. I'd filled in a questionnaire and she went over that – and, in general, I was OK – with the exception of my foot, which is still painful and inflamed. She gave me a bit of a roasting about my weight and alcohol intake (I had been honest) – but I got to 'half-time' with reasonably good news.

The second half was not so good. After a while for them to process the blood sample, I was ushered in to see a proper doctor – and you can imagine my surprise when I met her. Yes, her. A lady, and a spectacular one at that.

She was almost as tall as me, and as black as pure ebony. She reminded me of a woman from those nomadic, regal Tuareg tribes and I obviously looked a bit flustered as I sat down. She instantly put me at ease, explaining that they would normally match a male patient with a male doctor, but as I had made a late appointment she would be very happy to do my consultation – provided I had no objection.

I think she took my silence as a nod.

We started with a physical examination – and, once I got over the obvious challenge about my feet ('I fell onto some iron railings'), I got a shock. She suddenly looked up from banging my knee.

'I want to check this with you first in case you have any embarrassment as I am a woman doctor. Are you comfortable with my examining your testes?'

'My what?'

'Your testes.'

'Wha . . .'

'Your testicles.'

'Are they . . .?'

'Yes. I need to examine them.'

'I . . . I mean . . . by all means. Go ahead.'

There then followed the most extraordinary minute of the (nearly) seventeen and a half million minutes that I have manifested myself in this guise on this planet. I can recommend it. In all honesty, she could have examined them for several hours without as much as a murmur from me – although, in fairness, during the brief examination I did (apparently) make a sound.

Anyway, the bad news: I am still creating uric acid at the rate of the pissing camel and a number of my key ratios are 'outside the range we would consider normal'. I got yet another diet sheet, a lifestyle sheet and a detailed breakdown of all my results. I have scanned these and sent the lot off to the SCSC – and I am expecting a new regime anytime now. I suspect, more discipline will be needed from me, and more sanctions will be heading my way from them if I fall short. Gout indeed.

It's catch-up day today. Having been away, I've got laundry and mail to tackle – and I need to put some time in on my Charter and some more background reading. Cori has left me with a lot of thinking to do, and I have no ready answers – it may well be I have to take another project trip to get the thinking-juices going.

There's a nice note from Cide on my mat – asking me to join him and the 'Three Stooges' (?) for a beer in the Whalley Arms on Tuesday night – the day after tomorrow. I assume that the Three Stooges are Sid and Co, and I'd be delighted – it's time I caught up with these guys. Time is passing and I need to figure out if they are appropriate for my Team – and, if they are, how I get them in it.

»

19 February

18.23.45 GMT

To: All Constellations

Today has been notable for two things. First, as I thought, I got a whole new set of dietary and lifestyle programmes from the SCSC. They want to 'blitz' this gout thing with a heavy programme of anti-inflammatory tablets for ten days. If that fails I am 'warned' that I will have to take on a programme of daily drugs that will turn me from a mammal into a bird – or at least that part of me that seems to be producing this uric acid. Birds, apparently, do not generate uric acid – and I guess I haven't seen one with angry red toe joints.

On top of that, there's another exercise plan – to do one of the 'cardio-vascular' workout 'options' three times a week. I must also cut right back on alcohol and caffeine, eat dark berry fruits and drink at least TEN glasses of water a day.

This is getting ridiculous. We have never had any trouble like this before, and I have enough to do and think about without pissing every twenty minutes.

There was a second thing. What was it? Oh, yes – I have started my Charter. It will be a seminal document, and I will be sending it in draft form to the SCSC before I do anything with it. However, despite the ground I am going to have to cover, I am going to try to keep it to ten points or less and fit it on one page.

When I say I have started it, I went out and bought a pad. I just need some inspiration to get those first few (but critically important) words down on paper.

»

20 February

12.45.56 GMT

To: All Constellations

On impulse, I saw Bash again last night. I haven't seen him much since I got my own car, but I do not want to lose touch with him as he is the only Muslim I have in my circle. I fancied a curry (and a few Boddingtons to be truthful – but I know I can't drink it as it's hundreds of calories per pint and alcohol is bad for the gout). I called Bash and he drove me to the Raj Gate – an Indian restaurant that I've come across about five miles up the valley – which gave us a bit of time to chat.

He was on good form generally – as he tends to be when his cricket team are doing well back on the sub-continent. Like most taxi drivers I've come across, he is a talking machine, but reluctant to offer views on the Big Issues. However, I managed to get out of him his view that the Muslim world is as divided amongst itself as it is with the rest of the planet. Sunni is still pitched against Shiite, extremist against moderate, reformist against reactionary. He reckoned a billion Muslims, a number which included him, would just like to get on with their lives – but it was getting harder to avoid the rhetoric and keep out of the heated debates. They feel they are being pushed and pulled towards the extremes of their own religion. It wasn't what I wanted to hear, and I ordered my 'poppadums' and 'chicken jalfrezi' with a heavy heart.

Tonight I'm seeing the 'gang' in the pub. I expect I'll hear another side.

»

21 February

12.45.23 GMT

To: All Constellations

Ugh. I had got out of practice. I have a hangover to top all hangovers – but it is so important that I not only understand but involve myself in the cultural 'tapestry' of the community. I mentioned before that a good shorthand way of condensing the complex mix of big and small issues of the day into an agenda that interests ordinary folk is to capture one of Sid's rants. Here's last night's (you miss something if you break the flow – so I've put some explanatory notes in *after*):

'*What's pissing me off? I'll tell you what's pissing me off. Here's what's pissing me off. Debt. That's what's pissing me off. Everybody's in debt up to the maker's nameplate (*1). Nobody saves for anything. Nobody. If you want summat today, and you haven't any folding stuff, you just borrow it. They're lending money to kids. They're shovelling money at college students. They're spreading credit around like a mad woman's shit (*2). When me and Betty started out, if we didn't have something, we waited till we could afford to buy it wi' cash we'd saved up. Didn't even use the HP (*3). I nearly had a heart attack when we borrowed money to buy our council house, but it's all paid off now and we owe nowt. Credit cards and them TV loans – no problem: if you've got yourself in the shit, just borrow more money and either get yourself deeper in the shit or lose your house. It's all goin' to blow up . . .*

*'And another thing – fookin' men's hair. What's that all about? Dyeing it blond? I mean, a few of us used a bit of Grecian 2000 (*4) round the sides when the grey bits came along – but for fook's sake. You seen that Rio Ferdinand? (*5) He's got plaits. That's the England centre half. We're not talking some Arab chutney-ferret (*6) poncing about at inside forward, we are talking about an Englishman playing centre half. And he's got plaits. You see this hair o' mine? My dad parted it this way seventy-seven years ago just before we went to church one Sunday and it's stayed that way ever since (*7). If it's not broke don't mend it. That's what I say. It were good enough for my missus, and it still is, and I never got the piss tekken out of me, that's for sure . . .*

*'And another thing – have you seen what they've done to a Mars Bar? (*8) They've tekken quarter of an inch off the size of it every year so's you don't notice but the price has gone up fifty times since I were a lad . . .*

'It's all bollocks.'

That was exclaimed on the back of one breath. It's impressive – and here are the notes to help you with bits you don't quite understand:

*1: I think this means 'high up' on something – anything.

*2: I have no idea. I assume this means quite widespread and out of control.

*3: HP is short for 'hire purchase' – a way to buy products by paying a little amount regularly instead of all at once. In principle you rent the product, and buy it with your last payment.

*4: A lotion applied to the hair which disguises the appearance of greying.

*5: An England soccer international team member.

*6: I have no idea. Just no idea. I think it has some vague homosexual implication.

*7: Sid's hair has a 'parting' down one side – rather like mine had (in the middle) before I went spiky. Time has affected Sid's hairstyle – there are about four (short) hairs on one side of the parting and about three on the other.

*8: A chocolate bar – a long-time favourite.

Now I'm going back to bed. I feel awful.

»

22 February

09.15.23 GMT

To: All Constellations

Great news last night to cheer up my suffering day. Xabi phoned from Malaga to say he is definitely coming over to England next month and would love to meet up. We are both enthusiastic in principle. He's going to finalise the dates and arrangements as soon as possible. I have a spare room here if he wants to come up north – although I'll have to invest in another bed.

This development reminds me that I need to up the tempo on putting my Team together. I have a number of interesting possibilities – but 'possibilities' are a long way from being a joined-up and dedicated team of followers. I feel I need to make some initial moves on this before the end of next month – within my six-month target. This puts a high priority on shaping my Charter – this will be the glue that holds them together.

More bad news on my health. The anti-inflammatory tablets are making me EXTREMELY constipated. Sparing you the really intimate details, I must report that I have just visited the lavatory for the first time for nearly three days. I have no practical experience of it, but I imagine what I went through must have been akin to giving birth. My tear-ducts are now clean and clear.

I was disappointed, after this seismic event, to record no weight loss.

»

23 February

11.25.56 GMT

To: All Constellations

I've just had a phone call from Cide – with some good news and bad news. The good news – I think – is that there is a golf tournament for Members and guests on Sunday (the day after tomorrow) and he's invited me to be his guest. I've not played a round yet. In fact, I haven't picked up my golf clubs (the steel bats) since I left the hotel. He told me not to worry because it was just about 'having fun and a piss-up' – and that if I turned up half an hour early he'd put me through my paces in a net they have for practising.

The bad news is that they are all worried about Skins. I did think he had been a bit quiet when we met up a couple of nights ago. Apparently he has not been feeling well for a while – but all of a sudden his doctor has started wanting things doing urgently. He's had some blood tests and they'll get the result tomorrow – which is incredibly quick for the public health service down here – and everybody's a bit scared about what the outcome might be.

»

24 February

17.23.34 GMT

To: All Constellations

I've felt a lot better today, although I'm still crapping big – I mean BIG – hard stony pebbles at irregular intervals. I decided to sit down and begin to shape my Charter this morning and, although I have nothing tangible to show for a lot of thinking, I believe I made progress. Here are some of my early thoughts.

Whatever the length of this thing (and I'm hoping to keep it to one page and a maximum of ten inspiring ideas) the opening will be crucial. I have seen enough of this planet (again) to realise that some things don't change – you need to GRAB people's attention right at the start. Of course, some of the ways that that manifests itself have changed – I read yesterday, for example, that many shoppers make their minds up about a retail business within two seconds of entering a shop. They can (and do) change their minds later – but those first impressions are deeply rooted. I must therefore get my opening right: high power and impact.

An example of what won't work is the opening line of a piece of (supposedly) seminal work which has been handed down, in the name of one of the Deities – the one that believes all human misfortunes can be traced to two ancestors eating some exotic fruit. Here's how it starts:

'Our Father, which art in Heaven.'

Now that sort of thing is just not going to get the job done here and now. As Cide would say – it's OK, but a bit like kissing your sister. It's like banging on the window with a sponge. There's no impact, no emotion – and nothing to grab.

My targets are the senses of 'alienation' and 'loss' that almost everybody I've met seems to feel to some degree – and my target audience will be the young people of the planet. We've agreed my work (and my Charter) cannot try to piggyback on any single one of the accepted 'big religions' because the divides are now too deep and advanced. That's the chord I need to strike in my first line. I need something to hook that lot. Of that I am now convinced. Of what it might be, I have no idea. Yet.

»

25 February

07.45.34 GMT

To: All Constellations

It's still very early – but I've been up for a couple of hours. Golf clubs, and the bag they come in, are quite a size and my new house is quite small – but that didn't stop me losing them. I have only just discovered that I actually left them in the boot of my Mini. I've just had a couple of swings in my little hallway, and tried some putts on the carpet in the living room – and I feel far from confident. I've got to be there (the golf course) at half past eight, so I'd better fly. I'll let you know how I get on tomorrow – but, just to warn ALL audiences (including the Corner Office) there will be little work done on my Charter today.

»

26 February

12.34.23 GMT

To: All Constellations

I survived. Just. Let me tell you about golf. There should be some more rules – one of which should be that you must not play if you suffer from gout (particularly if your golf shoes are new). I spend three of the four and a half hours the 'match' took to complete in absolute agony. This was despite the fact that I had a little trolley to carry my clubs on. Anyway, the game itself was not bad, and – amazingly (according to Cide) – I acquitted myself well. We eventually won, with Cide obviously doing all the scoring for us – and our victory was in spite of our two opponents blatantly cheating both individually and collectively. This became clear on the first 'hole' where one of our opponents hit his ball way out to the left of where it was supposed to be. There was a watery winter sun out at this time, and I saw the sun reflect off his golf clubs as he swung them about eight times as he progressed, almost out of view to the rest of us, up the left towards our target flag. And yet, when he got there, he said he had only taken four shots so far.

I mentioned this to Cide between the holes and he smiled and told me not to worry – but to do a bit of cheating myself. This is obviously in TOTAL conflict with what I stand for and the principles of my mission. However, it obviously had to be done and turned out to be quite fun. I scored 112, which Cide said was quite good – but he won the prizes for us by scoring a 73. He didn't seem to need to cheat like the rest of us.

Later on in the evening I had to go up to the stage to collect a bottle of Sherry for our team prize – and I got a smile and a quick hug from Nuala who popped in only briefly because she was on duty. She has lovely teeth as well as those green eyes that seem to follow you everywhere. I don't know if I've mentioned that.

One interesting item came up in the bar chat after we'd had quite a few of the Boddingtons. The Golf Club has a charity dinner event coming up in a few weeks and Cide mentioned that they had just had a message from the guest speaker (or 'turn') they had booked to say that he was cancelling. He was, apparently, another son of another famous ex-footballer. This seems a well-trodden career path for 'turns' – but does not seem to me to be an exceptional claim to fame. It indicates to me, however, that they may be looking on the lower slopes of the guest speaker market. Sounds like they do not have much of a budget.

I wonder . . . could I get myself and my message in shape to take on that kind of audience? I said nothing, but I'll keep watching this.

»

27 February

10.23.50 GMT

To: All Constellations

Listen to this:

'Madman drummers, bummers and Indians in the summer, with a teenage diplomat.'

I do not care what constellation you receive this in – if you hear those words at the opening of anything, you will take notice of what comes next.

I found them (the words) while I was browsing through the music on this gizmo I have been given that has been rigged up to look like an iPod. They are the first few words of a song by somebody called Bruce Springsteen. The song is called 'Blinded by the light'. It supports the theory I have picked up about the crucial importance of initial impact in modern life – where customers make their mind up about a shop within two seconds of entering the place.

The Springsteen opening got me spending several hours listening to music –and emerging with the theory transposed to music and firmly intact. I heard a song by someone called Chuck Berry called 'You never can tell.' The first line goes: '*It was a teenage wedding and the old folks wished them well.*' There you are. Wham, bam: the whole story is lined up and you are hooked. I kept listening, and was just nodding off to sleep when a woman started singing. Her name was Sarah McLachlan. The first words of the song 'Angel' grabbed my attention: '*You spend all your time waiting for that second chance, for the break that will make it OK*'. I was wide awake within an instant, and hooked. What would come next? You remember me telling you about a weird guy called Tom Waits? Listen to these – the first words of a song by him called 'A little rain': '*Well, the Ice Man's mule is parked outside the bar*'.

The Ice Man's MULE?!

What's all this in aid of? It defines precisely what I need for my Charter. I need a punchy, hooky-type opening line. Something that grabs people and FORCES them to listen to what comes next.

Here's what I'm working on. I'm thinking of a single, opening line that reads '*If things don't change, they'll stay as they are.*'

That should grab 'em. What do you think?

»

February 28

08.12.45 GMT

To: All Constellations

OK. OK. OK. Enough. I get the message. You think it was crap.

I opened my message-mail about half an hour ago and there were forty-three new ones. It took me two minutes to pick up a consistent theme for the content – and twenty-five more minutes to confirm it. Message received. You do NOT like my opening line. Most of you were polite, including (rather surprisingly) the guys from the SCSC and Him in the Corner Office. Some of you were, shall we say, assertive in your lack of enthusiasm. A couple of you went, I felt, a little far. I will go back to the drawing board.

MARCH

»

1 March

10.34.23 GMT

To: All Constellations

What is going on? I put the TV on this morning to catch up with the news, and saw on the date-line it was the first of March. Last night, when I went to bed, it was the 28th of February. My understanding was that the months – as if this wasn't complicated enough – had EITHER thirty or thirty one days in each of them. Remember, I was part of the team that OK'd the distribution of the definitive thinking on this kind of thing via the launch of Newton's *Principa* in the seventeenth earth century and, even if I say so myself, was one of the few in the SCSC who understood what we were trying to get out into the public domain on this planet. So, I THOUGHT I knew what was going on here – but this losing an hour here and a couple days there is not a little confusing.

In truth, seeing the name of the new month gave me a bit of a scare. It has suddenly brought home to me that during the NEXT month I will need to be recording some substantive progress against my Five Key Goals. My six months will be up. So, between now and then, I need to complete my Charter, and get it out there – using the PR help if needs be. I also need to get some glue on my key relationships and a lot, lot more.

I would also like to cram in a visit to America, even if it is only for a short period. Apart from being a prime contender for an alternative location if this fails, it seems to me – from reading and watching the popular media – that, although almost everybody views everything American with cynicism occasionally bordering on hatred, it is a country that still has enormous influence on the rest of the world. Even if it is, as Cide says, acres and acres and acres of space surrounded by teeth.

A visit to India is simply not on – we need to push that back into the next phase.

After my panic attack, things got worse. I popped in to see Cide – just to 'explore' the idea of me taking the turn's spot at next month's charity evening. (I've become quite excited by this idea – it could be a low-key, low-risk way of me getting started in public.) I found him in very sober mood. He'd just come off the phone with Sid who'd told him that Skins looks as though he could be seriously – and I mean seriously – ill. It might be something called the 'Big C'.

I took the hint and left him (Cide) staring out of the window and nipped back to my house to flip through my briefing manual and notes to see if I could find anything on this disease – but there was nothing under that name. I'd asked Cide what the basic symptoms were – but all I got was a terse comment: '*Aah, he's wandering about his house not talking to anybody and trying to climb up his own thumb*'. This made the disease all the more mysterious. I'll find out more – but this sounds like it could be a big shadow over forthcoming events.

I've picked up that a lot of people around here will suddenly say the words '*I have a cunning plan*' – sometimes when (a) the circumstances do not warrant it and (b) they haven't. For some reason, everybody laughs. This I do not understand. But this I do: I HAVE a plan. It may or may not prove to be cunning.

I am going to take the next ten days to finalise my Charter, and I'm going to include one of the ten points, and some of the background thinking, in each day's bulletin. This piece of work is seminal to everything we have planned, and it is crucial that I take my time and share it with you as it develops. In that way, I hope you will feel some 'ownership' for the final Charter, which I hope to be able to summarise on a single page. The importance of both your 'ownership' and the ability to get it expressed on one page have been stressed by the SCSC.

There is also one more task ahead of me in this critical first six-month phase – and one that I hadn't planned on. I had assumed that all of you were aware that this wasn't my first attempt at returning here and starting over. It appears I had assumed this wrongly – and I have had a number of mailings which have asked me to clarify what happened, and why wasn't *that* 'Coming' given the label of 'Second'. I'm not going to do it in the next few days as my mind is focused on my Charter, but after that I will give a summary of the events – short as they were – and the reasons for missing it out of the sequence completely.

»

2 March

17.45.32 GMT

To: All Constellations

I've been housebound today, working on the opening of my Charter, so I have no further news about Skins – nor any further progress on trying to book myself as the Golf Club's 'turn' next month with Cide. More of that as and when I can add something.

I'm continuing to struggle with the opening of the Charter. I realise how important it is, and I've still got some of your (quite frankly) rude and unhelpful comments about my first attempt ringing in my ears. I feel rather like the guys who put together the American Constitution must have felt when they first stared at a blank piece of paper. I know that my Charter is, eventually, going to be one of the planet's seminal documents – just as they knew the same status would befall their Constitution. It's a hell of a responsibility.

Although I don't yet have the powerful 'hook' line to open with, I do know the principle and content. It came to me while I was having a fried egg sandwich for lunch. On the egg box AND on the egg itself, the providers had gone to the trouble of advising me that the egg had been laid by a chicken that (a) had been fed with organic food and (b) had ranged freely (somewhere) during its life. I know from my studies of the planet before I arrived, and from the research done by my back-up teams, that this kind of thing is new on earth. A while ago, in fact just a few earth-years ago, quite frankly, nobody gave a toss about what the chicken had eaten and where it played out. But now we all want to know that the chicken was happy when it laid its egg. Yes, I know it sounds odd, because we are eating its babies, but it seems it is important to us that we (at least) are told that the chicken was content. Here's the bit that I think is key and which I plan to steal: we need some sort of CONNECTION with the egg's parent.

This is my breakthrough, this idea of CONNECTION. I have told you that I will be concentrating on addressing the sense of loss and alienation that I see all around me, and I believe this is a way of providing a missing link for all kinds of people who are reaching out. A connection can be a bridge for people reaching out to find other people, for businesses trying to relate to customers, for politicians trying to attract loyalty and votes, and, above all, for message-givers seeking message receivers.

We have studied earth in great detail. There was an 'Age' which was dominated by the Hunter-Gatherer. This was followed by an Agricultural Age. Then came an Industrial Age, when mechanical and then electrical engineering drove big changes. The next – and last to date – new 'Age' was the Information Age, in which telecommunications and chip technology changed almost everything. But these big waves have all now hit the beach – the big gains from all of them have been banked and the planet is now looking for whatever comes next. And I think I have it, and I think it is in the *zeitgeist* of my fried egg sandwich. It revolves around the world's need to connect and my wherewithal to enable that connection. I am so excited.

»

3 March

12.04.24 GMT

To: All Constellations

I've still not been out, although I've just heard the noon-time news and there's not much happening out there. On the little screen on my BlackBerry Look-alike, I got a message this morning from Nuala, which threw me a bit because I don't know how she accessed it – and if she can, how secret can it be? The only possibility I can think of is that – because I'm a bit forgetful – I have the earth access number of my BLa written on the back of it, and I suspect she must have seen it during one of the times we have been together.

The message itself was strange – in some kind of code I think. I've tried most of my software slang and code converters, but so far they haven't thrown any light on it. The message reads: '*Where r u? Send us a X. LOL, ☺ Nu.*' Can anybody throw any light on that? I only understand the words 'where' and 'send'.

Anyway, back to my important work. I'll come up with some powerful wording for my CONNECTION idea, which will be Number One on my Charter. For now, though, on to Number Two. This is one of those concepts we've recognised for some time back at the SCSC, and one we tried to 'filter' in to this planet nearly half a century ago. The vehicle we chose was a popular book author called John Steinbeck, and in one of his works (a book called *Travels with Charlie*) we slipped in the idea that ***all people are to be admired, while all governments are NOT to be admired***. This is a simple but powerful idea on how this planet has lost the plot, and how a remedy might be shaped. It centres on the idea that people are fine until they start to organise. The seed we planted was limited to organising in a government, but the reality is that the malaise is much more widespread. Once an individual ceases to be so, and links with one or more individuals in any form of organisation, then the built-in goodness of the individual goes breasts-aloft. (Note: I am using the words 'breasts-aloft' to mean 'disastrously wrong'. It's my version of an expression used by Cide – 'tits-up' – to describe such a disaster. I've changed it to make it a little less crude. Although I know I need to master the local vernacular, I do actually find a lot of Cide's euphemisms quite gratuitously coarse.)

Back to the Charter, and this, my second idea. I can think of no finer example of the concept than to point out that most individual Jews are nice people. But when the individual Jews form an organisation called Israel, they and it seem to become arseholes of the highest calibre. The same thing happens with other Religions, with other nations, with all governments (at all levels), most businesses and with Manchester United (a local football tribe that is a particularly dislikeable organisation). Breasts aloft indeed.

»

4 March

18.45.23 GMT

To: All Constellations

I've still not been out, so I still don't have any news about Skins or anything or anybody else. But it's Sunday today, so I'm going out later. I'll see what I can find out. My continuing recluse-like status is because I'm getting really engaged with my Charter, and I'm now ready to share my third idea.

This is not new, and it is common (in some form or other) with most of you – certainly those in the more conventional constellations. In fact, all of us on the SCSC are disappointed that we have to include it at all given that it was originally launched on this planet over two hundred earth-years ago – and we thought it had achieved what we called 'critical mass acceptance'. Not so, it would appear. Large chunks of the North American population are not only defying the concept, but are actively engaged in trying to force the rest of the population into sharing their disbelief in it.

The idea is simple, powerful and (I suspect) you will know your own Constellation's version of it by heart. It is this: ***All organisms compete for resources, and those that have some innate advantage will prosper and pass on that advantage to their offspring. By such means will species continually evolve.***

Yes, yes, I know – same old, same old. We first got this idea out into the open on earth in the mid-eighteenth century via a mouthpiece called Charles Darwin – whose idea was simply that noted above (and actually contained nothing to do with the 'survival of the fittest'). It is the most powerful singular idea in the 4,558 million years of this particular planet's history. Boring and obvious it may be, but it is being challenged and will need to be aired (and re-committed to) again. In America, something called Intelligent Design is being proposed to account for the origin and evolution of all species (including human beings). Have you ever heard such bollocks? Intelligent Design may have resulted in the concept of the Club Sandwich (something I had when I was in London) but not this stuff.

Three down, seven to go.

»

5 March

11.45.34 GMT

To: All Constellations

A bit late getting up this morning – after another evening in the Whalley Arms. I felt I owed myself a night out after all my creative efforts and articulation on my Charter. It turned out to be a bitter/sweet evening, so I'm going to tell you about developments there before I get back to Number Four in the Charter tomorrow.

I got to the pub about 9.00 p.m. last night and immediately made my way over to Sid's realm – to find only two of the three regulars there. The other chair was just left there, empty. Nobody had attempted to sit in it or take it elsewhere (nor did they throughout the rest of the evening), despite the fact the place was full of people.

I had (rather embarrassingly) forgotten about Skins and his illness, so wrapped up have I been in my work. This 'Big C' thing, it transpires, is the illness called cancer. I had been briefed about this as it is a modern type of plague that kills hundreds of thousands of the planet's population every year, and so merits a lot of press coverage. It's one of the reasons that a cigarette package has writing on it that tells you you might die if you smoke its contents – a message I would have thought should have fatally damaged sales. Anyway, Skins, it seems, has been diagnosed with it. It is an unwelcome growth INSIDE the body, which eats the part of the body it is in, and then spreads indefinitely. He (Skins) will be going into hospital in Burnley early next week where they will find the extent of the growth and see what (if anything) they can do about it.

It sounds horrible, and Sid and Rhys were very low in spirit. Recently I have started greeting Sid by half-shouting '*And what's pissing you off, Sid*?' which would ALWAYS get him off into a rant. But not tonight.

I was feeling quite depressed myself when Cide came in for the last round of drinks – and things suddenly looked up. His mind was obviously elsewhere, and I found conversation difficult, but I managed to bring up the subject of the Golf Charity night next month. I've confirmed it's actually going to be on the 7th of April, and I asked him if he had got a 'turn' booked yet.

'Aah, Christ Tommy, don't remind me. I'm not in the mood for more bad news tonight. I'm pissing against the wind whichever way I turn. The budget's ridiculous – I've only got five hundred quid – so who do they expect? On top of that, it's a busy time for events and I've only got just over a month's notice to give anybody. I have NO idea where to turn, but I've got to sort it by next week 'cos the Committee want to do the invites.'

I took a deep breath

'I'll do it.'

'What?'

'I said, I'll do the turn.'

'Look, Tommy, it's just not that sort of night tonight. I'm not in the mood, what with Skins bein' ill and all that. Just don't be a wanker.'

'I'm deadly serious. I mean, that's what I do.'

'How d'ya mean?'

'I do "turns" – and I'd be very happy to do yours.'

There was quite a long silence. Both Sid and Rhys had picked up on the conversation and watched Cide's face intently as he chewed over this new and unplanned development:

'What, you do this kind of observational comedy thing? Like Eddie Izzard? We've never had one of them, and it might go over a few heads – but it would help drag the bastards into the new century. I've seen some of these guys on TV and they're funny if you are pissed enough – and these guys will be. Y'now, the more I think about it, the more I think it'll show 'em I'm a modern, can-do, go-ahead kind of lad as well.'

He fell silent for another whole minute.

'How much would you charge? I've told you the budget's REAL tight?'

'Tell you what. As it's you and your golf club, I'll do it for free – and you can give the fee to a charity.'

'Bloody hell. Observational comedy, eh? Like Eddie Izzard. You?'

It seemed (at the time) to throw only a minor shadow over the whole plan – the fact that I had no idea what 'observational comedy' is or who 'Eddie Izzard' is. That would be sorted out later.

'Absolutely.'

'Kin 'ell. You're on. April 7th. You get a free dinner and you'll be on about ten o'clock. About twenty minutes should do it. Kin 'ell. Observational comedy. Kin 'ell. Eddie Izzard. Wait till I tell 'em. Kin 'ell. Sorted. Awright, my round. Same again lads? Kin 'ell.'

It's now in my diary – in ink. I will be in front of the public early next month, well inside my six-month target. We agreed and recorded these goals, but I'll tell you what – I suspect that half of the SCSC and the entire Occupant of the Corner Office doubted I would achieve any of them after last time. Ha!

I say it again: Ha! This time I mean BUSINESS.

»

6 March

11.34.25 GMT

To: All Constellations

Bit of a problem emerged this morning. Apparently, according to the overnight research done by the folk back at the SCSC, this Eddie Izzard guy is a 'turn' who is a man dressed up in a woman's clothing. They are (I quote) 'deeply troubled' by any association I might have with this man (or whatever he is), let alone the idea of imitating him on stage, and what it might do for my longer term image. This 'transvestite' thing is not a widespread habit here on this planet – certainly compared to what we had to witness on Proxima Centuri, which is the only other real example of this behaviour on this side of the Oort Cloud – but it has very negative connotations with the population at large here. So, why is this 'man' so popular, then? I'm not that worried about this as I'm sure I can find a route around the 'negatives' BUT I am beginning to be a bit concerned about the other aspect of what I agreed – this 'observational comedy' thing. Here's the issue: I can find all sorts of references to the word 'observe' and the same for 'comedy' – but I cannot find any dictionary or reference work which has them both together – and neither can the SCSC (who have a lot more sources to refer to). Anybody got any ideas? This is something I will have to sort out, and SOON.

Anyway, back to the Charter, and on to Number Four. Number Three was based on the singular best idea this planet has ever had – the one on the origin and evolution of the planet's species. The problem that has emerged is that the idea has caused polarisation amongst the population – inasmuch as that IF you believe in this idea (which, if you remember, we put out via a guy called Darwin), then you feel prohibited in having a 'faith' or believing in a 'deity'. Number Four will, then, simply state that the two are not mutually exclusive: ***You can question (for example) the Old Testament, or any deity-based belief system – yet still have faith.*** They are not incompatible – far from it. The fact that this particular planet is 4,558 million years old (which everybody should know) and was not 'created' in a week DOES NOT mean that there cannot be a God or Gods or a Faith or Faiths. A billion years is a day in the life of one of these concepts and/or beings.

It will be hard to prove to the cynics. 'Miracles' as such won't work any more. There are people on this planet who are PROFESSIONAL miracle workers, who saw people in half and put them back together again or make small cards disappear and then re-appear in your ear. I can't do any of those stunts – it took me long enough to master the conversion of water to wine and that is still the only one I can do. And, let's be honest, it has a limited dramatic effect. But I will be able to offer something as proof of the existence of a higher force. If anybody on this planet takes a simple two-sided coin and tosses it up a few times, they will get an assorted and random number of each side landing face up. But if they do it ten thousand times, it will always end up being half of one side and half of the other. How do they think THAT happens? Do they really think it just happens? Don't they realise that such an occurrence requires unbelievably careful monitoring and a lot of effort on our behalf?

»

7 March

09.23.31 GMT

To: All Constellations

A quick update on some other stuff before I get on to Number Five. I've heard that Skins is going in to hospital tomorrow for the detailed diagnosis of his condition and to sort out what (if anything) can be done about it. Nothing more from Nuala, although the folk back at the SCSC have assured me that the message I received from her – rather surprisingly – on the little screen on my BLa is a quite normal way for younger people to inter-communicate on this planet. They have advised me to respond and given me some guidance as to how to do it – but I'll leave that for a day or so.

It occurs to me that April 7th is fast becoming a date between me and the destiny of this Mission. It is important, I think, that I get as many as possible of my potential supporters present on the night. This won't be too difficult (I hope) with those in this area, but Xabi and José are in Spain and London respectively and I'd like to get them here. My PR lady is also London based, but since she is being paid it shouldn't be a problem to get her here – which is something I'll sort out when I've finished my Charter.

OK: on to Number Five. When they see what I am trying to do, a lot of people will expect me to focus on (what this planet calls) the Middle East. Throughout documented history, this region has been tortured and stressed. Millions have died through natural and mankind-made disasters. Three (and the 'main' three at that) of the planet's belief systems try to sit down on the one seat (Jerusalem) each time the music stops, and then occupy it until one or both of the others proceeds to murder them.

Surely, any Charter such as mine would attempt to oil these particular troubled waters? The whole world is looking for an answer and to produce one would be a big improvement on not coveting your neighbour's ass – which was a Big Number in one of the previous manifestations. Well, here's my position. You can forget it. As they say up here, my name's not Billy Hunt.

This Region is a lost cause. So, too, are its embittered and polarised peoples. But that's not the end of it. What caused that position and now *makes it worse* is that those from outside the Region think they can solve its problems by intervening (constantly) or invading (occasionally). The solution has to be found by the Region's aboriginals – the rest of us must stay out and back no one. For sure, it'll get worse before it gets better – and it may end up being a desert for a while. But anything's better than where it is now and where it's going.

»

8 March

11.34.29 GMT

To: All Constellations

Good news on some other fronts. You will appreciate that bringing all this together, in this form, has meant me being housebound for several days. My diet has consisted largely of fried egg sandwiches, all of which (the eggs, that is) come from happy, free-ranging parents. I've also drunk a lot of water, which apparently has taken fifty million years to end up in these bottles I get from ASDA, so there's a CONNECTION there as well – I feel that it's honourable, hard working water that slakes my thirst. As a result, I have lost two kilos, and my gout symptoms have eased – certainly to a level where I can sleep soundly at night.

While I'm at it, for those of you who like background stuff, it is still very grey and 'wintry' outside, and still cold and wet (compared with where I have been before). BUT the days are staying lighter for longer and signs of life are appearing in the hedges and hills and grasslands of the area. There's a feeling of optimism around – and it's one we all need to nurture today as Skins will get his detailed diagnosis. I'll keep you posted.

With the sixth point of my Charter, I am stating the obvious – but you wouldn't think so on this planet. It is, literally, a Universal Law – and I can't think of anywhere where it does not prevail (although I recognise it was a bit controversial for a while on the star Fornax in NGC1365 galaxy). It is simply this: ***That which is hot will cool***.

There are no exclusions from its reach. It applies to volcanoes just as it does to nightclubs. It applies to coffee just as it does to wars. It applies to stock markets just as it applies to gout-ridden ankles. It applies to heat waves just as it applies to celebrities. It applies to anger just as it applies to passion. It applies to football clubs just as it applies to beliefs.

It is so obvious that it should not need to be re-emphasised – but people on this planet consistently fail to factor it into any planning. They assume something that is hot, where its 'hotness' suits them, can and will stay that way. This is much the same as the phenomenon where people who are in debt believe that borrowing more from somebody else (or 're-structuring your debts' as it's called on television) will provide a solution.

It needs to be addressed down here. Trust me. And I am the one to address it.

»

9 March

14.23.34 GMT

To: All Constellations

It's worse than we all thought. Cide called round at lunchtime (he's just left) and passed on the news about Skins. Sid had been to the hospital with him (Skins, that is) and the scans showed a growth – a cancer – in something called the pancreas. Quite simply, the doctors believe that it is inoperable, and that the two options for (unlikely) survival were either a fierce programme of debilitating drugs (which would have to start right away), or – as they put it – to go home and pray.

I'm giving you a summary here – which itself has passed through two mouths and minds – but the position seems quite clear, although a couple of aspects confused me. Why would they name a disease after a train station? (I'm sure I saw one in London with the same name as Skin's affected body part.) Secondly: what's with this praying business? With the best will in the world (at least in this one, anyway) that's a long shot. If I've read Skin's situation rightly, and I add to that what I know on the subject of praying, and the range of odds against getting a result from it, it's an option that demands a strong Plan B. And there doesn't seem to be one.

In the next couple of days I think I'll go around and see Skins for myself. He's become a friend and I think I'll find out for myself what he's up against and see if I can do anything to help.

Whichever way you look at it, it's depressing news and I'm not in the mood to blog for much more today. In fact, I think

I'll call in at the hotel later and catch up with Nuala, which sounds a much better plan than sending her a message on this little screen we have on our mobile communication units. In fact, just writing that (last) sentence has cheered me up. I haven't looked into those green eyes for a while (I don't know whether I've mentioned their colour to you before), so I'll bring you up to date with what's happening to her AND we'll hit Number Seven of the Charter.

»

10 March

09.23.37 GMT

To: All Constellations

Straight into the Charter today – I'm feeling really business-like. It is a simple statement (again) that the planet needs to recognise if it's going to get any sort of act together. That statement is: ***An 'adult male' is an oxymoron***.

You will remember from an earlier bulletin I sent that I mentioned that we had had some fun back in the SCSC by actually shaping three or four (I forget which) sexes on this planet, but then having the word spread that there are ONLY TWO. I suppose it was a bit infantile, but it amused us. It was similar in principle to the idea that we had to spread the word that the Jews were the 'chosen people' – and then we hammered the shit out of the poor buggers for two millennia. Both of these 'pranks' were designed and implemented by the SCSC – and it will come as no surprise that the SCSC's membership is dominated by the equivalent of this planet's alpha-male sex.

Throughout the recorded history of this planet, the male has dominated almost every form of life and progress. That there are a handful of notable exceptions indicates nothing more than that these exceptions prove the rule. There can be no arguing that the Ascent of Man has been generally impressive and sometimes specifically awesome – but there can equally be no doubt that the setbacks and stresses have been more than equal and opposite. The fact that the planet today is a mosaic of good ideas and good people being almost drowned by bad ideas and arseholes is, in no small measure, due to the fact that the alpha-male remains dominant. And the key to understanding why is to understand that the male of the species, while possessing good potential, is normally a puerile, asinine, childlike, shallow, power-hungry control freak governed for 86.3% of his waking hours by the blood flows rumbling through his penis.

(Note: these figures are provided by the research division of the SCSC, over a period of 23 earth centuries, and they are accurate to within two standard deviations. The only other recorded instances that come anywhere near these were recorded, over several billion earth years-equivalent, on the star Slipher, where a nodal score of 62.5% was notched up. And you all know what happened there.)

I don't think I'm going to be able to change it, but it is important for my Charter, and my Mission, that the planet recognises this – *and adapts its thinking accordingly*.

On to other things. Nuala was busy when I went in last night – too busy to talk much because they had a wedding reception to deal with. Apparently the 'cheese 'n' onion' pies hadn't turned up so it was all hands to the pumps to find alternative catering for 150 people. I saw the bride – she was a big lady in a very fancy dress made of frilly material that was a kind of sea-blue colour. The front of the dress was cut quite low, revealing a sizeable bosom valley. On one of said bosoms was tattooed some sort of design. It looked like a truck, but I may have been wrong.

The good news is that Nuala has Monday off (the day after tomorrow) – and she phoned and got us a table booked at a very successful and trendy restaurant just up the valley. It's called the Three Fishes, and I've been told I have to dress reasonably smartly!

I've also found the time to read up on Skins' plight – and the recommended treatments (radiation and chemotherapy) sound awful. Poor bastard. I'll call in to see him over the weekend, and see if I can do anything to help – and at least offer my support.

»

11 March

12.34.11 GMT

To: All Constellations

Sorry! Off at a tangent again. I've just put the phone down from a long chat with Xabi – and the exciting news is that he may be able to come to my debut 'turn' next month. He has been making final plans for his trip to England for a while, and might be able to match up the dates.

What I did find out about him – which I did not know before (although, when I think back, I had missed a lot of 'hints') and which I found a little disconcerting – was that he travels around Europe quite a lot in his allotted holiday time, and he does this mainly for the purpose of

PROTESTING. He is totally against the power of global companies and their puppet governments and believes that they are shitting on the ordinary citizens of the world. Every time there is a meeting where the powers that be get together to (as he puts it) 'carve up the world's demand and supply markets', he joins up with a determined group of protesters outside the venue. This usually ends up in some altercation with the local police. With this in mind, he asks me about the vigilance of the British immigration authorities because he travels with his protesting 'kit' with him, and fears he might be intercepted at the airport if they find it on him. The 'kit' consists of a lemon and some vinegar, and a handkerchief to wrap around the face. These, he explained, enable you to withstand some tear gas. He also carries some fake blood in a travelling shampoo container – which, he says, is useful if you suddenly have to get through a crowd quickly. The emerging problem is that the immigration authorities in Europe have caught up with the recommendations of the (American-based) Ruckus Society and their 'guidelines' for these specific items and are on the lookout. I told him the truth – I had no idea, having not attempted to come through Luton airport carrying fake blood in anything.

He (and several hundred others – all linked by the Internet) are planning to 'protest' at a meeting to be held just outside the English offices of a corporation called Chiquita – which trades in bananas. The protest will be on the 4th and 5th of April, and he seemed pretty sure he could get another few days off work to come up for my 'turn' on the 7th. I said he could sleep on my couch-type bed, and it sounds like we have a plan.

The news about his activities worried me a little, but on further reflection I think it strengthens my potential Team rather than weakens it. It is important we have some other strong minds in the squad – and some who are also driven by the need to change the planetary status quo. We may clash a bit on HOW to achieve our goals, but I suspect we have much else in common.

»

12 March

20.45.13 GMT

To: All Constellations

Just got back from Nuala's house – a lovely day and I'm not in the mood for any Charter stuff right now.

She picked me up around noon and we drove up the valley to the restaurant. The spring season is beginning to take hold and the whole place looked lovely. The hedgerows are beginning to green up, and quite a few flowers and blossoms are splattering vivid colours around the place. It is as though the country is waking up, cleaning its teeth and washing its hair.

The restaurant was excellent – and gave me more evidence about my seminal 'connection' idea. On the back of the menu was a list of every supplier that provided the items that featured on the front – however indirectly. In many of the cases it also included photographs of the person involved – the farmer, the butcher, the fish merchant etc. I had a piece of roast belly pork, and it was strangely comforting to feel a bond, a closeness, a connection with the man who had raised my pig and expedited its early death.

Anyway, enough of that. What happened next – after the lunch – was much more exciting, if a little bizarre.

We went back to Nuala's place for (her words) 'a cuppa tea and a catch-up with yesterday's papers'. She made the tea and sat me down at one end of the sofa, arming me with the sports section of the paper – and then lay down *with her head in my lap* and proceeded to start reading the magazine. This was not what I was expecting, and I confess I kept reading the same line over and over again. As it happens, I couldn't see her face as my newspaper was blocking it, which was as well because I suddenly realised that there was movement in the area where she was resting her head. When I say movement (and I'm blushing at the memory as I write this), I mean movement of a growth type. Part of me was getting larger. Unbelievably, I was experiencing a penile erection. And, judging by the pressure and tightness I was feeling the area where her resting head was constricting this ill-considered growth, I was not the only one feeling it.

Frankly, I froze. I tried to think of something that would lower this embarrassing state of arousal, in the hope that it might go away and we could get through this episode without having to react or talk about it. The subject I thought about was elephants, which I thought would be harmless and get the de-arousal job done, but suddenly my mind swooped from envisaging a quiet herd of them chomping vegetation for their lunch and (from nowhere) produced a picture of an elephant's penis several metres long. At that juncture, my own penis actually levered Nuala's head off my lap. I was ACUTELY embarrassed, but – let's be honest here – THAT TAKES SOME DOING.

There seemed to be no other option. I would have to move and explain what had happened, and I slowly lowered my newspaper. I was greeted by a sight which I will treasure for a long time in my memory, not just for its aesthetic serenity, but for the relief it provided me. Nuala was asleep. A ray of spring sunlight had fought its way through the lace curtains and was just catching her face. She looked so beautiful. For some reason (a dream, I expect) she was smiling.

After about ten minutes my genitals had reached some sort of neutral state, and I decided to quit while I was ahead (so to speak) and moved so that I would 'accidentally' wake her up. At which stage, we both shifted position to finish our cups of tea, and the rest of the afternoon passed without incident. She dropped me off at my place about a couple of hours ago, and gave me a gentle hug and a kiss on the cheek as I moved to get out of the car. She did say something strange – something about me having a 'fair old piece of furniture down there' and that she would enjoy 'polishing it one day' – but how the subject of (I presume) my new sideboard came up, I don't know.

»

13 March

09.23.31 GMT

To: All Constellations

Right. Bright and early, and back to business – my Charter. I must get this finished and off to the PR lady within the next couple of days – plus, of course, pulling it together and asking for your feedback and constructive (PLEASE) comments.

This (Number Eight) is another one that we have already pushed out into the public domain on earth. Again, like we did with the Steinbeck thing, we used a popular author, and, again, we misjudged its potential traction and popularity with the public. So it's down to me.

It is a slightly more sinister and focused version of 'that which is hot will cool'. It concerns all societies, of whatever size, location, history, culture or religion. It has been consistent throughout history, and WILL REMAIN SO. It is an inalienable fact that ***all societies contain the seeds of their own downfall.***

We got this out in a book by a guy called Jared Diamond, leaving it as late as the earth year 2005 to do so – hopeful that the key points were by now all but clearly visible for all to see. No such luck, so here they are again – the five 'seeds' of societal self-destruction:

1. Self-inflicted environmental damage
2. Climate change
3. Hostile neighbouring societies
4. Decreased support by friendly neighbourhood societies
5. Society's inadequate response to its problems

There they are. It is not my job here to document the evidence, but a five-minute scan through any history book of this planet shows that a mix (and sometimes all) of the factors have played a part in the downfall of every (once) successful and prosperous society. As noted earlier, there is only one 'superpower' on the planet today – the United States of America – and all of the above are present and correct there. They are doomed, and this knowledge MUST be factored into my thinking.

»

14 March

07.23.54 GMT

To: All Constellations

Look at the time!! I've got the bit between my teeth here – so I'm doing this before my breakfast. Number Nine today and the last one – Ten – tomorrow, and then I can pull them together in my Charter and start working with it. It'll be good when it's done – I have a lot to do before my 'turn' on April 7th, including (if I can fit it in) a short trip to America. It's just too big for me to say that I have achieved my FKGs without having some personal experience of the place – even if it's just for a couple of days.

Right. Number Nine. I want this one to 'blow up' one of the stupid, misguided, trite concepts that is forever being trotted out as some sort of template or panacea for a model way of life on this planet – even to the point where you can buy a card-game named after it. Earth needs to recognise something, and recognise it fast: ***There is no such thing as a Happy Family.***

I saw a model of this misguided idea in the Sunday newspaper magazine (which I brought back from Nuala's). It had a lot of photographs of a husband and wife, and two appallingly docile and camera-friendly children. They had acquired an old vicarage somewhere just outside of London and (seemingly with an unlimited budget) converted it into a 'designer-home'. The four of them, occasionally accompanied by their dog, posed for photographs in every room, and emitted signs of rapturous happiness, both individually and as a unit. They smiled at each other in every possible combination. They smiled, solo, for the camera. The dog smiled. I think one of the kitchen cabinets smiled. Oh, happy days. Oh, happy family.

I decided to use this as an example and got the SCSC research guys to do some in-depth stuff for me. Here's what this 'happy family' is made up of:

- The husband was made redundant seven months ago from his job as a Customer Service Manager for a large supermarket chain. It happened two days before his forty-eighth birthday. He has had no success finding a job since that time – or, at least, a job that 'matched his aspirations'. He has sent off 262 job applications. His wife does not actually know he lost his job as, every morning, he leaves home at the normal time and goes to the supermarket's outsourced out-placement centre. The Customer Service function he managed became automated, and all personnel were to be based in Ireland from then on. He has all but spent his redundancy money on the house and living expenses, and now owes £17,349 on his credit cards, and £256,238 on his (joint) mortgage – a loan which is secured by the property. He began an affair four years ago with the National Sales Manager for the company that supplied his supermarkets with cereal products. The good news – the only good news – is that she was a female executive. She won't go away, and is currently threatening to phone his wife if he does not hold to the promise he made her after only two months in a stolen night at a Travelodge Hotel. His doctor has him on some anti-depressants, but these have made him come out in blotches and accelerated his hair loss. He is also embarrassingly and painfully constipated. He refuses to answer the phone in the house, and has his mobile phone permanently switched off.

■ The wife has put on ten pounds in the past twelve months, and grown another chin. She desperately wants – NEEDS – some cosmetic surgery. She does not consider this a discretionary spend, and is aghast that her husband is holding out for budgetary reasons. She has taken – understandably in her mind – a liking to a mid-morning shot (or two) of vodka. She suspects her husband is being unfaithful, but has no proof. To get her own back, only last week she tried to sexually conquer the young man who came to repair her dishwasher. In fact, she walked in on him all but naked, clad only in her new (and secretly bought on her own credit card – current outstanding amount £12,307) tantalising (so it said on the wrapping) black-lace half cup bra and matching thong. The guy barely noticed, told her to act her age and that she still owed him the £45.00 minimum charge for the call-out. In fact, and to be truthful, her vodka intake was a lot more than two shots per morning.

■ The son, aged thirteen, hated his hair that his mother insisted was kept long and clean and curly. That was not the only thing that bothered him. Masturbating was all the rage with the boys in his class at school, and a few 'porno' magazines, well thumbed and unnaturally sticky, were doing the rounds to help the processes involved. The problem was, when he was locked up in his bedroom and all ready to go, the 'smutty' magazines didn't seem to help the situation. What helped the situation was him closing his eyes and thinking of a particular boy in his class.

■ The daughter, aged fifteen years and eight months, had not slept for three nights. This insomnia had been brought on by her home-pregnancy testing kit showing positive. She had only had sex twice, which seemed so unfair. There was, therefore, a fifty percent chance (by her calculation) that the father was that Jamaican lad who sold those pills outside school, and who had just been awarded his third anti-social behaviour order.

There is no such thing as a happy family. It is a false brick on which to build the foundations of a calm and successful society. Every family unit is riven with a mixture of angst, mood swings, infidelities, illnesses, peer group pressures, quirks, oddballs, impossibly high aspirations and sheer incompetence. I need to get that message over. More importantly, I need to provide another foundation stone.

»

15 March

09.23.29 GMT

To: All Constellations

Here we go. Last one: Number Ten. Then I can pull them all together and you can fire in the comments.

The last Charter point is powerful, albeit negative for much of the planet. It has wide-ranging implications for my Mission.

Democracy has been present on this earth, in some form or another, for at least two millennia. Contrary to popular belief, it is not just present in so-called Christian societies. The very first Islamic state – Medina, founded by the Prophet Muhammad some 1400 earth years ago – was an example of a free and just society. But, whatever its definition, the perception is that it has 'won' over alternative philosophies and structures, and is now the predominant and desirable state for all societies. Even if some of them are holding out, they just don't know what is good for them.

Against this background, my final Charter point is dynamite. It is that ***Democracy is NOT a solution, at least not in its current forms.*** It is impotent. What this planet calls democracy today is really governance of the entire world OF (international) corporations, BY (international) corporations and FOR (international) corporations.

The powers that be, heading these corporations and their puppet governments, do not give a shit about free people. What they give a shit about is free markets and free capital flows. The idea that an individual can change things by exercising his or her right to vote for some sort of representative in government would be laughable if it wasn't so terrifyingly pathetic. So, they are catching on; they are stopping voting.

Something else is needed. Another force; another way of thinking. My mission is to make people realise this harsh fact, and help them find another way.

»

16 March

11.34.23 GMT

To: All Constellations

This is the exciting bit, and I thank you all for your patience. I felt I had to expand a bit on each of the points so that you would have some of the background thinking available – but the real power – the BRUTAL power – of this Charter is in its summarised simplicity. It is designed to be memorable. Before I came here I was briefed on the potential impact of what they call 'sound-bites' on this

planet – particularly if you envisage extensive media work and coverage. There is no point at this stage being over-modest – I think this piece of work scores highly against all our pre-set success criteria. What I suggest you (all) do is digest it for a day or so (I need a day to catch up) and then let me have your feedback. At this stage the only other person down here to receive this will be my PR lady – who, I'm sure, will give me another dimension of feedback.
My early thoughts are this will not see the light of day in public until my 'turn' at the Golf Club next month. Here goes. No, wait a minute, I'll see if I can find a fancy script for this. Right, that should do it:

The Initiate's Charter

1. There is a universal sense of loss and alienation on earth. New Age winners will help people re-connect to what's lost and distant.

2. All people are to be admired. All governments are not to be.

3. Organisms that have an innate advantage will prosper. By such means all species have evolved and always will do so.

4. But you can still have faith (or a Faith).

5. Intervention in, or invasion of, the Middle East by outsiders always makes it worse. Learn the lesson. Stay out and support no one. Let the regional aboriginals sort it out. It'll get worse then better.

6. That which is hot will cool.

7. An adult male is an oxymoron.

8. The seeds of self-destruction are sewn in every society.

9. There is no such thing as a happy family.

10. Democracy is impotent. It is a world of international corporations, governed by international corporations, for international corporations.

I am feeling strangely calm. I have, for the first time, just re-read it in its Charter form. I think the font makes a big difference – not that the content is anything but substantive in its own right. One last check. One last deep breath. And here I go – I will now press the 'send' button.

»

17 March

13.45.26 GMT

To: All Constellations

A day of anti-climax. I was not expecting any responses (having asked you to hold back) and received none. Frankly, I had a lie in this morning – going back to bed with a flask of decaffeinated tea (apparently, so my last health guide from the SCSC tells me, this helps to limit my uric acid generation), three fried eggs on three 'oven bottoms' and my newspaper. Bliss.

I eventually got up about 11.00 a.m., and had a weigh. That was a bit disappointing, as I thought I might have lost a bit with all this cerebral effort, but not so. Maybe I shouldn't have had that third egg sandwich, or maybe I should adapt Cide's policy, which is only to weigh yourself just after you've had a crap (and don't forget to take your glasses off), but really these are small issues in the grandeur of my overall position. Yes, I feel pretty pleased with myself. This afternoon I will clean my house – which looks as though a hurricane has passed through. There are papers and books strewn everywhere, lots of screwed up bits of paper where I was trying out different formats for my Charter, and an embarrassing amount of half eaten meals and dirty dishes. There is a clever machine down here that uses a basic manufactured vacuum to clean up dirt and stuff. I've got one (somewhere) and, if I can find it, I'll try it out. My only other plan for the day is to try to find out how Skins is getting on. I might drop in to see him tomorrow. Oh, and I must book a flight to America.

»

18 March

08.23.16 GMT

To: All Constellations

You're probably not aware of this, but I've got myself a conventional computer/communications set up here as well as the one I use for this blog. I sent a copy of the Charter to Cori – the public relations agent I have 'retained'. Most of you will remember that this was not my idea, and I remain unconvinced that the idea in general, and she in particular, are needed – but I bow to the wisdom of the SCSC. I guess, after the last fiasco, I'm not in a position of strength to argue.

Anyway. I had some of your replies and feedback to my Charter – and I'm generally encouraged. But I'm most unhappy with this lady's. She replied using the same 'email' system, and I think the best thing to do is to scan it in to this system and let you see the full copy. Here goes:

Subj: Your 'Charter'
Date: 16/03 17:45.38 GMT Standard Time
From : cvialli04@aol.com
To: tramsbottom1@aol.com

Hi Tom:

Just got your email. Sorry in a rush – just going out to theatre (Spamalot!). Had a quick read and REALLY like the font. As to rest of it, got some probs. Will give it some more thought but initial response is WHAT THE FUCK IS IT? Sorry about earthy lang and I should add lots of !!!!!! but I suspect you didn't send me the whole thing and I've read it out of context. But not sure (genuine) what it is meant to be and (more 'portant) what u want me to do with it. Is it a sort of song lyric? Like Bernie Taupin used to fax to Elton John? In which case I need to find a melody writer to match you up with – but quite honestly you don't (my view – lots of !!!! again) give him (or her! Oops!) much to work with. Or is it a kinda Peter Kaye thing? He's always doing stuff like this on the Net and he's v. successful (as you know !!!) – but he's got a lot of profile already. Sorry if this sounds gloomy and I know it's a bit abrupt as I MUST MUST MUST go now. But need more inf if we are to put a budget together and get it out there. Whatever it is. Love the font tho.

Chat soonest. C.

I really don't know what to make of this – although it doesn't sound very positive. In fact, I don't understand half of it (who or what is an Elton John? What has this Peter Kaye got to do with it? Do I know Spamalot? What's with the melody writer thing?). I'm just sharing it with you at this stage in the interests of total transparency. I'll do a bit more 'finding-out' and get back to you. I suspect, though, I'm going to have to go to London to explain this to her – but I think I will need her help to make sure I get enough impact with this when I do my 'turn'.

That vacuum thing is brilliant by the way.

»

18 March

15.34.15 GMT

To: All Constellations

Right, I've done some research. Elton John – he's a bloody singer and a homosexual who has to be delivered to parties in a huge vehicle to accommodate his outrageous clothing. Now I'm totally confused – I'm going to have to sit down with Cori, across a table, and sort it out. I'm planning to make that happen by flying to America from London, which will give me the chance to take a bit of time to see José and Cori before I go. I would like to get them both up here for my turn, albeit in very different support roles.

I've still got your feedback dribbling in, so I'll wait until I've got the full picture before commenting – but so far it looks as though most challenges are semantic and I won't have to make substantial changes.

While we are waiting, let me clear up one thing that's recurring. I assumed that most of you (all of you, in fact) were aware that this was not my first attempt at a Second Coming. However, the Project Team title – the SCSC (Second-Coming Steering Committee, if you remember)

– has confused some of you. How can this be a SECOND COMING if there has already been another one after the first? Shouldn't this one be the THIRD?

Those of you who know all this, sign off now – the rest of you, please digest (or re-digest) the following. Yes, I Came, with a capital C, again, and (we thought) it was well researched and that we had learned lessons from the first one. It transpired not to be so. It was such a disaster that we decided to (sort of) re-write history and re-classify it as a PILOT Second Coming, as if we didn't really mean it. For those of you who have forgotten, let me remind you of the painful details. When I say painful, I mean painful (as ever) for yours-bloody-truly.

We left it nearly an earth millennium and a half before attempting another Coming in this format – although, clearly, our parallel system achieved a lot of traction in Medina in about half that time.

I came as a guy called John Huss, and operated in what was then called Bohemia. Well before the middle of the fifteenth century Anno Domini, as they classify it here, I was already REALLY annoying the incumbent Pope (John XXIII) by pointing out, to increasingly large and wildly enthusiastic audiences, the corruption and greed that existed at every level of the church. I had almost finished my Charter (I've actually just read it again and it seems terribly dated) and was on a roll.

Remember, this was well before the so-called Reformation down here, and, quite frankly, and to use a modern earth expression, the Pope got the hump. He had a big hissy-fit. The bastard ex-communicated me.

I was required to defend myself against charges of heresy before the Council of Constance, and was guaranteed free passage by the Holy Roman Emperor *in situ* at the time – Wenceslaus, another bastard. When I arrived, they only refused to honour this promise, took me prisoner (the double bastards) and on June 6th in the earth-year 1415 sentenced me to be burned at the stake for heresy.

On July 6th (these bastardy bastards didn't hang about) my head was shaved and a tall cap placed on it – with the word *heresiarch* embroidered on it. They tied me to the stake, and then noticed I was facing east, so untied me and then re-tied me facing the other way (so I would not have the 'honour' of facing the sunrise), and burnt me to death.

Let me tell you about burning. That nailing bollocks is a piece of cake compared with this. Last time, pierced only by four six-inch nails, I was able to compose some serene and meaningful words about forgiveness as I went back down the tunnel – but not this time. Absolute, excruciating pain. My last words were unholy and uncompromising. I called them every vile, insulting name I could think of. And very loudly.

Two things emerged from this 'pilot' Second Coming. First: there were lessons to be learned again. More planning was needed. A lower profile was called for. I allowed myself to be over-influenced by a 'celebrity' of no standing whatsoever (John Wyclif). We needed a better support infrastructure to be in place, both back at the ranch and on the ground, before making enemies in high places. These are lessons we believe have now been learned.

The second fall-out from this sadly fated mission was that I spent nearly five hundred earth-years undergoing skin grafts. The first two hundred were in the actual Universe Central Burns Unit itself, covered in thick petroleum jelly. Deep joy. So, next time you are thinking of giving me earache about something, just remember what I've been through to get here. And who I'm doing it for.

Where was I? Oh, yes. I'm going to call in the Whalley Arms tonight, catch up with what's gong on and see if it will be OK to call in and see Skins sometime soon. I should have gone today, but thought I'd get this out of the way. What we are on now is the definitive Second Coming.

»

19 March

12.34.27 GMT

To: All Constellations

A bit late starting this morning – I keep forgetting how a night in the Whalley Arms takes it out of you. Still no Skins, but the others were coming back to form and I got a peach of a rant from Sid:

'Evening Sid, so what's pissing you off, then?'

I ventured this without much hope of much in reply. But I got a beauty – maybe with some extra from some pent up feelings. Again, I'll write what I remember without interruption, then I'll add what explanations I can.

*'What's pissing me off? What's pissing me off? (*1). Just look on that table. What do you see? A pack of fookin' crisps (*2), that's what. That's all I fancied, just some fookin' crisps and what do I get? I get "Kettle Fried Lamb and Rosemary Crisps with Sea Salt Flavouring". And what do I pay? Not thruppence, oh no. I pay about a working lad's wage forra week . . .*

*'And another thing: tomatoes (*3). When did you last taste one that tasted like a tomato? (*4). Nah, they LOOK brilliant but they're fookin' strip-mined (*5) in Peru or summat –*

*'And look at this – what the fookin' 'ell? It's a MENU, that's what it is. In the Whalley Arms!! Food in't' pub. What bollocks is that? And have you read it? Listen this – STEAK PIE! Can you believe it? I'll tell you about this steak pie without even seeing it – the first time the pie will meet its crust is when it comes out of the kitchen door (*6). And – you ready for this? listen up – this is what it says about the red wine: "subtle flavours of buttered toast". Buttered toast! So, the wine tastes like my fookin' breakfast, 'cept mine's usually burnt . . . and that's supposed to be GOOD. Oh, wait forrit, here's the best – look at this – veal escalope drizzled in a reduction of its own "jus". What the fook; I mean what the fookin' fook? I got drizzled in a reduction of me own jus (*7) once when me missus got carried away and it hit me right in the eye but I never thought of putting it on a menu in't' Whalley Arms . . .'*

That's all I can remember – but I feel it's so important for you to get as much of this kind of thing as you can. This is how a lot of the ordinary folk talk around here – and what they talk about. These notes may help:

*1: It essential when you are starting off on one of these rants to repeat yourself. Everybody knows what's coming then, so you can gear up accordingly. This a different sort of repetition to the normal, rather odd, habit of repeating the personal pronoun at the end of the sentence – for example: 'I'm going out, me'. After a while you CAN tell the difference.

*2: Crisps are cold fried potatoes sliced very thinly and often served as a snack while drinking. Apparently they used to be cheap and simple. They are salted simply to get you thirsty so you will drink more.

*3: These are a red fruit, which was not available during my first visit. It was imported from the Americas a few hundred years ago and has become very popular – but mass production has favoured looks at the expense of flavour.

*4: Yesterday, and I confess I quite liked it when I clearly should not have done.

*5: This I do not understand. I think he was being facetious.

*6: This is a Big Issue here. Apparently a proper steak pie should have pastry on the bottom and sides welded (somehow) to a pastry lid. It is near heresy around here to drape some pastry on top of a bowl of beef stew and call it a pie.

*7: I have honestly no idea what this bit is about. None whatsoever. So don't bother asking.

All in all, we had a good evening, and I called Bash to take me home. He was on good form, complaining only about his national cricket team – which is another sport I have only seen on the TV because it doesn't start here until the summer. I brought up the subject of my 'turn' at the Golf Club next month and asked him if he'd like to come as my guest. He seemed really keen – but told me that he couldn't afford to lose a night's earnings as he was saving up for a trip back to Pakistan with his family (his wife, mother and two children). This gave me an idea – which I kept to myself for the time being. What I might do, if I feel his support will be important on the night, is to simply book his taxi – and tell him to leave the fare meter running. That might prove a bit expensive, so I'll hang back before deciding.

I've a lot to do tomorrow, so the rest of today will be spent compiling a 'To Do' list. At least, that's what I'll do when I've had a kip.

»

20 March

17.34.05 GMT

To: All Constellations

What a productive day! I hit my 'To Do' list first thing by getting a haircut. (I confess I've let myself go a bit recently with the effort I've put into the Charter.) Again it took TWO HOURS to get sorted out. TWO HOURS! I had to have all the highlights re-done. However, I honestly think, if I am to be a modern media-aware person, it's worth while.

Straight after that, I organised my tickets to visit America. I used what they call a 'travel agent' for this because I didn't want to make any mistakes with so short a time available to me. So, I fly to a place called Miami on the 29th of this month, and return on the 2nd of next month. We chose Miami because it seems a very popular destination at this time of year, with the weather forecast to be sunny most of the time. The ticket seemed very expensive, but it has to be done. I do not think I could go through the first (crucial) six months without having SOME direct experience of the only real superpower left on the planet. Maybe I can get some understanding of why America seems universally disliked.

My next job was to phone Skins and arrange to go and see him. I spoke to his wife (Doreen) – who seems very pleasant – and I'm going round to his house on Wednesday lunchtime (the day after tomorrow).

Then I spoke to Cori – my PR 'agent' – on the phone. Something is clearly troubling or confusing her. She has had a copy of my Charter for several days now, and still hasn't come up with any really groundbreaking ideas as to what to do with it. In fact, she is still claiming that she is not sure what it is. I explained it again, slowly – and with not a little irritation creeping into my voice now and again. All I could get from her was some confused comments about 'White Rap' not being a mainstream channel in the UK. In turn, I've no idea – NONE – what that is all about, so I decided that the best plan was to leave it until we meet – stressing that we had a good budget available (which seemed to cheer her up a lot). I'll go down to London (which is where I fly from to go to America) a day or so early and see her on the 28th for lunch.

I've also (what a busy day!) agreed to meet up with José for dinner on the 28th – although that itself caused some confusion. This island has some strange differences. I am only about 300 miles away from where José lives, but he has dinner in the evening, whereas around Whalley we have dinner at lunchtime. That got me and José a bit confused for a while!

»

21 March

12.34.23 GMT

To: All Constellations

Life's a bit frenetic at the minute – but I just want to pause and cover a couple of pieces of feedback I have had from you about the Charter. They are not really challenges, or strong demands that I make changes, but a couple of you, using your own experiences, have suggested ideas that – even if they are not formally included in the final version – still bear thinking about.

There was an interesting idea from Verunakk. Now I know a lot of you will think that irrelevant, but in fairness it's nearly as big as Pluto's moon – and we should be prepared to consider ideas from minorities. The idea was quite simple – that we should ***re-discover and celebrate silence***. Yes, quite. Obviously, their own experiences were important in defining this priority, but there is an issue to be addressed here on this planet as well. People do seem addicted to noise. The news and entertainment media never stop. Music invades lifts, toilets, restaurants, pubs, and almost every public facility. Personal telephones wail everywhere, and people seem to feel the need to raise their voices when talking on them in public. The younger generation are rarely seen without earphones. We have lost, it seems, the ability to enjoy silence. More important, we have lost what comes with it – the ability to pause and reflect and calm down.

I guess the source of the next 'input' is even more contentious – coming as it does from one of the Cephids. However, I'm going to include it anyway – as it has much relevance for my mission. Stated simply, it is this: ***we do not learn from our history***. Obviously, when we consider what happened to the Cephids, we can see why this is a Big Issue there, but its relevance on this planet is also huge. We DID try to get the message out here (via the writings of a German Philosopher called Hegel) – but he has been largely written off down here as a gloomy bugger. But when you think about the current planet-wide problems caused by localised conflicts in Afghanistan, Palestine and Mesopotamia, you can see the point.

At this stage, I intend to do nothing more than make a note of these. But they are both valid and helpful – and I thank those who took the trouble to input so positively.

»

22 March

17.23.56 GMT

To: All Constellations

What an awful day. Just terrible. I'm just back from my visit to see Skins – which was only supposed to be a half hour or so. It lasted until just about half an hour ago, and has left me very deflated and – for the first time – really questioning what I can do down here.

Let me start at the beginning. Skins only lives about a ten minute walk away from my house, so I ambled over just after twelve noon.

I was not unprepared. I had looked up his sickness in the reference section on my computer – and the guys from the SCSC had done some more work on it. I knew he was in serious trouble, but that cures were not only possible but were beginning to move into the 'probable' category thanks to the march of science and the ability to diagnose these diseases quite early. What I also knew, however, was that the cures – heavy radiation and chemotherapy – were awful. They were long, drawn-out, debilitating and hugely unpleasant – and I saw one of the purposes of my visit as being doing what I could to arm Skins spiritually for what lay ahead.

It was a pleasant, sunny day – and I was feeling quite optimistic as I knocked on his door with the brass knocker provided for the job.

The door was opened by a strange looking woman. She had a kind of hawk face, heavily lined and with the pallor that I have come to associate with a lifetime of smoking cigarettes. Her grey hair was pulled tightly back from her face and tied in a pony-tail at the back. Her body was bigger than her face justified – a disparity not helped by the fact she was wearing a kind of pink track-suit made of a velvety-type material, the top of which failed to meet the bottom by about four inches around the midriff. The fashion mistake was unheeded as it was not visible from her vantage point. She had a rather large bosom, and the track-suit top was unzipped enough to reveal the upper slopes of two industrial-sized breasts, the left one of which (that is, the left one as she would look at it) included a tattoo of what looked to be a short length of barbed wire. Any sexual nuances that might have been signalled were diminished by the fact that her waist was actually larger than her chest. The outfit was completed by running shoes, which had some sparkling stuff on their sides, and by a cigarette held in a long thin tube-like thing.

'You Tommy?'

'Yes . . . I ha . . .'

'Come on, come on; in you come. He's expecting you. I've just got a brew on – you want some?'

I thanked her and said yes to her huge backside as we went into the house.

It was of a pretty standard design for the houses I have seen around here – with just two rooms downstairs, one of which led onto a small kitchen. Or, at least that's what I thought at first.

I was still trying to get my bearings as she poured the tea into a mug and handed it to me.

'He's through in th' Oasis.'

'Sorry?'

'Th' Oasis, it's his room he's built on't' back.'

With that she pointed to a door that had been mystifying me, and left me to find my way.

Feeling a little nervous, I knocked, but got not response of any kind. So I opened it – and walked into quite the weirdest place.

It was a decent sized room, which had been built on the back of the house. The first thing I noticed was that there were no windows. The second thing was that every inch of wall space was taken up by an assortment of pictures and posters. The third thing was a full set of drums in one corner, with the seat unoccupied. The fourth was Skins himself, sitting – or rather sprawling – in an old armchair, with his feet up on a stool in front of him and with HUGE earphones on his head, which were wired into a sound system the size of my car.

I was taking all this in when he noticed me – and got to his feet, rather painfully, while removing his earphones. He was thinner, and the artificial light gave his skin a rather yellowish tinge, but he seemed cheerful enough. He pushed his rather large footstool over towards me.

'Tommy! Great to see you and thanks for coming. Don't get many visitors, and when I do I don't normally let 'em

in here – but plonk your arse down and drink your tea. I was just listenin' to Wayne Fontana and havin' a laff to meself – he stole a bird from me at a party once and soon after he went bald and a bit daft. Hee Hee.'

The Oasis was his room. Despite his pop music background, it was nothing to do with the popular singing group of that name (of which even I had heard!), but the name of the Club in Manchester where he and his group (the Four Leadbellies) got their first booking in 1963. His drum kit, rarely used nowadays (and not likely to be any more so), stood proudly in one corner, and the stuff on the walls captured the popular music scene in the short and rather uncelebrated time of the Leadbellies' success. There were photos of Skins in the group, who seemed to be four sombre looking young men with high collars and hair like mine before I had it sorted. There were posters for concerts featuring the group – usually positioned some way down the billing. And there were photos of Skins without the group, but accompanying an assortment of (I presume) 'stars' of the time. Some of them were signed: Alma Cogan, Pete Murray, Freddy Garrity, Terry Dene, Wee Willie Harris and some others I couldn't read.

The pair of us sat down and chatted about something and nothing for a few minutes before I took a deep breath and asked how he was doing with his illness.

He was very 'matter-of-fact' about it. I know it annoys the Corner Office, but it is important you all realise (if you are going to UNDERSTAND this place) that the ordinary people use oaths a lot. It is just commonplace and it SEEMS inoffensive to most people. In a short speech about how he felt and what life was like Skins used the word 'shit', or a derivative of it, as a verb, an adjective, an adverb and a noun. The more remarkable thing was that he showed no negative emotion, and his voice was as if he was reading the weather forecast.

I took another deep breath and started. I was about to tell him that I knew what was ahead of him, I understood how miserable the treatment programme might seem, but that all of us – his mates and his family – would support him through this tough, tough programme. I got about five words into this loosely prepared speech when he raised his hand and stopped me. What he said next stunned me.

I should try and capture his speech verbatim for you, like I do with Sid's rants. But, in truth, I cannot remember much of the detail. He made the principle clear from his first few words – that he was having none of the cure. He was going to let nature (and presumably the illness) take its course. He'd had enough. He'd talked it through with Doreen (and, interestingly, Sid) and they both understood and supported his position. They had promised not to grieve while he was still alive. If things got really bad, they would do what they could to end the misery for him.

I stared at him throughout this monologue. I had no words at that stage.

Eventually, I put some thoughts together. Surely, now that science offered a cure, he should take it? What about the sanctity of life? If there was a chance – any chance – didn't he owe it to himself to give it a go? He could have ten, twenty years of life left.

He explained it in the most astonishing way. He reckoned it was the most SELFISH decision he had ever taken, and was embarrassed because it was so. I looked confused. Selfish? To abandon your own life?

He explained that he was a coward, and that he had no stomach for the pain and misery ahead. But then he added that the idea of the 'reward' of extra years had little appeal to him, and it was only at this stage that I began to see the real logic. His theory was that his had been a golden, blessed generation – and that the generations before him AND the generations that were following him had a shitty deal. The years ahead offered (in his eyes) unfettered terrorism, rogue states with nuclear arms, no proper jobs, people with debts up to their armpits, no proper pensions, unaffordable housing, the earth wrecking itself and shitty music.

In contrast, he pointed to one of the pictures on the wall. It was of somebody called Gene Vincent. Apparently, he (it was a 'he') was a pop music star of the 1960s. It transpired that Skins had gone to see him at a club called Mr Smiths, and during the interval had gone to the gents. While he was relieving himself, the 'man himself' walked in (limped actually, he had a bad leg) and proceeded to pee in the next urinal. As if that wasn't enough, somebody called Graham Nash, of a group called the Hollies, walked in and proceeded to relieve himself in the urinal on the other side of Skins. Now THAT was a golden period, in Skins' eyes – and if a cure were about to offer him ten more years of the 1960s he would go for it. He did not envy the young their future, he just envied them their energy and recognised his would never come back. A cure that offered him ten more years of the 21st century, with him heading into his seventies, bald and miserable, feeling crappy and with no guarantee that his cancer was beaten, was simply not attractive. Enough. His time was up. There was nothing to grieve about. He'd had a great run. The time was right.

The rest of my time with him was occupied by him going through every photo and poster with me, plus endless scrap books, while his Dansette 'radiogramme' sound system (which looked nothing like mine – it had an arm thing that seemed to scrape across a plastic disc) played what seemed an endless supply of tinny thumping music.

I went through it all feeling numb. If this approach to life and death was widespread, I had a bigger job on my hands than I first thought.

I'm back at my base now. I still think that.

»

23 March

08.40.32 GMT

To: All Constellations

Not a good night's sleep. I was thinking and then re-thinking over the afternoon with Skins. Running through my mind was the idea that, somewhere in that conflict of emotion and activity (or lack of it), was something very important for my Mission. Around 4.00 a.m. this morning, I think I found it. It is important enough – at least I think so – that I should have addressed it in my Charter, but what I do about it now I don't quite know.

It is this: if I am to succeed on this planet, on this Coming, I will have to ***rekindle optimism***.

I had not noticed just how widespread pessimism and negativity has become on this planet. People don't vote in their democracies. Suicide rates are higher than ever. Depression itself is now recognised as a widespread and definable disease. Euthanasia is debated openly and increasingly sought as a right. Advances in science and nutrition have produced large pockets of the earth's population in their seventies and eighties – but a younger population coming up behind them that is not excited by the thought of an endless old age.

It is not a dearth of happiness. It is a widespread lack of optimism.

It's taken a while, but at least now I see it. It was not a challenge I faced before, and I recognise it will be tough to address. But address it I must if this Mission is to succeed.

The only other happening 'of note' to record is that I have had another of these written messages on the small screen on my phone – from Nuala. I think it's in code again – I cannot make head or tail out of it – here it is in its entirety: '*Where R U? had a few bevvies and feel a bit ratted. Answer me a ? next time U C me. When U look at me what do U C?*

Don't ask me what this means. I have no idea.

»

23 March

13.34.26 GMT

To: All Constellations

I also had a bit of a panic this morning as my thoughts got back to more 'normal' agenda items. When I get back from America I will not have a lot of time to get my presentation-speech ready for the 'turn' at the Golf Club. I have been reminded this morning by the SCSC that I need to do some work on it – given that it's been a long time since I held a crowd.

I find this a bit unnecessary. I mean – I'm the guy who invented rhetoric, way before anybody put a name to it. I ended up being renowned for my ability to hold an audience – and here are these clever buggers telling me I have to 'research' the science.

First thing I did, however, was give Cide a call on the telephone. I needed a bit more information on this 'observational comedy' – and wanted to pick up a few more bits and pieces of information about the audience and what will and will not work.

He was very helpful. He said this lot always like a good golfing joke – and suggested one: 'Old golfers never die. They just play in front of you.' He said I'd probably want to stick the 'F' word in to spice it up a bit – given the audience and the occasion – and he clearly found this very funny. I've made a note of it – but I don't see anything funny about golfers with eternal life.

Anyway, anything for a peaceful life. To keep the SCSC happy, I've ordered, via my computer, some books on public speaking for express delivery. I've got a long plane journey to America – and whereas I was going to use it to do some more reading about that particular nation and its history, I will bow to the direction of my betters and read up on some twenty-first earth century public speaking skills. For the record, I've ordered *The Oxford Union Guide to Speaking in Public*; a book by somebody called Mitch Murray (*Handbook for the Terrified Speaker*) and Barry Gibbons' seminal bestseller on the subject entitled *Speakeasy*. Let no man or spirit accuse me of not putting in the hard yardage.

»

24 March

09.34.16 GMT

To: All Constellations

Up early this morning, and I have already sorted out my accommodation in America. The hotel I use in London – the Marriott – has a branch in Miami where I am flying to in America. It's in a place called Coconut Grove, which sounds exciting.

This travel thing has brought up a snag however – and I'm not sure of its significance. But it has made me very annoyed. Let me explain.

When you travel by air on this planet, you have a variety of 'classes' of travel. It was all explained to me by the travel agent, and – once you understand it – it's not that complex. If you don't have much money, you can travel 'economy class'. That's not very comfortable or luxurious, but it's the way that most people fly. If you have more money, you can fly in what they call 'business class', which upgrades all aspects of the flying experience. Finally, if money is no object, you can fly 'first class'. This, apparently, gives you the height of luxury, with a full-length bed if you need to sleep and top-quality food and drink.

Frankly, I spent very little time on my decision in the travel agent's. The fare for economy class from London to Miami and return was £599. For business class it was £4,200, and for first class it was £7,600. Naturally I chose the latter. Given the importance of my mission, the urgency of the time frame, the need to stay as fresh and de-stressed as possible, I chose the class that would – in my view – be most appropriate.

It appears I made a mistake. My first inkling was a short communication from the Operational Shift Manager of the SCSC, indicating that a whole SECTION of my operations manual covered travel expenses and what would be allowed for flights and for per diem expenses etc. etc. While, in certain extreme circumstances, I could justify business class flying, on no account could my Mission justify first class. I was requested to go back to the agent and make the appropriate changes.

To cut a long story short, I refused. And I refused rather rudely. It is true that I could have been a bit more thorough reading the ops manual, but it was a genuine mistake, and I thought the circumstances (notably the critical importance of my Mission to the whole planet) warranted it. I am also getting a bit tired of these unhelpful interventions by these control freaks – most of which I don't tell you about. I'm out here, flying solo on the front line. Those guys are sat on their lard-arses, shuffling paper and staring at screens all day. Why they bother about money, I just don't know – they've teams of people doing sod-all but make virtual money cards and fictional bank arrangements for me. Hints about all this were included in my impolite reply.

Oh my word – did I ever upset somebody, notably Him in the Corner Office. This is nothing about money came the hissy-fit message, this is about me keeping an appropriate 'profile' for the Mission. This is about moving anonymously until the time was right. This is about me remaining a 'man of the people'.

Man of the people? Do you know, I nearly resigned. What utter bollocks. Man of the people? Does 'He' realise who I am and where I've been? Has 'He' any feeling for the pain and suffering I've had? Endless months in the burns unit; holes the size of earth worms in my feet. Has he any REAL idea of what's ahead of me?

Man of the people, my arse. Think about it. I am a man FOR the people.

I've said my piece in no uncertain terms, so this whole thing may be aborted. Let's wait and see.

»

25 March

07.34.51 BST

To: All Constellations

Crisis over. Everybody has cooled down. I think I got a lot of grievances off my chest just by writing down what I did and firing it off. And, not for the first time, He has shown quite Infinite Wisdom in suggesting we just 'park' this issue and calm down – we can review at the end of the first, crucial six-month stage. In the meantime, it would do both of us good to have read the other's point of view. There's a couple of things there that both sides could digest.

It's early morning on a Saturday, and it is a lovely day here. The early morning sun is up already and I've just made myself a sausage sandwich, on which I've learned to spread red ketchup quite thickly. I'm armed with a big mug of tea, and – with the crisis with my home office over before it's really begun – I'm feeling quite pleased with myself. I've got to do a medical update tomorrow (due back with the SCSC before the end of March) so I think I'll give the pub a miss tonight – but I may pop in to the hotel to catch up with Nuala to see what all these coded messages are about.

I think the rest of the day is going to be about cleaning my house up. The sudden appearance of bright sunlight is making everything look dusty and dirty. If I'm still in the mood I might even give my car a going-over. You can barely tell what the external colour is just now – but a bucket or two of water will solve that.

It's a few minutes since I wrote that last bit and I've been reading the paper. Here's something weird. Apparently, and I have no idea why, tonight we simply change every device which tells us the time – moving it forward in complete unison by one hour. Everybody does it together, and tomorrow morning we all wake up and our common time has just lost an hour. Does anybody know what this is about? Is it the *Principa* or that space/time continuum that we let Einstein come up with? Didn't we do something like this on Linulk 4S once? It's not a big deal, but I'd be interested. If I'm to sort this planet out, I need to get my head round this stuff.

»

26 March

18.17.45 BST

To: All Constellations

I had a quiet day planned, but it turned out quite busy and productive. On the spur of the moment I called Nuala to see if she'd got time for a cup of coffee or something – and we agreed to meet up at the hotel in her afternoon break at 3 o'clock. I thought I'd use the visit there to catch up with Cide on one or two details about the upcoming event – and he told me he'd be in the Pro's shop all day – so I popped in just after lunch.

He threw me a bit at the start – showing me the promotional brochure he put together for the dinner on the 7th of April. The cost for the dinner and 'famous' cabaret act was £25 per head, and on the first inside page it explained what the choices of meal were. On the other inside page it listed the Golf Awards that would be made that night. I thought it looked very professional and was about to give it him back when I turned over onto the outside back page. There I read about the 'famous' comedian Tommy Ramsbottom – who (get this) '*has been having northern club audiences in stitches for years with his hilarious observations of everyday life*'.

I was just about to let fly at Cide – but he intercepted me. He told me to stay cool – that everybody used a 'bit of poetic licence on these things', otherwise you wouldn't get 'bums on seats'. It was designed, he added, to give me loads of flexibility – and that he knew most of the audience personally and they would be just great with me.

I confess to still being a little concerned, but suddenly realised that this reminded me that I had to sort out seats for my 'guests'. I started to list them, and that's when he told me of their special offer – that if you booked a whole table of ten, instead of £250 it was only £200. Well, I am hoping for nine (although I admit I have still work to do) – Xabi, José, Bash, Sid, Rhys, Skins (if he can make it), Cori, Nuala and myself. Cide suddenly grinned (always worrying) and told me that he could make up the tenth place for me – that Debs (remember her? Ugh!) wanted to come – and she'd be great fun on that table.

I was far from sure about that – but it seemed sense to book the table anyway. That's one less job to do.

When I caught up with Nu, she was looking a bit drawn and tired – but so, so pretty. We grabbed a coffee and sat in the residents' lounge. I asked her about those two messages she had sent me on my phone screen. She smiled and I could have sworn she blushed slightly – but said she'd forgotten the first one and was a 'bit tiddly' when she sent the second one, so I should just ignore it. That was a bit of a pity because I had rehearsed – at length – what I was going to tell her about what I saw when I looked at her. Pity. No matter.

Anyway, I told her about my progress with the Golf Dinner – and showed her the brochure. She is a bit of a worrier – and was a bit concerned about the way I had been 'bigged up' (Cide's poetic licence), but I assured her that Cide knew what he was doing. I then received her 'considered opinion' that 'that would be a first' – but I chose to ignore it.

What came next was very helpful. She told me that if any of my guests wanted to stay that night, she could offer a special low rate for bed and breakfast because it was a weekend and no weddings were planned for that particular night. It was only £35 for bed and breakfast – and this immediately struck me as a better idea than trying to jam them all into my place. So I booked rooms for Xabi, José and Cori – for the magnificent sum of £105. Add this to the £200 I am paying for the table and it comes to the HUGE total of £305 – against which can be offset the £500 fee I am getting and giving to charity.

So what have we got? A breakthrough, high-profile 'turn' within the six months, as promised – at a 'cost' of a net investment of £195 in charity. And I'm irresponsible when it comes to expenses? Eat your shorts pal.

I got another bonus from Nu. She had been to Miami for a holiday a couple of years ago and, although she had stayed by Miami Beach, she was able to give me a good list of things to see and do. Very helpful – and I agreed that, as soon as I was back, we'd get together and I'd tell her all about it. I don't know whether I've mentioned this before, but she has quite, well, sort of attractive green eyes

So, there you go. It started out as an ordinary day – and I ended up by getting a lot done. Now I've got to make a list of what I have to do tomorrow – it's my last day before I set off for America.

»

27 March

18.45.23 BST

To: All Constellations

Another quite successful day. Nu had given me a list of things she felt I'd need to get for my trip to Miami – including things like little gadgets that enable you to use the electrical machines that we use over here when they are plugged into the American electrical system. No, I don't understand why they are different either. I've also got, on her advice, some cream to put on my skin to protect me from the much stronger sun I'll experience over there (what a joyful thought) and some spray to ward off nasty insects.

I've also bought some lighter clothes and some SHORTER leg trousers. These come down just below the knee and have (I counted) thirteen different pockets in them, of which eight have zips on them. This struck me as daft but I was assured by the sales assistant that they were being worn by all 'modern' men this year and I don't want to appear different. I also bought what they call a 'carry-on' bag – again on Nuala's advice. This means that you take your luggage with you on the plane so you never lose sight of it – as Miami airport is renowned for losing baggage.

I've just got all my travel documents together and checked the 'passport' I've been provided with. Apparently, Americans basically don't want anybody to come into their country since they had some explosions caused by foreigners recently – and if your travel documents aren't exactly right they turn you back. I can only hope that the SCSC research team got these right.

I've had a practice 'pack' and it's a bit tight – particularly if I am to get my books on public speaking in – but I'll get what I can in tomorrow and we'll see what gets jettisoned.

An early night for me. I've a lot to cram into the next few days.

»

28 March

17.34.21 BST

To: All Constellations

Now I'm back down in London, in my room at the Marriott Hotel. I got the train down this morning, and have just got back from a meeting with Cori Vialli, my so-called PR agent.

I'm getting more and more unhappy with this arrangement, but the SCSC are insisting that I get some 'professional' help in 'shaping my proposition' and getting the 'right profile'. Quite frankly, I don't think I've been doing too badly on my own, but the message comes over loud and clear: this is a very different world than the one I knew (or the ones I knew depending on your definition of these things). What worked then will not work now.

The meeting started badly. She had a copy of my Charter, and – to be honest – I had expected a PR plan, or at least some ideas on what to do with it. All I got was a confused look – and what I thought was a rather lame explanation for her lack of progress. It was, she said, essential that we have a face-to-face 'engagement' before she put an action-plan together – in order that she could understand the 'goals' and 'success criteria' of the project.

We were getting nowhere until I brought up the subject of a budget. She cautiously explained that she would need a 'substantive' fee (called a 'retainer') each month, and then funding for some 'direct programmes' using a 'multiple-media' approach. I asked what retainer she was thinking about. She replied rather quickly that she was thinking about £3,500 each calendar month – and she set off on what was obviously going to be a long justification of such an amount. I cut her short. I told her that the retainer would be SEVEN THOUSAND a month; that my first 'turn' was booked for the 7th April; that I would expect her there; and that she should take that as a base position and then plan a programme of activities. I would be available from then on to give my full support.

There was quite a long silence. She seemed (I thought) quite nervous, and suddenly in a rush to get back to her office – explaining that she would send an agreement along these lines to my hotel tonight.

That's how you deal with these people. Decisiveness and assertiveness wins the day, I find. I just have to get approval of these sums from You-Know-Who and the whole thing is up and running.

The agreement has not arrived here (the hotel) yet – so I'm just going to have a rest and then I'm going to meet José. He's got a night off – and we've agreed to meet at a restaurant called Joe Allen's near a place called Covent Garden. My objective tonight is to get him to agree to come up for my 'turn' – which reminds me, I need to telephone Xabi to confirm his plans as well.

It's all go. I fly out of the London Airport (which, strangely, isn't in London at all) tomorrow at 10.15 a.m. – which means I have to be at the airport (for some reason) at 8.15 a.m. I'll sign off now and update you when I can tomorrow.

»

29 March

12.34.23 BST (07.34.23 EST)

To: All Constellations

This is unbelievable. I'm up in the air writing this, in the first-class section of a plane flying to America. More of my meeting with José in a minute (it went well) but first let me tell you about this.

First things first: get a load of the time on the top of this communication. Well, I should say – get a load of the TIMES!! Yup, there are two of them. The way the earth orbits the sun (and all that other stuff) has implications (which we never thought of) if you want to have a reasonably constant spread between day and night throughout the planet. It means you have to alter the times in different places – so that the start of the daylight occurs at roughly the same time wherever you are. Brilliant! Why didn't we think about that on the Draghij XK Group?

And if you think that's brilliant, wait till you hear this. Obviously if you are a being that eats solids, you've got to get rid of them. In most places that's a bit of a mucky business – but down here they've moved on from using a dedicated hand to clean yourself up afterwards to providing little rolls of paper specially provided and situated right next to the place where you do your 'number twos' (as they call it rather quaintly on this planet). I personally find this system much better than the old way. Now then, hear this. In this plane, in the first-class lavatory (from which I've just returned), they provide some things called 'moist wipes' to do the job! Moist wipes!! I know I've become a bit coarser after six months in Whalley – but can you imagine? Six months ago I wouldn't have dared to write down the words 'moist wipes'. How everything has changed, including me.

Back to yesterday. I got the agreement from the PR lady delivered to my room, so I signed it and (with a bit of help from the hotel staff) got it posted back to her. She'll be coming up for my 'turn' on the 7th, and we'll take it from there. Later I got a message from her saying she's booked in the hotel – so all that's confirmed.

The even better news is that I used the time before I met José last night to firm up on some other arrangements. I phoned Xabi, and he has taken up a room at the hotel for two nights, one either side of the 'turn'. I had also asked Cide to offer three of my ten seats to Sid, Rhys and Skins – at my expense – and they all said yes (Skins with the obvious qualification that he would come if he could).

So, I was in a good frame of mind as I turned up to meet José. It got even better very quickly. Once he heard that there is a golf course attached to the hotel he booked for the whole weekend after the turn. Apparently he has just taken up the game and is mad keen – but finds it very expensive around London.

Our evening was going really well when I had one of those moments – those incidents if you like – when I realise, sometimes, just how close I come to being exposed. You know by now that this Coming was meticulously planned and researched, and that I am very VERY careful not to expose myself to people or circumstances where a sudden 'black spot' in my knowledge or manufactured background blows my cover. Wow, I came close last night. I was just about to take a bite of my pan-fried calf's liver, when he put his fork down and looked at me:

'Here we are, having dinner and a great time. It's hard to remember, isn't it, that barely twenty-five years ago – well within our lifetimes – our two nations were at war. What do you think about it, looking back on it? Isn't it weird? Wasn't it weird?'

It may well have been. It might well be. I had no idea on either. My comprehensive briefing as a result of all the comprehensive research had missed this one. I didn't even know who had won, or whether this 'war' had resulted in some sort of score-draw.

I got out of it with a clever mix of a few things. First (and I claim no credit for this) was José's love of alcohol – so I bought a bit of time by refilling his glass with some of the red wine we had ordered. Second: (and this was clever) – I have noticed on TV that there are a number of clichés that everybody uses in all fields when they want to say something and nothing at the same time. So, I made up this amazing rambling sentence, which included the phrases 'draw a line in the sand' and 'time to move on' and 'life is a game of two halves'. It seemed to do the trick. I wasn't really sure about the last one (the 'two halves' bit) but I'd seen some guy on the TV use it after a game of football – which seemed like a war – so I chucked it in. Whatever. We were able to carry on with our meal – albeit with him a bit wistful for a while.

I do like José. He has a sense of humour very similar to mine – and it was a really good end to the night to confirm I had him, the last member of my Team, enthusiastically agreeing to come and support my 'turn'.

He is, however, hard to shake off when he's drunk a few glasses of wine. I had to be very firm in refusing his invitation to go 'clubbing' after our meal. I knew I had an early start the next morning, and all his entreaties to join him at this 'private dancing' place where the 'birds' had nipples like 'the hat-pegs in the *Iglesia de Santa Cruz* in Buenos Aires' fell on deaf ears.

Even so, it was hard work this morning getting to the airport and going through all the bother of getting on the plane. But I'm here, in mid air, and my moistly wiped fundamental orifice feels fresh as a spring daisy.

America, here I come. By my calculation I've about four hours to go.

»

March 30

09.34.26 EST (14.34.26 BST)

To: All Constellations

Oh dear, I am all over the place with this time-adjustment thing. I was wide awake at three o'clock (Miami time) this morning, so I have used some of the time to go over in my mind exactly why I am here and to put together some things I wish to do and see. But first, let me bring you up to date on my arrival yesterday.

Miami airport is a zoo. In my (let's call them) two-and-a-half Comings I have been nailed up like a picture and burnt like corn stubble. In both instances I felt only marginally less welcome than I did arriving at Miami. The processes to get in seem endless, but once you've got through all that, there's another treat in store. As you emerge through the glass doors to get a taxi, you leave the air conditioning and enter what I can only describe as a steam bath – and my £50 spiky hair-do suddenly permed into a mass of limp curls.

As you can imagine after the long day, the long flight and the long queues through immigration control and customs, I was not at my best, so it was a bit unfortunate that I got a real 'Mr Happy' as a cab driver. I was full of questions, but he wasn't full of answers. In fact he wasn't full of anything, including information on how to get to my hotel. He was from an island called Haiti, and if he is representative of the bad humour and the task-skill shortage of the rest of the population, I'll give it a miss.

We got there, eventually, and I was too tired to do anything but collapse on my room bed and watch TV. I thought that would be a useful way to learn at least something about this place, but all I learned from Channel 7 News was that almost every scene involved somebody with a microphone standing in front of some yellow tape describing a violent death.

Heeding Nuala's advice, I tried to stay awake until 9.00 p.m. local time on my first night but I drifted off to sleep well before that – hence the 3.00 a.m. wakening.

My plan this morning is to go to one of Nu's recommendations for a late breakfast. It's on a place called South Beach and it's called the News Café. Beyond that I can't remember much, so we'll take the day from there.

First – let me share my thinking, in as brief a way as possible, about why I'm here – even for this short time. I am aware that 'things' may well happen quickly after my 'turn'. I feel well prepared, but (on the advice of the SCSC) need to make sure I am ready for anything. With that in mind I believe that I must get some sort of 'feel' for America – its culture, its thinking and some early ideas on how it might react to me. Fact: it is the planet's only superpower. Fact: it is not alone, but it is the recognised headquarters of Christian Bigotry. With the latter in mind I want to get as much information as possible on the Bob Jones University in Greenville, South Carolina, and the Westboro Baptist Church in a place called Topeka, Kansas. (More of them later.)

Let's face it, when my profile explodes onto the world scene (please remember – this could be no more than ten DAYS away), there will be much in-fighting between the world's Faith systems. They will argue as to who was right and who was wrong. They will move into different 'response modes'. However brief and inadequate, I must get SOME idea how this nation will feel and act.

I had too much to eat yesterday – too much of the wonderful food (and drink) on that luxurious flight – but I'm hungry now and ready to get on with my Mission. I've looked out of my window and it appears to be a glorious day. I've asked the hotel reception to get me a taxi to go to South Beach and they've told me it will be here in a few minutes. About half an hour ago, I saw an animated cartoon show on the TV featuring a little character called Top Cat. He woke up one morning and lifted his dustbin lid up and proclaimed, to no one in particular: 'I greet the new day unafraid'. I could not put it better myself.

»

March 31

07.23.16 EST

To: All Constellations

I feel so bloated. I don't think I have ever eaten so much in my life, and I only had two meals. I thought Whalley was bad for the size of the food portions consumed at each meal, but I realise now that I know nothing.

I got a taxi to South Beach yesterday morning – on a lovely, lovely day. Blue skies, bright sunshine, and a temperature you'd love to follow you everywhere. When I got to the News Café, I bought the local newspaper to give me something to read while I had my 'breakfast', and I managed to get a seat on the pavement terrace which gave me a great vantage point from which to watch this new world go by.

When the waiter came to take my order, I didn't recognise much on the menu, so I pointed to a good looking meal somebody had on the table next to me. The waiter told me it was something called 'corned beef hash' – so I ordered it, along with some 'home-style fries, two easy-over eggs and whole wheat toast' that he recommended as suitable accompaniments. I don't want to spend too much time on this stuff – so let me summarise my seminal findings from the next hour I spent at the café:

1. American newspapers, like American TV, show no interest whatsoever in anything outside America. This, I think, will have significant implications once my Mission gets going.

2. It seems that every American is enormously fat or very thin. There is no in-between size. The fat ones wear very tight clothes, the thin ones wear very loose ones. Odd.

3. If, as a male, you whiz past the News Café wearing only tight shorts and shoes that have little wheels on them, with a yellow living writhing snake around your neck, nobody (apart from me) bats an eyelid.

4. Corned beef hash, with two eggs, home fries and wheat toast weighs (by my guess) approximately 3 kilograms.

I finished all my food, as I have been brought up to do. It was only then that I saw that nobody else ate more than half of theirs, so I would add another summary point: this is a land of waste.

I was so exhausted by my eating efforts that I just walked across the road onto the beach and, even though it was still before noon, I fell asleep on the sand. Big Mistake.

I had forgotten to put on the cream that Nuala convinced me to buy to stop the sun burning my skin. I awoke about 90 minutes later, and was immediately aware that something was wrong. My face hurt, particularly my nose. It was that old familiar (for me) burning sensation. Would you believe it? The sun had burnt my face quite badly. When I saw it in the taxi mirror, it was a fierce red colour.

I had a quiet afternoon. I got some more soothing cream from a pharmacy, which you put on AFTER you have been burned and went back to the hotel and watched TV. They were showing a game called basketball. I found this very simple to understand: five very tall black men ran up a wooden court and threw a ball through a hoop into a small net. Then five other very tall black men, dressed in different coloured shirts, ran up to the other end and did the same. This was fine, albeit a bit predictable, but then something weird happened – with just one minute to go in the game, the whole thing entered some kind of space/time warp and the last minute lasted for about a quarter of an hour. What a strange phenomenon – but it is this kind of thing I must understand if I am to become a globally populist initiate.

At about 7.00 p.m. I decided that I had better go and get some more food. I'll be honest, I wasn't hungry – but I had a target list of restaurants to visit so I ordered another taxi and set off for a place called Versailles.

Much of this city has what they called a Cuban influence. Cuba is an island about 90 miles off the coast, and has thoughtfully deposited thousands of refugees and criminals in Miami, and they have shaped much of the city's culture. Versailles is one of its *typico* Cuban restaurants – and I had been recommended to order the roast lamb.

You would have thought I would have learned something from my morning experience. The roast lamb, when it came, could have fed six people, but it did not come alone. It came with bread, fried plantains (banana like things), rice and a black-bean gravy.

I tried my best, but it was with a heavy stomach that I crawled into bed after my first full day in this fascinating country. The even worse news is that those black beans are still 'with me' this morning, but unfortunately I cannot open the windows in my hotel room to ease the problem.

Saturday today, and I have a full programme lined up.

APRIL

»

April 1

09.34.25 EST

To: All Constellations

I feel a tingle as I look at the date that appears automatically on the top of these communications. It is April. This is the pivotal month, the month of my scheduled breakthrough.

I am also aware that I am in a bit of trouble with the SCSC. I was supposed to give them an update on my medical condition before the end of March – but have just not had the time. Anyway, I was not able to bring all the bits and pieces I need to do it with me because I was a bit tight on luggage. I'll do it as soon as I get back.

For the record I was not able to fit my 'public speaking' books in either, so I will have a lot to cram into the few days before my 'turn'.

Right, yesterday's report. Here's a weird thing: I went for an early lunch to another (Nuala) recommended place called Joe's Stone Crabs. I have a number of eating places on my list, and I'm not going to get around them all – so I chose this one because it sounded a bit lighter on the food side.

There was quite a queue when I got there, but I eventually got a table and ordered with the help of a waiter. Now, here's the odd thing – you don't get the whole crab. You just get a claw (which is a leg). Here's the bit that's weird – when they take the claw off a crab, IT GROWS AGAIN. Now, this is against everything I have come across in my researches on this planet – and I am beginning to wonder if Stone Crabs are some sort of rival Initiates in themselves. Do you remember those little bastards on Frogah–Da45? They looked a bit like earth crabs, didn't they? Do you remember what they turned out to be and what happened there? I mean, it's some miracle to grow your own leg back. I must watch out for this species – once I'm out in the open, they might be forced to make a move.

In the afternoon I went to a local baseball match. It was at the University of Miami, and I had noticed in the paper that they had a match against another University. As I am aware from my pre-reading that baseball is a big element of the cultural *zeitgeist* in this country I went along. Without getting too complicated, the afternoon was notable for two things:

1. When I went for a glass of beer to cool down as the afternoon temperatures soared, I was obviously served by someone who was only partially sighted. In human form, in all fairness, and understandably given what I have been through in this form, I look my age. I could be mistaken for somebody ten years older. I could not be mistaken for somebody fifteen years younger – but it transpired that I could not get a beer until I produced my passport to 'prove' I was at least twenty-one. I would have thought it was risky having nearly blind people serving beer.

2. Baseball may be a cultural cornerstone of America, but it is achingly, numbingly, mind-alteringly boring. A man on a little hill throws a little ball at another man who has a stick. He swishes and misses. This is repeated again and

> again and again and again until one of them hits the ball and attempts (for some reason) to run around a circle. There is wild excitement at this juncture, and many of the men who had been standing about spitting streams of dark brown liquid onto the floor and scratching their scrotums suddenly jump about and wave and run. Then it goes back into the cycle of throw-swish-miss for a few more hours. This is a strange nation.

By 6.00 p.m. I had had enough – and I had filled up barely half a page of my 'America' notebook. I have no idea what the score was (or is – they may still be playing).

Before I left, I had a 'meal' of something called a 'hot dog'. Again, this was driven by my need to understand as much as possible of the culture here in the short time I have at my disposal. It is a strange thing: what you do is get a piece of bread and split it down the side. Inside you put a sausage, which sounds pretty good. Then you put on some fried onions – which also sounds good. To complete the offering, you then add some RED sauce and then some YELLOW sauce, which you think will take the base tastes of the first three ingredients and explode them into some sort of culinary firework display. This makes the fact that, when you bite into it, you cannot taste ANYTHING AT ALL, rather mystifying.

When I got back to the Marriott, I had had enough. I tried to watch some TV, but after seventeen more crime scenes on Channel 7 News, I dozed off.

Tomorrow I must watch TV for the Sunday Church services, so I'll have another busy day. First stop will be breakfast at a place I've found myself called Starbucks. It's probably a one-off, so it will be nice to explore somewhere that only a few people know about.

»

April 2

15.23.16 EST

To: All Constellations

It's mid-afternoon and I'm heading off to Miami airport in a few minutes to catch the plane back – so this will be the last communication on this EST nonsense.

I'm not going to spend much time on yesterday – it ended up being just a succession of restaurants and food and drink and more food and more drink. Here – quite unbelievably now I look at it – is an 'inventory' of what I ate and drank yesterday in some sort of chronological order:

1 large double shot decaffeinated skim milk latte (a kind of coffee)

1 blueberry muffin (a kind of cake)

1 Corona beer (self-explanatory, but with a bit of lime stuck in the bottle neck for some reason)

1 portion chicken *fajitas* (about 2 lbs of cooked chicken mixed in with another 2 lbs of onions and peppers wrapped in several pancakes)

1 Awesome Blossom (an onion which had been splayed out, covered in batter and fried)

1 half-pint of ketchup accompanying the last two.

1 Haagen Dazs ice cream, *tres leches* flavour (this was completely unnecessary, but – as history indicates – I can resist temptation only up to a point)

About thirteen Fried Pork Chunks, with rice and black bean gravy

Garlic bread (three pieces)

Fried plantains (about eight)

1 flan (a dessert made from cream and eggs)

1 *café cubano* (a VERY small cup of coffee with about half its size and weight made up of white refined sugar) – this did not help me sleep.

When I couldn't sleep back at the hotel: 1 packet of Pringles Crisps; 1 bar Toblerone Chocolate and 1 packet Oriole Cookies from my mini-bar in the hotel room.

I am catching on to the American way of life.

Today I have had but one meal – a lunch at a Cuban place where I had something called *fabada*. Unfortunately, this delightful soup, which contains chunks of ham, also contains more beans. I really am becoming embarrassing. I would not like to be sitting behind myself on this plane tonight.

Enough of food and drink.

Lets turn to one of the prime reasons for jamming this trip in – religion. It is a Big Deal here, but (a) very confusing and (b) very misinformed and misguided. Here's an example of the confusing bit: at the airport I saw a magazine called, strangely, *The Onion*. It had a big banner headline, which read: **God Answers Disabled Little Boy's Prayers. 'No' says God**.

What do you make of that? I don't remember that (and I'm sure I would have done), and I suspect it might have been made up. But why? Beats me.

On to the misinformed and misguided. I watched TV all morning (today is a Sunday). There are many TV channels here, but it was almost wall-to-wall religion – all of it some version of Christianity. There were, however, only two common elements: (a) all the men 'presenters' have wild staring eyes and strange *bouffant* hairstyles and (b) they all solicited money.

Frankly, I got more and more annoyed. I have already mentioned a couple of the organisations I want to explore further, one being the Bob Jones University. This fascinates me because it is obviously a young people's haven, and (I believe) it will be the young people who carry me to success. But here is a University (motto: brains are no substitute for God) where alcohol, cigarettes and fornication are willingly banned and – get this – it was only three earth years ago where segregation between black and white humans was revoked. Basically, they have micro-analysed their 'Bible' to find supporting words for their selective distorted views. They cheerfully ignore the Big One we DID leave lying around: LOVE THY NEIGHBOUR.

Brains are no substitute for God? They believe that everything was created by this God thing. I scream at the TV. No it wasn't. It was a combination of climate and earth movements that did it. We should know.

And as for those mental spastics in the Westboro Baptist Church, well – I just give up. America is, apparently and according to the members of this church, doomed. And why would that be? Because it is (increasingly) tolerant of homosexuality, that's why. So these church 'soldiers' take every opportunity, including the funerals of soldiers who have died in combat, to scream and pour out their vitriol at anything and anybody that passes. Hey, I have news for the zealots in Westboro. This God entity doesn't hate homosexuals. HE WAS PART OF THE TEAM THAT CREATED THEM.

My view? I am not personally attracted to all that bottom stuff, but they strike me as far more balanced and attractive than anybody I witnessed in Westboro.

My short visit has left many impressions. This country is a living paradox. Full of delightful people who are also paranoid, gluttonous, wasteful, bigoted, divided, insular and who consistently have the leadership they deserve.

I will have to progress here once I make the breakthrough. It is just too big and influential to ignore. It will take some careful planning. I suspect I will also have to tailor my offering to offer benefits to people with those characteristics.

»

4 April

08.23.54 BST

To: All Constellations

The more alert amongst you will have noticed two things: (a) we are back on GMT (i.e. English time) and (b) I have missed a day. What happens when you fly back from America to England is that, on account of that time changing stuff, you LOSE five hours, so I got back early on Monday morning – and by the time I had got back into London and then got a train back up to Preston and then got a taxi from Preston to

Whalley, most of the day had gone and I was really tired. So I thought I'd get an early night – and then set about my many tasks today feeling refreshed.

So, here I am, ready to go. It's Tuesday today – and on Friday evening this mission of mine will explode into life.

I've a lot to do before then, including a medical report back to the SCSC who are getting very VERY worried about my image and appearance when I 'go public' for the first time (and are letting me know these views at about half-hourly intervals). I have also got to work on both my speech content and speaking techniques, using these self-help books I have bought. The Charter will form the 'main thrust', but I cannot just read it out – I must add to it with entertaining anecdotes and examples. I'd like to catch up with Nu, just to feed back, as promised, on my American experiences. Also, she knows this kind of audience well and may be able to help me with both content and style tips. I need to check my wardrobe and make sure I have the right outfit for the occasion – and, if not, to head into Burnley to get fitted out.

Before I do all that, let me just pause and ask you to reflect on a couple of things. It is several months now since I outlined – openly and honestly – my Five Key Goals for the First Crucial Six Months. I won't repeat them here (you will find them under the daily blog for earth date 24 October). All I would say is that I felt almost overwhelmed when I formalised them at that time, AND I know, I just know, that many of you felt the tasks were wildly over-optimistic. With that in mind, let's all just pause and reflect on progress. Take the first one: to develop a very limited number of key personal relationships. On Friday evening I will have a table of TEN attending my first public outing – of which eight could fall into that category (never, never will I consider Debs as one of them – she is just there to make the numbers up, a fact that I still find worrying). Remember the first time? It took more than three decades to get twelve Team members, and one of them turned out to be complete shit. I am a 'can-do' Initiate by any definition – and it would be nice if an occasional communication of recognition headed my way from You-Know-Who because you can track the same sort of progress on the other four of the FKGs.

Right, breakfast finished and Blog done. I must get on.

»

5 April

11.34.26 BST

To: All Constellations

Yesterday did not go as planned. I have watched a lot of TV and reached a decision that I should wear a dark blue casual suit with a plain (lighter) blue open necked shirt for my breakthrough event. That seems to be the 'uniform' for male TV celebrities who want to combine entertainment with some substantive content. Most of them also parade quite bright red socks worn with shiny black casual shoes with tassels on, so I thought I'd better set about getting them as well.

Of course, I have such a suit – so I thought I could just tick that off then head out to get the rest. Disaster ensued. I (wisely) decided to try it on (just to be sure) and found that I could not fasten the trousers at the front. At least, not for a few minutes – during which I pulled and contorted until at last I got the top waist button through its little hole. At which time the whole of one trouser pocket split. This thing has obviously shrunk really badly in the wardrobe – presumably because of the damp or something.

So I headed into Burnley needing a new suit as well as the rest of the stuff – and there was a lot of choice. I found a big place called 'My M&S' (do we own that? I thought we stopped doing that after the Co-op went bad down here) and they had everything – but here's the strange thing. When I tried on the trousers with a 34" waist, they wouldn't fit either – and I ended up having to buy a pair with a 38" waist. I don't know what's happened here, but I assume it's something like they do with the hours now and again – that they must all agree to change waist measurements at midnight on a given date or something.

Anyway, I got everything else and headed home – to be greeted by what I can only describe as a vitriolic communication from the SCSC guys. They monitor all my movements with what they call a con-Stellar Webcam, and had witnessed the trouser-dance I had performed earlier when trying to get into my suit. It was not, they opined, a shrinking of the cloth. Nor was it a universal conspiracy to change measurement systems at midnight on the equinox. It had a much more simple explanation: that, on the eve of my great breakthrough, which had been planned and worked for earth centuries, I had allowed myself, despite their constant guidance and entreaties, to become (and here I quote) a Fat Bastard.

Well. All I can say is that somebody could control their temper a bit more. But it is true that I seem to have a fuller face and that my clothes have been getting tighter – but I have paid no real (serious) attention to it until now. The outcomes of this 'exchange' of views were twofold: first – I haven't eaten or drunk since and, second, my medical report is now a priority.

If I can find the stuff, I'm off to do it now. The good news is that all my new clothes fit properly, albeit with more material involved – and they look good. That said, I'm not sure how I can show off the red socks.

»

6 April

12.23.17 BST

To: All Constellations

One day to go! The excitement is almost unbearable. We will then move instantly and (I hope) seamlessly into a second phase of fame and exposure. My views will be sought and analysed to the point of exhaustion. I will cease to have a private life. Cameras will follow me everywhere – something I have not had to put up with before.

There is no doubt that the whole Home Office team are worried as to how I will react – with celebrity status coming much more quickly and being so much more extensive and intrusive this time. I, however, am supremely confident.

But first things first. My medical. It was not good. Oh, there were some elements that were OK: notably my blood pressure (measured here as 132 over 86), and my uric acid creation was back within an acceptable range (which eases that gout problem). BUT BUT BUT – big problems are emerging: My weight has BALLOONED to 94 kilograms and my cholesterol level has done the same – up to 6.1. I can only put that down to four days in America – which must put a question mark against it as a possible Plan B location. There were one or two other lesser worries (for example, my renal function – whatever that is – was slightly abnormal).

You know what annoys me with all this? Some of these results signal that my health is being threatened, mainly by the sedentary and glutinous lifestyle that has overtaken this planet – but are 'they' worried about that? No, they are not. They are worried about how I look, and the threats to my 'image'. Apparently, if and when I appear on TV, the cameras will mysteriously add about 5 kilograms to my appearance. In their eyes, the result is an Initiate taking on a Second Coming looking like a 100 kilogram lard-arse (as Cide would say).

There's nothing I can do now of any substance between now and tomorrow night – except continue not to eat or drink. Now I must sit down and spend the rest of today (and some of tomorrow) reading these books on speaking skills. I was hoping to see Nuala, but that will have to wait until Saturday.

The good news is that I have heard that Skins is going to try to make it. I may have a full table.

»

7 April

17.34.56 BST

To: All Constellations

We are almost there, and I am beside myself with excitement. I am dressed up and ready to go to the hotel. I feel a bit odd, probably on account of the fact that I have not eaten or drunk for two days now – but I think my speech is in good shape.

I found it hard to sleep last night. Maybe it was the lack of food and drink, maybe it was just the excitement. I had quick chats on the phone with José, Cori and Xabi who have all arrived and are all set. Bash is going to come round in a few minutes to take me to the hotel – and he doesn't know it yet but I'm going to get him to leave his meter running and come in and join us. Cide is bringing Skins, Rhys, Sid and (ugh) Debs. Nuala will miss the dinner because she is working, but will join the table for the speeches. Cide will be on the top table, but join ours when he has introduced me.

All this had been sorted, but I just couldn't sleep – so I went back to my books on speaking techniques, just to hone this thing to perfection. As I intimated yesterday, I ended up spending about three or four hours going through them. The biggest challenge I have is that Cide has insisted I only 'do' twenty minutes. His point is that it will be much better for me (and for the audience) if I leave them wanting more – rather than overstaying my welcome. This seems sound advice (and is generally echoed in my formal books on public speaking) – but it presents me with a problem. What I did this afternoon at the start of this exercise was to stand in front of a mirror and give my proposed talk, timing myself exactly. What resulted was a rather disappointing (and somewhat frightening) two and a half hours – and that involved being a bit abrupt on the last couple of points of my Charter. Clearly there was much 'editing' to do, so I settled down with my books and a notepad.

I found much of the content of these self-help books rather childish and obvious. It is not as though I am a stranger to this stuff. Many's the time I have had an audience in the palm of my hand, but I do appreciate the importance of this particular occasion and I recognised that I had work to do to get it down to something effective and efficient for the particular occasion and audience. I ended up with these important lessons learned for modern audiences:

1. Steven Spielberg, who is a big name in the world of entertainment down here, is adamant that if you want to ENGAGE an audience, you must ENTERTAIN them. I feel this is important for me. My Mission is serious, and so is my speech content – but I must lighten it a bit so it will be enjoyable and memorable. I'll take Cide's advice and start with a humorous joke. The one about the old golfers will do – just the right audience.

2. It seems vital that a speaker should check his equipment before he starts. These days, they have machines down here that magnify your voice so you don't have to shout to audiences that number more than twenty – which will be a first for me. I must remember to check it all works beforehand.

3. It seems that stance and posture is important for effective speaking – which is something I've never considered before. I think it comes naturally to me – but some of the points are worth remembering: breathe slowly at the start; stand away from things like lecterns; use your mobility (particularly arm movements) for effect and emphasis; rest your elbows on your diaphragm when you are not waving your arms about (which helps with your breathing); make early eye contact with a friendly face in the audience; don't pick on individuals with your jokes – and when you finish just summarise the absolutely key things you want your audience to remember and ABOVE ALL finish on time.

4. Try to avoid using copious notes – or visual aids of any kind that cram too much information on them. Both these

factors mean you lose eye contact with your audience, and this is stressed by all the books as a No-No.

5. There were several sections about handling what they call 'hecklers' (these are rude people that shout things from the audience), but the general consensus in all the books was that the vast majority of speakers would not face a heckling problem. It just doesn't happen outside professional theatres. That's something of a relief because it used to be an occasional problem for me. In fact, that's very good news – it sounds as though the march of time has brought some positive changes in society.

Even with all the learning and several more rehearsals I couldn't get it down to much below an hour (after all, I have ten key points), but I think that once I get started I will be able to hold them for that kind of time. This is a unique occasion in the history of this planet and I am sure they will cotton on to that. If not, I'll just adjust my timing while I'm on my feet. No problem. I used to do it all the time.

I hear my front door bell – that must be Bash. Here we go.

****

You will notice some little stars separating this part from the previous one. This is not a new day's blog. I have just put those markers on the page to indicate that this is a follow up on the same day. Yes, it is still April 7th, but midnight isn't far off, and I have been back in my room, at my house, for nearly an hour.

It has not been a happy hour. In terms of physical pain, the hour I have just spent compared favourably with being burnt or nailed. In terms of mental anguish, however, it has, I believe, seen me at my lowest ever. For some reason I cannot think about the events of this evening with my eyes open. It is only with them firmly shut, as if I were somehow cut off from everything and everyone, that I can begin to piece together the events of the Golf Club Awards Dinner and Charity Evening.

It is hard to define exactly where it started to go wrong. It certainly started well – Bash being quite enthusiastic about the idea of having a free dinner while his taxi meter kept running under the supervision of the hotel security staff.

The place was absolutely full, with every seat taken. Clearly, I had drawn the crowds in. This was only to be expected (I'm guessing that some rumours have spread as to who (or what) I might be and what I might be talking about). A full house is always a confidence booster, and it was with a light heart that I welcomed everybody to my table. There was a bit of reticence (shyness I suppose) as they got to know each other – but that soon melted away. The only tiny snag was Debs' appearance. If you remember, she is a BIG girl, and she was wearing the tiniest skirt you could imagine. The top edge of the skirt failed by several inches to reach the bottom edge of her, well, I suppose you could call it a blouse. The resultant gap was occupied by what the Americans call a muffin-tin overflow of skin – that is, a waistline that overhangs the bottom garment rather like a muffin cake overhangs its baking tin when it is cooked. Her blouse, which seemed to be made of moist wipes edged with lace, was wholly inadequate for the task it had taken on, and José, who was seated directly opposite her, was left with little option but to stare at the tattooed upper slopes of her breasts all night. At least, I assume he had no option because that's what he did.

The first signs of something going off-plan? That's difficult – but I did begin to be aware of the huge amounts of alcohol heading for each table. The entrance ticket entitled each table of ten to a bottle of white and red wine between them – but both ours had disappeared before all ten of us had sat down. You could then order extra wine or beer from the waiters, and this our table, along with every other one it seemed, proceeded to do at a quite astonishing rate.

It was here that I made my first mistake. I'm admitting this because, when we review this evening when deciding whether to abort or try and rescue the Mission, I want to take my share of responsibility. I am not one to shirk. You will remember I had not eaten (or barely drunk any liquid) for about three days before this event in an attempt to slim down a bit. I'm not sure it made much difference, but my already high level of self-confidence was raised even higher when Cori, who had thoughtfully bought a photographer with her to record highlights of this breakthrough event, complimented me on my appearance. Feeling good, I had two rather large glasses of something called *Concha y Torro* Cabernet Sauvignon red wine. This on a completely empty stomach. I immediately felt a bit light-headed, and this may have contributed to what followed later.

What followed immediately, however, was a pleasant meal (which I ate) and some pleasant drinks (which I drank) and some pleasant conversations (which I joined). I failed to notice that the noise level in the place was rising steadily, and that things were getting, well, a little raucous, until a bread roll, from an unknown and undetectable source, hit Xabi on the side of his head. At that stage, I began to look around, and the first seeds of doubt and worry were sewn. Only about half the people were still sitting down – the others being at the toilets or outside, smoking or standing at the bar.

At that stage two things happened. Cide stood up, banged his glass with a spoon and announced that the

Awards Ceremony would begin in five minutes, so would people please fill their glasses and make their way back to their seats. The second thing that happened was that Debs, who, at the time, had made her way around to my side of the table and was standing next to me, and was trying (I think) to put her tongue in my ear, was sick down the left-hand side of my hair, shirt, suit jacket, suit trousers and my left shoe. The only thing that escaped on the left-hand side of my body was my left red sock, protected, as it was, by being invisible.

I confess, I was within an inch of panicking – but it is at these moments that true greatness reveals itself. Nuala, who had not yet joined us to sit down, but who had been monitoring our table closely, was by my side in seconds – and grabbed me by the ear and whisked me out to the kitchen. In fairness, she did a great job with the tools to hand – endless pieces of paper kitchen roll, cold and hot water, dishcloths and a pan scourer. Throughout it all, she was silent, respecting I suppose the urgent need to get me back in some sort of shape. On reflection, I think it took about ten minutes to get me in the best shape possible, and then she uttered two sentences. The first one covered her views on Debs, and her presence. I can't remember it verbatim, but it included the idea that Debs was as much use to life generally, and me specifically, as a 'barrel of cold piss'.

Her second, short, sentence was built around the concept that I wasn't much better, that enough was enough, that I needed someone to sort me out and take me in hand, and that she was that someone and that before the clock struck midnight tonight she would prove her case in a way that made my eyes water.

I had no time to digest this information. We needed to get back out. The end results of her efforts were amazing.

With my suit being dark you couldn't tell unless you were really close up (or, indeed, wearing it) that the left half of it was wet. The only really visible clue was my hair, the left side of which was spikeless.

When we got back in the main function room, Cide was just getting to his feet to announce the awards. For the first time I felt my confidence falter. I don't know whether it was the wet feeling of my clothes or the fact that the room looked, felt and sounded more like a fish market at peak trading time than a room suitable for the delivery and receipt of keynote speeches – but I do know I began to feel very nervous.

Cide's opening remarks did not help. I felt the situation needed some *gravitas*, and was hoping he would provide it. But he opened by saying he had some 'housekeeping announcements' – included in which was an entreaty, on behalf of the Golf Club Committee, that those present would refrain from 'pissing in the car park' on the way out.

This was not what I had in mind at all. Not at all. With an increasing churning in my stomach I tried to listen to the awards as Cide fought valiantly to be heard over the increasing drunken din. This process was not helped by Cori trying to brush and spray the left side of my hair into a shape that bore some relation to the rest of it. José had temporarily disappeared with Debs, but frankly that was something of a relief. Xabi was trying to commit Bash to join him in some anti-America protest that he was thinking of organising tomorrow outside a McDonald's in Burnley. Skins, bless him, was slumped in his chair taking little notice of what was going on around while Sid was eating both their desserts. Rhys had nodded off, despite the noise.

At this stage, the last award was announced, and Cide stood up again to announce the 'turn'. I can remember his exact words. I will remember them always:

'Ladies and gentlemen. LADIES AND GENTLEMEN. Oh, for fuck's sake, can you lot just shut the fuck up for a minute or two while the "turn" comes on.

'Now then. We are always being asked to do shit for charity. Only last week, a scout group came up to me and asked if I'd run a sponsored half-marathon for charity. I told 'em to sod off. My knee's bad. But they kept asking – so I kept telling 'em to sod off. Then one of 'em said it was for partially sighted and blind children. And d'you know what I thought? I thought: fuck it. Partially sighted and blind kids? I'll have a chance. Put me down for it.

'Now, tonight's "turn" is doing this for charity. He's promised to donate his £250 fee to a local cause, so I'd like you to put your hands together to give a warm Whalley welcome to somebody who has had them rolling in the aisles in northern clubs for years now . . . Ladies and Gentlemen . . . Tommy Ramsbottom.'

Let's face it, I was not in good shape for this speech before this announcement. After it, I was about three times worse. At the end of that terrible, sick (and, I thought, unfunny) story about the poor blind children, there was an absolute uproar – and it was only when I looked around and paid a bit more attention that I realised that these people were *laughing*. What on earth had I let myself in for? If this was the material that got a response from this audience, I was doomed before I began. I only had one joke, and that was lame and tame by comparison, even if I put 'F' words in all over the place.

I started to walk towards the microphone. My mind was just a writhing mass of jumbled thoughts, when suddenly something else became clear. A fee of £250? The bastard. The fee, which I had promised to give to charity, was supposed to be £500. Cide was obviously trousering the other £250.

Somehow I got to the microphone, and turned to stare at a sea of faces and a wall of noise. I looked back at my table, for my carefully collected team of supporters. I needed eye contact with some friendly eyes – but I couldn't make anything or anybody out as the main lights were being dimmed.

I launched straight into my joke about old golfers never dying, and smiled and waved my hands about as I delivered the punch line. It had no effect whatsoever. None. At this stage I saw Cori, who had left our table and manoeuvred herself into a position where I could see her plainly. She was motioning something with her hands and arms. It took me a good thirty seconds to work it out. I was talking WAY too fast, in spite of all my rehearsal. I had completely wasted my one and only joke by talking like a chipmunk.

With a heavy heart and a feeling of impending doom, I launched into my Charter, starting with the first Big Point about 'connection'. I abandoned eye contact, and stared downwards. I gripped the lectern, in a way I had trained myself not to do. I just half closed my eyes and set off.

And then something strange happened. Gradually, ever so gradually, the din level dropped. It was only a bit at first, but then it was noticeable. I raised my eyes a tiny bit, hardly daring to look out – but when I did I saw something amazing. The room was like a war zone, but most of the people were back in their seats again, and they were staring at me. There was no applause, no chatter, no bread-roll throwing, no nothing. And for a moment I thought I was winning. And then it happened.

I had noticed earlier that one of the guests on another table was a blind man, sitting right at the front. He was accompanied by a dog, presumably to help him find his way about. It was because of his presence that I was particularly surprised at Cide's joke about blind children, but I noticed he laughed as loudly as anyone. I gained in confidence as the silence spread, I found it strangely comforting to look at him in the audience.

In hindsight, I misinterpreted the growing silence of the audience. Given the seminal content of my speech, and its potential impact on the state of all nations, I assumed it was a mixture of growing acceptance and respect. I was wrong. It was a growing incredulity. It was growing as would the mass of water, fed by a quiet but substantial river, behind a dam with structural weaknesses. At some stage something small was going to break, and within seconds there would be catastrophe.

The 'something small' was provided by the blind man. I had reached the end of my second Charter Point ('All people are to be admired. All governments are not to be'), and I was using the Jewish race as a thoughtful example, when there was a particularly quiet moment. You could hear a pin drop. All of a sudden, the blind man shouted:

'This is fuckin' rubbish. Gerroff.'

There was absolute silence for between three and four seconds. I know exactly how long it was because I have relived it a dozen times already. During that time, the audience froze all movement as well as sound, and I struggled to remember anything from my books about handling hecklers. Nothing came to mind. I do remember opening and closing my mouth several times, but no sound was coming out. With masterly timing, the blind man then turned to the man next to him and said, in a loud and clear voice:

'*Has he fuckin' gone yet*?'

If the 'something small' was provided by the blind man, the 'catastrophe' was provided by the rest of the audience. The silence and stillness lasted for another two seconds and then exploded into a wall of noise and movement. It wasn't just laughter, it was hooting and shouting and waving and drinking and getting up and sitting down and, in some cases, standing on chairs.

I froze. I scrambled desperately to reorganise my thoughts, but I simply could not remember what came next on my Charter. I pressed my elbows into my diaphragm, to no avail. In fairness, I don't think anything would have worked or even helped. As it was, I remained as a distressed statue, albeit one with its mouth opening and closing with no sound coming out.

A sort of rescue came in the form of Cide, who appeared from nowhere, drying his eyes with his handkerchief. Grabbing the microphone, he shouted something about thanking me, and that now we would get on with the final part of the evening and have some fun. He then switched the microphone off, and whispered in my ear:

'Tommy. For Christ's sake head for the exit and let me tell a few jokes. Then I'll play some records over the sound system. If I don't, they'll burn the fucking place down.'

With that, he gave me a polite shove in the back, and I began to make my way through the tables, some of which contained people who seemed to be crying with laughter. As I passed my table, I heard Tommy's first 'joke':

'D'you know, I have a lot of friends. One of them has a nickname. It's "Shagger". And I have to tell you she's not very happy about it.'

At my table I saw Sid banging his beer glass up and down in merriment. Skins had not moved. Both of them looked the other way as I passed. Rhys was still asleep. Bash and Xabi had joined Debs and José in being absent. Cori was nowhere to be seen. I saw Nuala in the distance carrying a tray of dirty dishes. She didn't see me. As I made my way out of this bedlam I heard Cide's last effort:

'I've been trying to get my bird into bed for ages. So, I tried a bit of subtlety. She was having a late night coffee at my place, so I said "How d'ya fancy your eggs in the mornin'?" Know what she said? "UNFERTILISED!"'

I could still hear the laughter as I made my way outside the building. In truth, I could hear it echoing around my head all the way home in the strange taxi that got me there – Bash having disappeared.

That was an hour ago. I'm going to put some more of these whatsits in while I have a think about what to say next.

****

It's all but midnight now, and I'm tired – although I doubt sleep will come. I know I am guilty sometimes of ferocious mood swings. In a recent appraisal (we do them every hundred years or so) I was told that my highs were too high, and that my lows were too low. But this is a new low. I am absolutely rock bottom. I suspect that I will get a torrent of negative gobshite from the SCSC tomorrow, and probably a personal one from Him. It will be about lack of planning and professionalism. I will have made poor choices and prioritised the wrong things. I will have been deflected and my judgement of people and events will have been sub-standard. Again. Oh, yes – the 'again' bit will be stressed, you can mark my words.

But you know what? I am down but not out. This particular Mission must now be aborted. My team (such as it was) is now non-existent or in disarray. Tommy Ramsbottom died tonight. In fact, he died twice. He died, as they say down here, on stage. I accept that now, but it is an event that will have been forgotten by nine out of ten of the audience by the following week. But Tommy Ramsbottom also died in a second way. He will simply cease to be. This disappearance will also have little or no impact on the local people in Whalley – or, indeed, the wider population of the planet. Perhaps a handful will wonder what happened, and why and where he went. But they will soon forget. That's the only good news. Given the strength, I will Come Again, and the slate will be clean.

I would ask you to ponder and reflect. I would ask you, when the time is appropriate, to review with me what went well and what went badly. This has implications for all of us. But I warn you, I am about to press the 'send' button on this communication, and after it has gone so will I be. And I will be gone for some time.

Hang on, there's somebody knocking at my front door. That's weird – who comes calling at 11.58 p.m. at night?

Ah, well. I'll just press 'send' and go see who it is.